TOUCHED BY ICE

New York Times & *USA Today* Bestselling Author

CYNTHIA EDEN

Published by Hocus Pocus Publishing, Inc.

Copy-editing by: J. R. T. Editing

DEDICATION

For the incredibly thoughtful and always
amazing Michele H.

CHAPTER ONE

Brutal. There was no other way to describe the night. The discovery. The pain of seeing those tiny bones being unearthed. The pale, pink blanket. The dirty, small, stuffed rabbit that had been left with the bones...

Weariness and sorrow pulled at her, but Antonia Rossi—Tony to her friends and colleagues—kept her spine stiff and her shoulders squared. She couldn't leave the scene, not yet. Even though every part of her just wanted to run away as fast as she could. This particular scene stirred too many of her own long-buried secrets.

The van's back door slammed. The sound jolted her, and she stiffened. The driver turned toward her, tipping his head. A sign that he'd be pulling out soon. The remains would be taken in for review by the medical examiner.

Beside her, the police chief exhaled on a long sigh. "This property had been searched before. Right after the disappearance. All the properties that belonged to the family were searched, just as a matter of course. How the hell was this missed?"

This...the body of an eight-year-old child. A death that had occurred over twenty years ago. All but forgotten by everyone.

But not by me. Because Tony's job was to work the cold cases. To keep hunting when others stopped. "It's possible the body was moved here after the search." More than possible. She suspected that was exactly what had occurred. "Forensics will be able to tell you more." Though she had plenty of suspicions on her own.

Forensics would also confirm the identity of the victim. But based on the remnants of clothes—the little blue jeans, the tattered yellow shirt, and the very distinct shoes, blue converses with yellow laces—Tony felt certain she'd found her girl. After all, Meridian Duvane had last been seen in those exact clothes so very long ago.

Banshee, Tony's German Shephard, brushed against her leg and stared up at her with worried eyes. The dog had caught the tension in her voice. Banshee always knew when Tony was upset. *Dammit, I hate finding the kids.* When you didn't have a body, then you could still have hope. You could still think...*Maybe she's out there. Maybe one day, I'll wake up and she'll be back home.* But that hope was gone now. Because little Meridian had been found.

The van pulled away, and Tony's head tilted as she watched the taillights fade into the distance.

"Yeah, forensics will have a field day," the chief agreed. "Especially with that blanket and the damn bunny. Killer had to touch them, right? Maybe his DNA is on them."

She hoped like hell it was.

"You okay?" the chief asked her when she remained quiet. Chief Hardy Powell. Fairly new to the job, only in the position about six months. Sounding shaken. Nervous. Probably his first time to find one of the kids. They were always the hardest.

So she decided to be honest with him. Maybe he needed some honestly. "I'm not." Her lips curled down. "You're not, either, and that's okay. That's what makes us normal." If they were both completely okay with digging up a little girl, then there would be a problem. Slowly, deliberately, she gave a long exhale. "I'll be around if you need me." Since only bones remained—and bones were her specialty—the chief medical examiner very well might need Tony's services. She didn't have plans to leave Biloxi, Mississippi, anytime soon. When she'd come down for the case, she'd rented a house near the beach. She'd planned to work the case and then take some long overdue personal time. Her fingers sank into Banshee's coat. "Come on, sweetheart, let's go."

She and Banshee turned for her rental car, and Tony's long, black braid slid over her shoulder. It wasn't a particularly cold night. Did they even get cold nights this close to the Gulf? There was definitely no chill in the air. Quite the opposite. The air felt humid. Heavy. A hot breeze blew over her cheeks. A breeze that swept away the tear that had leaked from her left eye. Dammit. She hated crying at a scene. So unprofessional. But Meridian had been so small, and when Tony had seen those bones unearthed, she'd been shoved right back into her own past.

"Dr. Rossi?"

At the questioning male voice, Tony stiffened. Escape had been so close at hand. *Denied*. Thinking it was a cop or one of the members of the crime scene team trying to get her attention, Tony turned around and she even had her game face in place when she looked toward the speaker. Points for her.

But she didn't find herself staring at a cop or one of the crime scene analysts. Instead, a tall, broad-shouldered male in an elegantly cut suit stared back at her. He gave her a quick smile.

She didn't particularly like smiles at murder scenes. Half of his face was in shadow, half spotlighted by all the illumination the cops had brought in for the investigation. He looked sinister when she suspected he'd meant to appear charming.

"My name is Smith Sanders, and I'm here on behalf of my employer." He extended a business card toward her.

She took it automatically, but since she was a few feet away from the spotlights the cops were using, it was too dark for her to clearly read anything on the card. Tony just shoved it into her back pocket.

"My boss is Aiden Warner," he added. Then waited, as if the name was supposed to mean something to her.

It didn't, so she just kept staring back at him. Tony didn't exactly spend her time following the business world. So if his boss was a bigwig, the name didn't ring any bells for her.

"He wants to hire you," Smith continued determinedly. "I have a car ready, so if you will just come this way..." He motioned to the right. To the right, where a black limo waited about fifty yards away.

Tony blinked. "Uh, no." She would not be going that way. Tony had seen the limo arrive earlier and had figured it belonged to a local politician who'd wanted to get his name tied to the discovery of Meridian's body. Knowing the way politicians worked, she'd thought he'd rolled in to do a press conference about finally getting closure for the family. About never giving up on the missing. The usual spiels that she'd heard people in power say dozens of times.

Though since they didn't have the killer yet, she hardly thought there was any closure to discuss on Meridian's case.

"Excuse me?" Smith seemed to be struggling to get his words out. "Did you just say 'no' to me?"

She had. What Tony didn't get was why he seemed so surprised. With a shake of her head, she informed him, "Tacky to bring a limo to a crime scene. You should tell your boss that. Try arriving in something less flashy."

"I...will?" A question. "I'll, um..." He coughed. "I'll tell Aiden you think he's tacky."

She nodded. "You definitely should tell him. Less is more. And as to the offer of a ride, no, I'm not getting into a car with a stranger." Seriously? "That's not how my world works. Cute, though. Really." No, it wasn't. She huffed out a breath and fought to hold onto her composure. Meridian had gotten to her. "I'm not looking for a job at the moment. I'm just finishing up a scene." Which he should be able to tell—clearly—on his own. "So thanks, but no thanks."

Smith's mouth opened, then closed.

"Good night." She turned away. Banshee instantly turned with her.

"But...but people don't tell Aiden Warner no!"

"Really? That's odd." She kept walking. "Could have sworn I just did."

***

She wasn't coming to the car.

Aiden Warner watched as Dr. Antonia Rossi turned away from Smith and strode toward her small sedan. She opened the passenger side first and let her dog jump inside. Bending low, she spoke to the dog, rubbed it behind its ears, then shut the door. Moving with an elegant, if somewhat stiff grace, she headed around the car to the driver's side.

Got inside.

And drove away.

Well, sonofabitch.

So much for the first meet and greet with the doctor of the dead.

The back door of the limo opened. Clearing his throat, Smith slid inside. He tugged the door shut behind him.

Aiden's fingers tapped on his thigh. "She's not with you."

"Astute of you to notice."

He raised a brow. There was enough illumination in the back of the vehicle for Smith to easily see his expression. An expression that Aiden knew would clearly say...*What. The. Fuck?* Smith had been given one job. One.

Get Dr. Rossi in the limo.

"Ahem. Sorry, but she said no, boss." Smith shrugged. "Not like I could physically force the woman into the vehicle. Pretty sure that shit is illegal. There are rules, you know. Rules that even people with more money than God have to follow."

His fingers stopped tapping. "You mentioned me specifically by name?"

"Yeah, and I don't think your name did jackshit for her. Didn't seem to recognize it at all." Smith settled back along the leather seat. "I don't think you two run in the same circles."

No, they didn't. That was the point. "Her circle is the dead."

Smith reached for a glass decanter. "That's creepy as hell."

"*That's* the reason I need her." And she'd just fallen perfectly in his lap. Or, she should have. Because he'd been in Biloxi on business. Another casino opening. Another hotel acquisition. And then, as if fate had decided to smile on him, he'd learned that the target of his latest hunt was there, too.

Antonia Rossi. So he'd gotten her exact location. Easy enough when you had money to burn. And he'd gone straight to her. Since he didn't want any of the nearby reporters snapping his picture, he'd asked Smith to handle the meet and greet. A mistake, obviously. While his head of security—and best friend—excelled in many areas, clearly this was not one of them.

"I think she found the kid." Smith's voice was different. A little ragged around the edges. Very unusual for him. His fingers trembled a bit around the decanter. "Saw something— someone?—get loaded into the back of a black van before I approached your doc. And I swear, I think the woman was crying."

He stiffened. Aiden also noticed that her car had just driven away. *No, you can't run.* He leaned forward and lowered the privacy screen that separated him from the driver. "Follow her." A curt order. "Not close enough to scare her, but do not even consider losing her for a moment. I want her vehicle in sight at all times." He knew where her rental house was located, but what if she went somewhere else? What if she left town entirely? If she'd already closed this case, then she could disappear on him. Sometimes, she vanished from the spotlight for weeks. The woman had a tendency to go off-grid, and now that she was within his grasp, he couldn't lose her.

He *wouldn't* lose her.

"Are you sure this is a good idea?" Smith asked him. "Maybe you should just, you know, cool down a bit. Send her an email on Monday. An official notice with an offer of employment. Do something *normal*. Not like, oh, I don't know, stalking the woman to a *crime scene* and trying to get her into your car. FYI, I'm pretty sure she thought that was super creepy. And, ah, trashy. She definitely thought the limo was trashy. Or, actually, maybe she called it tacky."

"A limo? Tacky?"

"Tacky at a crime scene. The doc thought it was something one should not do. Driving a limo up when there was a murder. Just passing along her opinion. Not mine."

Aiden settled back in his seat. He'd had a reason for arriving in the limo. "The car would have given us privacy to talk. The last thing I wanted was for a reporter to film me trying to convince her to take my case." He kept his voice emotionless even though Smith, of all people, would know just how emotionally impacted he really was by the situation. *I need Dr. Rossi.* "I have emailed her, and you know that. I have also sent her several official letters offering employment. She hasn't responded." He got that the Ice Breakers were slammed. Their sudden notoriety had propelled them from the shadows straight into the spotlight.

The Ice Breakers. A cold case solving group that had started online. All from different backgrounds. All driven by, Aiden suspected, their own demons. He could certainly understand that. His dark demons tormented him every single day. Their group had come together to try and solve cases that had gone ice cold.

They'd had a streak of successes. Such big stories that the media had started to run profiles on them. And so big that everyone with a lost loved one or an unsolved murder in their past was clamoring to get the attention of the Ice Breakers.

Add me to the clamoring list.

"She seemed tired. Even as she, ah, politely said for you to go to hell."

He'd been in hell for a long time. "That's what she said?"

"Technically, she said to tell you 'thanks, but no thanks' but the rest of the message was in her tone. Hard to miss it."

"Her tone said for me to go to hell?" Why the fuck did he find that intriguing? *Because no one ever tells me that.*

"Yep." Smith took a long gulp of his drink. "I even mentioned to her that most people don't usually tell you no."

"I'm sure she loved hearing that," Aiden murmured. He found himself intently curious about everything Antonia—Dr. Rossi—had said.

"I don't think she's gonna take the job." A warning. "You need to move on and find someone else."

Hardly the first time that Aiden had been told to move on when it came to this case. But, as before, he wasn't in the mood to take the advice. There were some things that just couldn't be forgotten. "I've tried other people. They weren't her. They didn't get the job done." Because everyone knew that Dr. Rossi found the dead.

"You just gonna toss more money at her?"

Maybe.

"One day, you're gonna find someone you can't buy."

"Absolutely." He just hoped like hell that today wasn't that day. Because he needed Antonia Rossi, and he would do whatever it took in order to get her on his case.

***

She didn't quite understand why the casino was open twenty-four hours. When Tony walked past the rows and rows of slot machines, they were empty. The whole place seemed empty.

She'd gone to her little rental house, but hadn't been able to stay inside. As soon as she'd walked through the door, the place had felt chilled. Or maybe she'd felt chilled. Too dark. Too quiet. An escape had been needed. She'd thought the bright lights of one of the nearby casinos might push her darkness away.

But, instead, she just found more emptiness. Sure, there was plenty of light. Glaring lights. Too bright. And a few people sitting at the poker tables. That was it. Hardly the distraction her soul needed. But she'd take what she could get.

Tony sat down, not at a poker table, but in the blackjack section. Gambling wasn't a hobby. Wasn't a vice for her. Wasn't something she usually did at all, but what the hell? Why not give it a go?

The dealer exchanged her cash for some chips, and Tony glanced to her right as someone else sat down to play.

A familiar someone else.

Smith Sanders.

Fabulous.

He pushed some cash toward the dealer, just as someone else sat down on Tony's left. Her gaze slid to the left side, and she saw the black sleeve of a man's suit coat. His wrist. His long, tanned fingers. Her nostrils flared as she caught the rich, masculine scent that clung to him, and a sudden, almost dangerous awareness flooded through her. The kind of awareness that she suspected a deer felt when it was being stalked by a hunter.

The men put down their chips. The dealer slid out the cards.

Her gaze snapped back to the dealer. A blond woman, pretty. Maybe mid-twenties. With steady hands and bright red nails. A warm smile curved the dealer's lips, and when she looked at the man on Tony's left, that smile lit the woman's eyes. She leaned forward a bit, letting her cleavage dip. Was that flirty move because she was interested in the man? A man Tony hadn't actually *seen* yet. Not his face, anyway. She'd avoided looking directly at him. Instinct. Preservation.

But maybe the dealer was being flirtatious and sexy because she wanted to distract the guy. Distraction would mean he probably would be more likely to lose on his hand. Good for the house, right?

"Oh, my God." A sudden whisper from the dealer.

Tony had been looking at her own cards. A ten and a Jack. Not too bad.

"You're the new owner. Aiden Warner." Breathless. Husky. Awed.

"I am." From the corner of her eye, Tony saw Aiden wave his strong hand over his cards to indicate that he didn't want more.

"You're even better looking in person," the dealer told him in a rush.

Really? The flirtation was taking over the whole hand. Pain beat behind Tony's right eye. This was not the escape she'd hoped to get.

Smith tapped to show he wanted another card, and an elegant queen was placed before him.

"Bust," he groused. "The ladies always do me in."

Tony wanted the bout over. She didn't even care about her winnings. Fleeing was her priority. Standing quickly, Tony prepared to make a dash for the nearest exit.

"And the lady wins," the dealer announced.

All the cards had been turned over.

The dealer pushed the chips toward Tony.

"Thanks." She scooped them into her hands and turned from the table. She'd cash those babies out someplace else in the casino.

"What's the rush?" A deep, dark voice that belonged to Aiden Warner. "Aren't you feeling lucky?"

The low taunt stopped her as nothing else would have. In general, Tony wasn't a runner. She didn't flee from trouble. Not her style. She preferred to confront things head on. But this wasn't your typical night—not even typical in her unusual life—so she'd been having a moment of weakness.

She didn't like being weak.

Her head lifted and turned toward Aiden even as her hold tightened on the chips. "I don't feel particularly lucky," she informed him flatly. "Because two men are stalking me. That sort of behavior tends to make a woman feel exceedingly unlucky."

A sharp gasp came from nearby. The dealer. It was instantly followed by a passionate, "*There is no way Mr. Warner is stalking—*"

"Not two men," Aiden cut in smoothly. "Just me. Smith tagged along because he's my chief of security." He rose, too, and Tony realized that he towered over her. Power and arrogance in a too expensive suit. A man who spent too much time at fancy offices and in towers looking down on the rest of the world. A man who probably had no idea of just how violent and twisted life was for most people.

For her.

She could see the strength in his shoulders. They stretched out his suit coat. A faint line of stubble covered his jaw. She was sure the dealer found that stubble sexy. He was tall, dark, and handsome, the old stereotype to a perfect T. His thick, dark hair was lighter than her own, almost more brown than black with faint highlights that were caught by the overhead lights. His amber eyes stared back at her with a faint hint of curiosity.

And with far, far too much satisfaction.

Just what did he have to be satisfied about? She was preparing to leave him in her dust.

"I have a business proposal for you, Dr. Rossi," Aiden told her.

Goose bumps rose on her arms. His voice was really quite something when he pitched it so low. Deep and rumbling, it slid over her in the best— no, correction, the worst—way. She didn't want to find anything about this man to be arousing.

Yet, she did. Because when she looked at him, one thought slid through her mind. *Sin.*

This man is built for sin.

Temptation. Recklessness. Passion.

In other words, a born heartbreaker.

"I have a room upstairs," he continued.

Well, of course, he did. He owned the casino. Hadn't that been established already by the helpful and flirtatious dealer?

"I would very much like to talk privately with you."

"Sorry, but it's past my bedtime." Such a lie. She had trouble sleeping most nights. The dead had a tendency to haunt her. Wasn't that one of the reasons she was out right then? Because she didn't want the darkness to surround her.

"I will triple the winnings in your hands if you just give me five minutes."

Tony glanced down at her winnings. "Triple, huh?"

"Yes." Confident. Casual. As if money meant nothing to him. Probably because it didn't.

"Can you hold out *your* hands for me?" Tony asked him sweetly. She could do sweet. Occasionally. Her friends would say that when she did sweet, though, you really needed to watch out.

A frown tugged at his rather noble brow, but he lifted his hands and offered up his palms to her. The calluses that she saw on his fingers surprised her, but only momentarily as she deduced their source. *Probably from working out.* That would fit with his lifestyle. She lifted her own hands and poured the chips into his palms. "There you go," she told him with a cold smile. "Payment for you to leave me alone."

Another gasp from the dealer. It absolutely sounded as if the woman might be choking this time. Mildly concerned, Tony glanced back at her.

"You—he...*it's Aiden Warner.*"

Yes, she knew exactly who the man was. Tony focused on him once more. "No more stalking. It's an exceedingly unattractive thing to do." With that, she marched away from him and headed between the line of slot machines. She'd take the elevator back down to the lobby and get the hell out of there. Surely, there would be a cab waiting. It had been easy enough to snag one on her way to the casino. Correction...casino-slash-hotel. The mammoth building was both.

But when she slipped into the elevator and turned to jab the button for the first floor, Aiden stepped into the too tight space with her.

Tony noticed that he'd ditched the chips.

Ignoring him, she crossed her arms over her chest.

"I haven't made a good impression on you."

The doors slid closed.

"No shit," she replied. Tony could feel his eyes on her. The elevator just needed to go down three floors. Three little floors. How long could that possibly take?

"I apologize. I understand that I approached you in the wrong manner, but you had been ignoring my emails and letters, so when I realized we were in the same city, I seized the moment."

The elevator was far too slow. Three floors should not take this long.

"Have you read my emails? Or the notes?"

"No." Truth. "I've been working three cases, and the group has been inundated. You can't even imagine how many people have been contacting us." This was something that ate at her and wouldn't stop. *So many are lost*. Her head jerked toward him. "Every single year, over 600,000 people go missing. And I wish—*I wish* I could help find them all, but I can't." Her arms dropped to her sides. Her hands clenched into fists because she'd just had an image of too small bones being uncovered from black dirt. *Dammit*. She blinked quickly. Tony absolutely refused to cry. Especially in front of strangers. Aiden Warner definitely counted as a stranger.

"My twin brother is one of those missing."

More blinking. Her gaze shot to the floor so she wouldn't have to look at him. Wasn't this what she'd been afraid of? Hearing about his victim. Because when she heard about the victims, as soon as someone became personal to her, she was hooked. Another lost soul to haunt her at night. "I'm sorry," she said, and Tony meant it.

"He disappeared when we were seventeen, and despite the thousands and thousands of dollars that I have spent hiring private investigators over the years, he has never been found. It's like he just disappeared from the entire face of the planet one day. Disappeared while life kept going for everyone else."

The elevator dinged. The doors opened. She should walk through them. She *should*. But it was already too late. It had been too late the moment Aiden Warner stepped onto the elevator with her.

"I can have a driver take you back to your rental house."

All she had to do was walk out of that elevator. Stride boldly forward. But she'd already made a fatal mistake.

Tony had found out about the victim. There was a reason someone else in the Ice Breakers read the emails and the letters from families and desperate friends, even when the notices were addressed to her. As soon as a victim became known to her, as soon as the person whispered through her mind...

His twin.

Swallowing, she glanced over at Aiden. She studied his handsome face. The high cheekbones. The long, strong nose. The jaw that seemed carved from granite itself. Window dressing. All of it. Gorgeous, sexy window dressing. What really mattered to her were his eyes. And when she looked into his gaze, she saw pain staring back at her. Pain and grief and a dark, simmering rage.

Aiden Warner was angry at the world.

She could relate to that.

"Was he your identical twin?" A careful question.

"Yes."

So she was staring at an exact copy of the victim. Victims always became personal for her, but this was different. A whole other level of different. Because she was staring at him and imagining this man...

Small bones covered in dirt.

The elevator doors began to slide closed.

Aiden threw up his hand to stop them. "I won't trouble you again."

He wouldn't. But the ghost of his brother would. "Take me upstairs."

She saw him tense.

"You can have five minutes, free of charge." Such a lie. Tony already knew she'd be giving him far more than five minutes.

But Aiden didn't move.

So she did. "Don't make me change my mind." Sighing, she reached for his arm so that he would stop blocking the elevator doors from closing again.

Except, when she touched him, something happened. Something she didn't expect and something that spelled trouble for her. A shock of awareness. A bolt of almost electric tension. She touched him and knew that her world was about to change.

When she'd poured her chips into his palms, she hadn't actually touched him. She'd been very careful. This time, though, her hand curled around his arm. Even through the fabric of his coat, Tony could feel the heat emanating from his body. That heat slid around her. Through her. It warmed all the cold spaces that she kept locked inside. Slipped past the ice that shielded her from the rest of the world.

"Oh." A breath. Her hand fell away from him. "That could be problematic."

He stared at her, never once changing his fierce expression. Without another word, Aiden pulled a keycard from his pocket. He slid it over the small, black screen on the elevator's control panel, and then hit the button for the top floor.

The doors closed.

Her fate had been sealed.

CHAPTER TWO

"What made you change your mind?" Aiden was genuinely curious. One minute, she'd basically gone from telling him to kiss her ass to...well, giving him a chance.

And, yes, he'd screwed up. Handled things in his usual bulldozer manner when he should have tried some finesse. But finesse had never been his strong suit. That had been more his brother's domain. His brother had been a king when it came to charm. No one had ever been able to resist Austin.

"I haven't changed my mind. Yet. I'm not saying I will help you. I'm just saying..." She ignored the giant windows that looked out onto the city and eased down onto the couch. "I'll hear your story." One sneaker-clad foot swung back and forth. "I didn't say I was taking the case. As I told you—"

"Six hundred thousand people go missing every year." A statistic he already knew. Not like he hadn't done his homework.

"The longer a person has been missing, the more unlikely it is that you will find that person alive." Her voice flowed, low and clear. Not husky.

Not breathy. More like almost somber musical notes.

He paced closer to her. Over the course of his research, he'd seen numerous pictures and videos of Antonia Rossi. He'd even watched quite a few of her lectures online. She was brilliant, no doubt about it. The woman possessed a true fistful of degrees, but her specialty was forensic anthropology. Or, it had been, until she and her cadaver dog, Banshee, had joined up with the Ice Breakers. Now, she focused on the missing, and the dead.

Antonia was the person he needed. Aiden was certain of that fact. "Name your price, Dr. Rossi. I will gladly pay it."

Tendrils of dark hair had come loose from her long braid. "Two things. First, just call me Tony. Everyone does. I like that way better than Antonia or Dr. Rossi. Second, I don't have a price." Her eyes—the most magnificent, dark eyes he'd ever seen in his life—locked straight on him. "I don't have a price," she repeated. "I don't take cases because I'm being offered obscene amounts of money to do so."

He inched closer to her, unable to stop himself. "And you think I was going to offer you an obscene amount?"

One hand waved vaguely in the air. "I'm pretty sure this is the governor's suite or the presidential suite or something like that. We could have talked in a normal office, but you're not a normal guy. You wanted to remind me that you had money to burn, so you brought me to your fanciest room in an effort to impress me." A roll of one delicate shoulder. "So, yes, I suspect you wouldn't offer some nice, normal amount of money. It would have to fall into the obscene category."

"But you can't be bought."

Her head inclined toward him. Her lips—full and free of lipstick—curled just the faintest bit. Not a real smile. More like a tease of what could come. "You seem to get stuck on that concept."

Yes, he did. With good reason. "Because in my experience, everyone can be bought."

"Well, then it must be super fun for you to meet me, since I'm not everyone."

Again, he stepped toward her. The woman seemed to pull him closer with every moment that passed. He'd met more beautiful women. A reminder that he *had* to give himself. He had met them at some point, surely he had, because Tony wasn't beautiful in a conventional way. She didn't have glass-sharp cheekbones or a perfect, oval face. But, she was just...

Striking.

Vivid.

Bold.

And as he stared at her, damn if he could remember *anyone* who was more attractive. *I've met supermodels. Actresses. And I can't remember their faces right now.*

He could only see her. Her long hair—which he was sure would be incredible when it curled loosely around her shoulders. Her golden skin. Her wide, deep eyes. The intelligence that burned so brightly in her gaze.

She was nothing like he'd expected. Everything he suddenly needed to have.

"You are staring awfully hard." Her eyebrows rose in inquiry. "Is that something you typically do?"

She also called bullshit when she saw it. A trait he admired. "I'm trying to figure out how I can convince you to help me. If money doesn't work, I don't exactly have anything else to offer."

"You think the only thing you bring to the table is money?" A somewhat sad shake of her head. "That's not how you should see yourself."

It was the way the world saw him. Everyone came to him with their hands out.

A soft sigh escaped her. "Tell me about your brother. I'm running on adrenaline and trying to hide from the crash that I know is coming. You're currently a wonderful distraction, but I can only be distracted for so long."

His eyes narrowed. "Are you always this blunt?"

"I've found it saves time."

"Well, by all means..." And he sat down right next to her.

She stiffened. "There are like seven other chairs in this ginormous suite."

"And there is a couch that is plenty big enough for two." A pause. "Unless you're just uncomfortable being close to me?" He wanted to be close to her. Almost like a compulsion.

An obsession.

"No. Sit. Your suite, you can sit anywhere you want." She locked those eyes on him, and up close, they were even more intense. "Tell me your story."

"Most people know the story, even though it happened fifteen years ago."

"Fifteen years ago, I was in high school. My head was buried in a book, and I'm sorry, but I don't know your story."

Fair enough. "My twin brother and I went to our family's cabin in North Carolina. We drove out on our own that summer. We were just going to do some fishing. Jump in the lake. Get drunk on the beer we'd snuck up with us." An exhale. "Something went wrong. Only one of us came back from the trip."

Her gaze never wavered. "I'll need more than that."

The problem was that he didn't have a whole lot more to offer. "Friday night was fine. Totally normal. Saturday—I guess I must have had too much to drink because I passed out. Just remember bits and pieces of that night."

She nodded. There was no judgment on her face. No change of expression. Tony just waited.

"When I woke up..." *God.* Sharing this story, just pushing out the details in a cold tone felt brutal. But he finally had Tony there, and he wasn't going to blow his chance by holding back. She wanted the grim details? He'd give them to her. "I was upstairs in bed. I walked down the stairs, calling for my brother, and I stopped cold on the fourth step." He could still see everything. Remember every single moment of that morning. The night? Nearly gone completely. Small flashes. Bodies dancing. Voices laughing. Darkness.

But when it came to that terrible morning...*I can remember everything.* "The first floor of the cabin looked like it had been hit by a tornado. Furniture was smashed. Plates were shattered. Beer bottles littered the floor. The front door was wide open, and the window near it had been smashed." Aiden paused, remembering. "The curtains blew in the breeze."

She leaned closer to him.

His nostrils flared as he greedily drew in her scent. A scent that seemed to calm some of the tension in him. "My brother wasn't there. I called and called, but he didn't answer. I ran outside, I searched for hours, but even though the truck we'd driven to the cabin was still there, he wasn't." A deep breath.

"Why didn't you call the police immediately?"

Not like it was his first time to field that particular question. It was the one everyone always asked. "Because my brother often made...friends. Kids he'd meet that he'd like to party with. He had a reputation for being the wild brother, while I was supposed to be the good one." *But I'm not. I never was.* "Our parents were already pissed at him because he'd gotten in trouble at school right before the semester ended. I was a lightweight when it came to drinks. I thought maybe...maybe I just had a few beers and crashed hard, and while I was out, he kept partying with the kids from town. Trust me, it was not the first time my brother had a crazy party at that cabin. For all I knew, he'd gone to walk off a hangover. Or he'd gone to some pretty girl's house for the night. I didn't know, so I searched and I waited."

Her head tilted to the left as she regarded him with those deep, deep eyes of hers. "Just how long did you wait before you called anyone?"

Too fucking long. "I went back to the cabin, and I started cleaning up."

"*Dammit.*"

"Right. Yes. I was told that, later. That I'd compromised evidence. That I'd screwed up a crime scene. The local police chief chewed my ass out." His hands fisted near his thighs. "But when I cleaned up, I just thought I was helping my brother. Cleaning up one of his messes, you know?" But he hadn't been. He'd been getting rid of evidence. Helping to cover the tracks of whoever had hurt his brother. "And that was when I found the blood."

"How much blood?"

When he closed his eyes, Aiden could still see the stain in his mind. "Too much."

"That's not really a quantifiable amount."

His back teeth clenched. "Enough that I don't see how anyone could survive that much blood loss. Is that better for you? It was a giant circle, and it had sunk heavily into the carpet. I didn't notice it at first because someone had tossed a blanket over it. I only saw the blood when I went to pick up the blanket and when I lifted it, the underside of the thick blanket was wet and red and—*you don't survive that.*"

Silence.

His gaze locked on her face. "I called the police then."

"I assumed you did."

He couldn't read her, and that drove him crazy. There were no emotions reflected in her expression. No tells that gave away her thoughts. Did she believe what he was saying? "The police—the local chief told me to get out of the cabin. To stay outside and wait for him. He thought the attacker might still be there."

Her lashes flickered.

Finally. A tell. And, yes, he'd known this part was coming. It always did. At least from investigators. Over the years, he'd hired plenty of them. *But she will be different*. He knew that in his gut. "It wasn't me," he gritted out.

"Excuse me?" Polite. Careful.

"I didn't kill my brother." No sense bullshitting around this point. Better to get this part out of the way now. "I loved him. I would never have done something like that to him."

Her expression changed to show mild surprise. "I don't remember accusing you of murder. I just asked to hear your story. But I am glad you went ahead and cleared that up for me, though..." Her lush lips pursed. "If you don't really remember the events of that night, how can you be certain you *didn't* kill him?"

Cold pulsed through his veins. "I didn't have so much as a drop of blood on me. The police looked. No blood. No scratches. No bruises."

A roll of one delicate shoulder. "That's hardly what I would call overwhelming evidence of your innocence. Especially if you showered that morning. And I'm assuming you did. You woke up, you felt like crap. So you decided to hop in the shower to see if you would feel better. That's what most people do, and I bet you did it, too."

Yes, he had.

"So the blood would have washed away."

"The drains were checked, okay? There was a whole crime scene team who came out."

"Were they very thorough? Did they know what they were doing? Or were they from some small town that had never worked a major murder investigation before?"

When he didn't answer, she nodded. "That means, unfortunately, that despite their best intentions, they probably overlooked important elements of the crime. Things that could have proven useful, but now, fifteen years later, all those elements will probably be gone."

"I didn't kill my brother," he repeated once more.

"You don't remember if you killed him," she corrected. "That's probably one of the things that eats at you the most, isn't it?" And, surprising the hell out of him, Tony reached over and touched his hand. Her soft fingers curled over his clenched fist. Her touch seemed to burn right through him. No, not burn him. Mark him. "You worry," she added in the voice that would haunt him, "deep inside, you fear that you might have done something terrible to the person who was the closest to you in the world. And that's why you keep hunting for him. You hope so desperately that he's not dead. That some miracle happened."

Her touch made him feel too unsettled. But she was wrong about one thing. His brother had to be dead. "The blood was his."

"Yes, I'm sure it was tested. But even with that, the hope is still there, isn't it? The hope is always there. It clings so stubbornly." Sadness darkened her eyes even more. "The case I was on tonight...The mother never gave up looking, she never gave up thinking that her daughter would come home, even when I told her that I was going out with Banshee on my search." A click of her throat as Tony swallowed. "Banshee doesn't find the living. Banshee cries when she finds the dead."

"Do you cry, too?" A question that just came from him, unbidden.

"Sometimes. The girl tonight—small bones in the dirt—she wrecked me." A heavy sigh.

And damn if he didn't want to pull her into his arms and just hold the woman.

What the actual fuck? He'd been the one revealing the most painful time of his life, and now he wanted to comfort her.

"Do you have any wine in this pretentious place or do I need to go back downstairs and hit the bar?" Her hand pulled back.

Instantly, *his* hand unfisted and reached for hers. His fingers curled around hers. Swallowed hers.

"What are you doing?" Tony frowned at their hands.

"I have no fucking clue." Touching her. Feeling warmth shoot through his fingers, up his arm, and through his whole body.

Her breath whispered out. "When I took your hand, I was trying to comfort you."

"Why?" *And why do I want to take away all of your pain?* Pain that seemed to cloak her like a shadow.

"Because I was sorry you had lost your brother." Her gaze remained on their joined hands.

"I was trying to comfort you, too." At least, he thought that was what he'd been doing. "My timing was shit, wasn't it?"

Her long, dark lashes lifted.

He would *never* get used to her gaze. It hit him with the force of a punch.

"You went to hell tonight, and when you came out, I was standing there, demanding you help me." Aiden nodded even as he felt disgust fill him. "Ask anyone, and they'll tell you I'm a bastard. Cold to the core. I look after my own self-interests and tell the rest of the world to fuck off. But then, I guess you don't have to ask anyone, do you? I proved that to you from the very first moment." He let her go. Rose. Paced because he needed to put some distance between them.

But he could feel her gaze on him, and when he swung back around, she still perched comfortably on the couch, loose tendrils of her dark hair sliding over her cheek, as she studied him.

"Oh." She blinked. "I thought you were going to get my wine." And one hand made a *shoo* gesture, as if she were shooing him toward the promised wine.

He didn't move. "There have been plenty of other people who suspected I killed my brother."

"Um, and you said you didn't. Though you have no actual memory of that night so..."

So you might be guilty as hell. Those words hung in the air, unspoken. Understood.

His mouth opened. Then closed. Then opened once more as he struggled to figure out what to say to her. "And you're not scared? You just want to drink wine with me?"

Now she rose. Didn't approach him, but instead stood by the couch. "Do you intend to harm me?"

"*Never.*" And the idea of anyone hurting her made a rough fury surge through him.

"Excellent to know, especially because I am considering taking your case."

Now his mouth nearly hit the floor. "What?"

"That's a bar, right? Looks like a bar." She walked past him. Her shoulder brushed his arm. Heat lanced him. An undeniable, shocking attraction.

Fuck, that would be a problem.

She kept going, heading toward what was, indeed, a wet bar in the corner of the room. Four wine glasses waited to the left of the sink, and a refrigerator hummed softly from beneath the bar. Her hand reached out, and she opened the fridge door. "Hmmm." Tony pulled out a small bottle of wine. "I'm sure this will cost a fortune, but I doubt you'll even notice it."

Bemused, he watched as she opened the wine and poured the contents in two glasses. Tony picked up the glasses and turned toward him.

"Oh." A frown pulled at her full lips. "Am I supposed to be drinking alone? Because you're still standing there."

"I don't drink."

"You don't?"

"Not after that night. I never want to lose a night again."

And the frown vanished. "You certainly passed that test with flying colors." She put his glass down but saluted him with her own. Then she took a quick sip.

"You...tested me?" He couldn't quite figure her out. Usually, he was good at sizing up people. Figuring out their motivations. Then using those motivations against them.

"I test everyone. Don't even know how to stop doing it. But then, when you work in the business that I do, trust is hard, so you're always looking for lies. And, sadly, they are usually there." Another sip. "I don't drink a lot, just so you know. But it really has been a bitch of a day. First, I spent too many hours in the dirt and found too many of my own ghosts, then this demanding..." Her gaze darted around the room. "I don't know how much money you have—millionaire? Billionaire? Whatever—this demanding guy insists that I listen to his story. I was trying to avoid listening because the minute a case becomes personal to me, it's in my head. The case gets in there, and it gets stuck." Softer. Sadder. "It will haunt me from now on. They all haunt me." Another sip. She put the glass down. "I'll take the case."

"You will?"

"But I make you no promises. I am not a miracle worker. The longer one has been missing, the harder it is to—"

"Are you fucking serious right now? You'll take the case?" He bounded toward her. Way too eager. "Why? Because I passed some crazy test and didn't take a drink?" Aiden needed to know exactly what he'd done to win her over.

More, he wanted to understand her because he just didn't.

Tony's head tipped back as she stared up at him.

"I offered you any amount of money you wanted, and you said no. I turn down a drink, and you say yes. That makes no sense to me." She didn't make sense.

"I have been told that I don't always make sense to people. That's okay, most people don't make sense to me, either."

Bemused, he could only stare at her.

"I'm taking the case because you are real to me. I see your pain, and I truly am sorry for what you've lost." Her hand rose. Pressed to his chest.

Marked him straight to his soul. Every time she touched him, that was what it felt like—a mark.

"Whatever happens, don't expect your pain to magically end. If anything, it will probably get worse before this is all over," Tony warned him.

Doubtful. "Finally getting the truth won't be worse. It's living in the darkness and not knowing that's the hardest."

"I've been told that before." A half-smile lifted her lips, but the movement held only sadness.

"But those people were all proven wrong." She glanced down, and surprise flashed on her face, as if she hadn't even realized she'd touched him. Her hand quickly fell away. "Tell me your brother's name."

Pain twisted inside of him. "Austin."

"Austin and Aiden. Guess your parents liked A names, huh?"

"Austin was named after my father. He was the first born, I was the second." The so-called bad twin and the good son. One who liked to stir hell. One who followed all the rules, not that those rules had done much good.

She absorbed that information with a slight incline of her head. "I have some loose ends to tie up on the Duvane case. When I'm done, we can plan to meet again. I will have plenty of questions, and you'll have to make yourself available to the other Ice Breakers."

Whatever it took, he would do.

"I will want you to take me to the cabin in North Carolina," she said. "Wait, does your family still own the place?"

"I own it." There was no family. Not any longer. His parents were dead. His brother...gone. There was only Aiden.

"Good. If you have the space, I can stay there with Banshee."

He had nothing but space.

"I'll want a tour of all the property that you own near the cabin."

Sure. Done. But... "You're not going to find anything there. The land has been searched. There's a big, private lake near the cabin, but it was searched, too. Right after Austin vanished, my father hired divers to go in and look for Austin. They didn't find anything."

"You never know what I might find. If I were a killer and I was looking for the perfect place to hide a body, I'd probably stash my victim somewhere for a bit, and then, once a nearby lake had been thoroughly searched and was off everyone's radar, I'd weigh the body down and let it sink beneath the surface. After all, why would you ever search the same place twice?"

His breath froze.

"That's what happened tonight. Where I found my victim? The area had been searched before, so her killer had to bring her back after the initial search was concluded. He had to be watching. Paying such careful attention. That's what killers do, though. Especially when they're closer than you ever want them to be. They always keep watch."

He could not look away from Tony.

"Sorry." She grimaced. "I've been told that I don't have the best conversational skills in the world. You probably aren't interested in knowing what I would do if I was a killer. Or in hearing about how killers behave."

"I am interested in every single thing about you," he rasped. An absolute truth. She fascinated him.

"You're interested in knowing where I would hide bodies? Like that's not a red flag." Clearly, she was trying to lighten the heavy mood.

He didn't mind the heaviness. There were lots of red flags where he was concerned. She just hadn't seen them yet. Soon enough, she would. Though he had gotten very good at hiding most of his bad traits from the rest of the world. A necessity for survival.

"You should consider trying to lighten up occasionally." She studied him with her dark gaze. "If you don't, if you let the darkness pull you down too much, it will suffocate you. Trust me, I know what I'm talking about." She tucked a lock of loose hair behind her ear. "Thanks for the wine. And for the distraction. Time for me to go before I crash." She turned for the door.

She'd only taken two steps when Aiden heard himself say, "You can crash here."

Her shoulders stiffened. Her head turned as she glanced over her shoulder at him. "Is that a polite offer because it's so late? One of those, you-can-take-the-spare-room deals? Or are you offering me something more?"

Damn. A low whistle escaped him. "Your honesty is going to take some getting used to."

"I've been told that before, too. But I don't think people ever get used to me." She turned fully toward him. "And you didn't answer."

She was the most honest person he'd ever met. So he'd give her a bit of honesty in return. "I want you."

Her eyes widened, as if his answer had surprised her. Why the hell would she be surprised? She'd asked the question. But because he liked finally being honest with someone, Aiden continued, "Every time I touch you, I feel a surge of heat pour through my body." *And I feel like you're branding me.*

"Mmm. Sounds like you might be catching a fever."

Yes, he feared he was. "Do you have some rule about not sleeping with people you're helping?"

"I have a rule about not sleeping with strangers. And you, Aiden Warner, are still very much a stranger to me. Sex requires trust. I've never been the casual-hookup type. In my line of work, you see how that goes very, very badly, very fast." A hesitation. "So you were offering...sex?"

"I was offering you the spare bedroom. But, just so we are clear, sex will be on the table anytime for me."

What could have been a faint blush slid over her cheeks only to vanish in the next instant. "I don't think I'm really your type. You don't need to romance me in order to get my help. I already told you, I'm in."

Laughter broke from him. Real laughter. The kind that started in your gut and worked its way up in a fast explosion that you could neither stop nor limit. The laughter poured from him, and he couldn't even remember the last time that he'd laughed this way.

"Well, that's just fabulous. Always the reaction I like to elicit from a handsome man."

He should stop laughing. He should.

When she hurriedly made her way for the door and *opened* said door, he did stop laughing. And he rushed his ass after her. His hand slammed against the door, shoving it closed. "My apologies."

"For slamming the door shut? Yes, you should apologize. Clearly, I was on my way out."

She wasn't looking at him. He studied her profile. Memorized her. "I laughed because I don't think any sane man would ever *romance* you in order to get your help."

Her head turned toward him.

He got lost in her gaze. Dammit. *Focus. Speak.*

He didn't. He couldn't.

"You're staring."

"Because you're beautiful." A growled response.

"No, I'm not. Charm isn't necessary with me."

He sucked in a breath and could have sworn he tasted her. No, he *wanted* to taste her. "Fine. You're right. Beautiful is boring, and I don't think you can ever be boring. Not even if you tried."

"You have obviously never listened to my lectures on skeletal analysis."

His eyes narrowed. "Stop fascinating me."

"Stop being fascinated by skeletal analysis."

He almost laughed again. Dammit. "You're vivid and bold. Striking. You have the kind of face that will haunt a man." Aiden already knew she was going to haunt him. "I was offering the spare room, but any time you want more, all you have to do is say the word."

She...she leaned up on her toes.

He leaned toward her, thinking she meant to kiss him. But she didn't. And, yes, he'd been way too eager. Only instead of kissing him, her mouth moved toward his ear. Her breath lightly teased him as she whispered, "If I said the word, you wouldn't be able to handle me."

Oh, fuck.

She eased back. "Your hand has to leave the door so I can exit."

Aiden didn't want her leaving. But he lowered his hand because he wasn't the one who took what he wanted and said to hell with the consequences. That had been his brother.

"Thanks for the offer of the spare room, but Banshee is waiting at home. See you soon, Aiden."

She opened the door. Headed into the hallway. It was precious the way she strode so confidently down that corridor toward the elevator. As if he'd just let her walk alone into the night. He stepped into the hallway, shut the door behind him, and headed after her.

Tony paused. "Are you following me?"

He didn't pause. He kept right on walking until he passed her. He pulled out his keycard. "You mean am I gallantly escorting you down to the parking garage and then giving you a ride home? Yes. Yes, I am."

"There are taxis near the front of the casino."

"Not very many—if *any*—at this hour." He pushed the button for the elevator. Entered when the doors opened. Swiped his card and punched in the button for the parking garage. Without his keycard, the elevator would not start—not from that particular floor. "And without a taxi, as safety conscious as you are, do you think a stroll around two a.m. seems like the best plan?"

"Fine. You can give me a ride." She entered the elevator.

Her scent teased him as she passed. The scent had teased and tempted him before, too, but this time, he stopped to identify it. "Lavender."

Her head turned toward him.

"Light, but it's there." Sexy as fuck. No, it wasn't the scent of lavender that was sexy. It was lavender on Antonia.

"It helps with restlessness. Insomnia. Or it's supposed to."

"You don't feel helped?" The elevator had started to descend. He pulled out his phone and fired off a quick text.

"I'm here with you...at nearly two a.m. So I think you can figure out the answer to that one."

Aiden shoved the phone back into his pocket. "Got a deal for you."

"You seem to always have those."

"Maybe the next time you feel restless and you can't sleep, you try coming to me. Maybe I can help focus that energy. You don't need lavender to help you stay calm." Though on her, the scent was oddly seductive. So very feminine. It just added more to her appeal. "You can have me."

You can have me.

Words that he meant more than she might realize.

"Maybe you should just kiss me," she surprised him by saying. "We can see if this attraction is real or if it will fizzle out in an instant."

Again, she caught him off-guard. Again, she intrigued him. He stalked closer, and his hand rose toward her face. His fingers skimmed over her cheek as his head tilted toward her. "Thought you said I couldn't handle you?" Hadn't those been her seductive, taunting words?

"This isn't handling me. This is just a kiss. To see if there is anything we need to handle at all. Because you might kiss me, and neither of us will feel anything in response."

Aiden had no doubt that he'd feel plenty. After all, he already did. And he wanted her mouth. Those plump lips were slightly parted, and he wanted to taste her. Aiden lowered his head a bit more to close that last bit of distance between them.

The elevator dinged. The doors opened.

"Car's waiting," Smith announced cheerfully. "Good thing I was already down in the parking garage or else you would have been all alone when the doors opened."

Yes, such a fucking good thing.

Locking his jaw, Aiden stepped back. He held Tony's gaze. "We can finish this later."

"If there is something to finish." She side-stepped around him. "Thought you were the muscle," she said to Smith. "Are you his driver, too?"

"For tonight, I am." Smith held up the keys. "So, sorry, but are we all on the same team now? In the kiss-and-be-friends phase?" His dark brows wiggled. "Because I thought you were in the tell-him-to-kiss-my-ass phase before? Have we switched?"

"He caught me at the wrong time before." She marched from the elevator. Stopped at the limo that had been left idling. "Of course, you have to take me out in this beast. Not like a regular, small car would do the trick."

"Bulletproof glass," Smith informed her proudly. "You don't have to worry about a thing."

But her attention swung back to Aiden. "You have to worry about bullets coming at you?"

He had to worry about all sorts of things. Now wasn't the time to get into those pesky details. "Dr. Rossi is going to help me locate my brother."

Smith whistled. "Damn. That must have been some elevator ride."

Asshole. "Want to get behind the wheel?"

"Oh, yeah. Sure." But he didn't get behind the wheel. Instead, he rushed to open the back door for Tony.

She didn't enter the car. She did stop to stare at Smith. "I'm going to *try* and locate Aiden's brother. I make no promises about the success I might or might not have." Biting her lip, she turned her head toward Aiden. "You get that, don't you? This isn't some sure thing. I'm not a crystal ball. I can try. The rest of the team can try. But we may still turn up nothing."

"Hope for the best, expect the worst." Smith nodded. "The way I live every day."

"That's rather...pessimistic," Tony noted.

"Nah. It's just realistic. Bet you've seen plenty of the worst out there, haven't you, doc?"

"Yes." A soft and somewhat sad reply.

Aiden knew she'd seen the "worst" that night when she'd found her little victim. Wanting to comfort her—when he rarely felt that urge with anyone else—Aiden slipped forward. This was the second time he'd wanted to take away her pain. His hand moved to the base of her spine. He felt her stiffen at his touch. "Drive us to Tony's house," he directed Smith.

"Sure thing."

Tony ducked inside the limo. Aiden followed her. And Smith slammed the door behind him.

As soon as they were alone in the back seat, Tony said, "You need a twenty-four, seven bodyguard because you're...?"

"Filthy rich? Owner of half a dozen casinos and hotels?" He waited a beat. "And because I tend to piss people off with incredible ease. Actually, that's a family trait. When my father was alive, he excelled when it came to that skill."

The limo pulled forward.

"But Smith is not technically a bodyguard. He's my head of security. You won't normally find him sticking so close."

"Why is he close tonight?"

"Because he's one of the few people that I trust with you." *Because you are too important.* Because most people didn't know how obsessed he was with his past. Smith knew. Aiden's head legal counsel knew. Both were in his inner circle. As for anyone else...

Tony is too important. I can't let anyone fuck this up for me.

Her gaze darted toward the window beside him. "You and Smith both know where I'm staying."

"Smith and I both know a great deal about you. Necessary research." She sat across from him, looking cool and collected, and he still wanted her mouth.

Correction, he just wanted her, and they were
alone again. Not like Smith could interrupt while
the guy was busy driving. So Aiden kept his gaze
on Tony, and he waited for her attention to shift
back to him. When it did...

"So, want to find out what it will be like?" *Do
not sound too eager.* "Want to see if there's
anything to *handle* when we kiss? Because I sure
as hell do." Because he wanted her on the case,
yes. A million times yes. But he'd also
discovered...

I fucking want her. What he wanted, he got.
Sooner or later.

CHAPTER THREE

She'd waded into dangerous territory, and Tony knew it. She wasn't used to handling men like Aiden Warner. Not just because he moved in circles far away from the quiet life she chose to live, but because the man oozed an animal magnetism and strength. Too good looking. Too strong. Too sexy. He made her want to throw caution to the wind and just see what it would be like to let go of the control she treasured so very, very much.

Sin. Temptation.

But...

That wasn't who she was. She wasn't the woman who had wild affairs with gorgeous strangers. She played it extra cautious around strangers. Even if those strangers came with their own bodyguards. *Especially, if they came with their own bodyguard. Correction...head of security. And why does Aiden need a car with bulletproof glass?*

"Scared?" he challenged.

Now that was an interesting question. Tony leaned back against the leather seat. "Am I supposed to be scared of you?"

"No." An instant response. "You have absolutely nothing to fear from me. I would never hurt you."

No, but he just might destroy her carefully ordered world.

And, yet, she still wanted to kiss him.

She'd been bluffing before, when she gave Aiden that comment about him not being able to handle her. He'd probably had way more lovers than she had. Not that she wanted to compare numbers. But you didn't have to jump into the deep end in order to know that you might sink far and fast. You just had to look over the edge and take a quick peek...

I will sink far and fast with him.

"It's late," she finally decided to say. *Playing it safe, as always.* "And we're almost to my rental." Because it truly was just a short drive down the beach to her place. Biloxi was an interesting area. The sandy shores of the Gulf on one side of the road. An assortment of houses with waving oak trees on the other. A slowed-down pace. Casual. Easy.

Except for the casinos, of course. They tended to liven things up.

"I understand," he murmured.

Did he? Did he get that she was fighting a hard collapse from the events of the last twenty-four hours and she was trying desperately not to make a mistake that might come back to bite her in the ass? She'd already agreed to the case, and if she wasn't careful...

What? You think you'll agree to the kiss and want more?

Yes. She did. That was exactly what she thought.

"In case you change your mind," his deep voice rumbled, "you can kiss me anytime."

"Very, very generous of you." Confident. Bold. That was what he was. "I'm sure you say that to all the ladies."

The limo stopped. *Escape.* She didn't wait for Smith to come around and open the door for her. She leapt for the handle. Her fingers closed around it, but before she could exit the car, Aiden leaned toward her. *His* fingers curled around her wrist. "I don't say that to all of them. But I'm saying it to you."

His touch unnerved her. In a good way that was going to be bad.

She opened the door. Jumped out.

And heard Banshee barking.

Immediately, she froze.

She froze so suddenly that Aiden bumped into her when he exited the vehicle. "Tony?"

Smith climbed from the driver's seat. His head turned toward the house. "Guess your dog hears us, huh? Must be excited to see you."

"No." Her feet inched forward. "That's not her excited bark." She knew Banshee. Tony had carefully trained her dog. She'd spent endless hours with her baby. She knew Banshee's every mood. That was *not* her excited bark. "Something is wrong." Yanking her keys from her pocket, she bounded for the porch steps.

Only to find herself being swung up into Aiden's arms. He lifted her easily, sweeping her off her feet and up against his chest. "No way. You don't *run* inside if something is wrong."

You did if it was your house. If it was your dog in there. "Let me go!"

"Promise you aren't going in without me and I will."

She jerked but his hold was unbreakable. Mental note, he was even stronger than he looked, and he'd looked plenty strong. The kind of strong she'd originally thought he'd gotten from working out at some fancy private gym. "Let. Go."

"I'm coming in there with you."

"Fine, whatever." She could have gotten out of his hold, but it would have required hurting him. She'd been taught a few mean and nasty tricks by her buddy Saint. When it came to mean and nasty, Saint always excelled in those areas. A bounty hunter who'd joined the Ice Breakers, Saint knew how to put fear into the heart of any man. A trait she admired. "Down. Now."

He lowered her. Her body slid against his. His hands remained around her waist, seeming to scorch her skin.

Her breath heaved out. "You don't get to just *grab* me."

"You don't get to just run straight into danger."

"Fine. You run in with me, if that makes you happy."

Smith cleared his throat. "Better plan. Head of security, standing right here. How about *I* go in?"

Banshee barked, even louder.

"Good thing there aren't any nearby neighbors here," Smith continued. "Guessing they'd be pissed."

There were no nearby neighbors. An empty lot had been recently cleared to the right, and a for sale sign perched in front of it. To the left, an older house sat, windows dark, driveway empty. The house next door had been empty ever since she arrived. The rental agent had told her it was available, too, but not booked for this week.

"Banshee only barks like this when something is wrong." She had to get in the house.

"Or when she finds the dead. That's her thing, right?" Smith asked.

Tony crept up the front porch steps. "She cries then." Banshee cried for the dead. She didn't bark. Tony slid the key into the lock. Turned it. With a shaking hand, she pushed open the door. There was no security system at the house, something that had made her uneasy, but she had Banshee, and her German Shephard was often better than any standard security system.

That's why Banshee is freaking out right now.

Smith and Aiden didn't need to worry about going in first. As soon as Tony opened the door, Banshee came charging out.

But she didn't go toward any of them as they clustered on the small porch. Instead, Banshee shot around them and headed for the empty lot.

"Chasing a squirrel?" Smith queried.

A shadow moved from the darkness of that lot. A figure that had been hunched down near a half-demolished bush. The figure leapt upright and raised a weapon at the charging dog.

No! "Banshee, play dead!" Tony screamed.

One of Banshee's favorite games.

Immediately, the dog flattened. She went down on the ground, stiff as could be even as the blast of a gun thundered in the night.

"Not a squirrel." Smith bounded off the porch steps. "Bastard is *running*."

"*What the fuck?*" Aiden grabbed Tony and pushed her toward the safety of the house.

No way was she going in without her dog. Not when some asshole was out there, shooting. "Banshee, to me, *now!*"

Banshee immediately sprang to life, jumping back to her feet, but instead of running to Tony, she looked toward the fleeing, shadowy figure.

"To me!" Tony commanded.

Unable to ignore the command, Banshee surged toward her. She flew up the steps, and Tony crouched low to wrap her arms around her dog. The dog was warm and strong against her, and when Tony's hands flew frantically over the dog's body, she didn't find any wounds.

Someone was shooting at Banshee. Someone was...waiting in the dark? For me?

"Great. The dog's here, now how about you both keep your asses inside?" Aiden growled. "I'm going to help Smith."

"But—"

He was already gone so he didn't get to hear the desperate words she'd been about to say.

But you're not trained. You're not a hunter. Not law enforcement. Didn't matter. He was gone. Rushing into the dark. Tony hurriedly crossed the threshold of the house with Banshee. She closed and locked the front door. Banshee stayed at her side, her body tense and alert.

Tony glanced down at her dog. "How long was he out there?" Just how long had Banshee been barking because an attacker had been lying in wait?

***

"Where the hell did he go?" Aiden demanded when he found Smith spinning around in the empty lot.

"The fuck if I know." Frustration seethed in Smith's voice. "Bastard is fast." He grabbed Aiden. "By the way, are you *insane?* Why the hell are you out here running toward a man armed with a gun?"

"Uh, because you might need help?" An obvious answer.

"I'm the security guy, remember? You're the client who doesn't get his hands dirty. Or have you forgotten who you are *supposed* to be?"

He was not in the mood for games. Some jackass had been waiting for Tony, with a gun. If she hadn't been with Aiden at his hotel suite...*Do not go there. Don't.* "Did you hear a car drive away?"

"No. I think he's on foot."

Dammit. Aiden whirled around. There were too many shadows near the edge of the property. Too many places to hide. And was that an alley snaking back to go behind Tony's rental?

Smith clamped a hand on his shoulder. "You can't stay out in the open. You're putting a target on yourself."

"He's not after me."

"No, he's after *her*. And you need her, so how about you get your ass in that house and make sure she's okay? I'll hunt out here." Smith pulled his gun from the holster he kept strapped to his belt. The loose t-shirt he wore had completely hidden the weapon. Smith was always armed with a variety of weapons. "Gonna fucking shoot at a dog? Not on my watch, you don't get away with that shit."

Jerking his head in agreement, Aiden bounded back for Tony's house. He was getting her—and her damn dog—and they were coming with him back to his hotel suite. No way was he leaving her on her own.

And as he ran back toward her, he wondered...

Who the hell wants to hurt her?

***

Banshee tensed. A low growl built in her throat as she directed her attention at the door. Not the front door. The back door.

"What is it?" Tony whispered. She'd taken the liberty of grabbing a knife from the kitchen. Not like she was just going to hang around without a weapon while some crazy guy was outside shooting. She gripped the handle tightly as she stayed close to her dog.

Banshee growled again and took a few shuffling steps toward the back door.

Tony's breath shuddered out. Her grip tightened even more on the knife. "Someone's back there."

Banshee barked, then raced for the—

A fist slammed into the door behind Tony, the *front* door. She jumped at the pounding of the fist, and even Banshee whirled back around.

"*Antonia!* Unlock the door!"

Aiden. Right. Her breath shuddered out. But if he was at the front door...was Smith at the back? She kept the knife in her right hand and hurriedly flipped the lock on the front door with her left. The door started to swing open. Banshee bumped into Tony's leg as the dog crowded close to her.

Bam. Bam. Bam.

Tony screamed at the sound of the gunfire. Gunfire coming from the back of her house. Her head whipped around so she could peer toward the back door. The rental was a shotgun-style house. The rooms branched to the sides, and with a shotgun house, as the name implied and the old saying went, a bullet fired from the front door would go straight to the back, probably without even hitting anything else.

But the bullet is being fired from the back. Not the front. And it's being fired at the lock.

Fired to break the lock. And it worked because, in the next instance, the rear door was kicked in and a man stood on the threshold, thin tendrils of red hair shooting up from his head. An oversize jacket hung from his thin shoulders. And his hand still gripped his gun.

Her left hand had instinctively grabbed for Banshee. She held the dog's collar tightly even as she still gripped the knife.

"Why couldn't you leave her alone?" he bellowed as his face flushed redder than his hair. "*Why couldn't you let her rest?*" He pointed the gun at her.

"*Play fucking dead, Tony,*" Aiden snarled.

She remembered what she'd told Banshee. Remembered the way Banshee had dropped before the bullet could hit her. And Tony dropped. She hit the floor, and as she slammed down into the wood, she heard thunder echo over her head. Thunder that had come from *behind* her.

Because the man with the red hair and red face hadn't shot at her. Instead, the gunshot had come from behind Tony. *Aiden had fired.*

His bullet slammed into the man's right shoulder and the gun fell from the intruder's fingers to hit the floor even as he screamed in pain. He grabbed for his injured shoulder.

And then—then his whole body jerked and spasmed. More screams tore from him, right before he fell, face-first, onto her floor. When he hit, he kept twitching.

"Taser," Smith said as he stepped inside and pushed aside her broken back door. "Non-lethal method, but sure, you go with the gun, boss. You do you." His gaze swept to Aiden. "All good here?"

"No, nothing is fucking good here," Aiden blasted back. "That fucker just tried to kill Tony." His hands closed around her shoulders, and he hauled her up and turned her toward him. "Antonia?" Softer. More careful. "Are you hurt?"

She still gripped the knife in her right hand. She was surprised she hadn't dropped it when she'd hit the floor. But other than some bruises on her knees and a heart that still raced too quickly, she was perfectly fine.

Banshee bumped Tony with her nose. Her gaze flew to the dog, and Tony scanned her for injuries. "Fine," she breathed. "We're both fine."

A long groan came from the man on the floor.

Her head whipped toward him. Smith had grabbed the guy's discarded gun and tucked the weapon into the waistband of his jeans. "Who the hell is this bastard?" Smith wanted to know. "Any clue?"

Tony swallowed to ease the dryness in her throat. She knew that man's face. "More than a clue." Hadn't she feared this, from the moment she'd seen the tiny bones...and the dirty, small, stuffed rabbit with the bones? A frayed blanket had been wrapped around the bones and the rabbit. A sign of care. Care even when the body had been dumped and hidden. As soon as she'd seen them, she'd suspected...

Meridian was put here by someone who knew her. Someone who had...loved her?

Love could twist and turn. It could destroy.

Sometimes, it could just be sick.

"Who is he?" Aiden demanded. He'd moved to stand protectively between Tony and the groaning man.

She eased to the side so she could see that man again.

His head lifted. Tears streamed down his face. "*Why?*" he gasped. "She...should have just been left alone."

"He's her father," Tony said. "Meridian Duvane's father. The little girl I found." She had to swallow twice to get rid of the lump in her throat. "And I think he's the man who put her in that grave."

A sob broke from the fallen man. He began to bang his head into the wooden floor over and over again. "Should have left her alone. Should have left her alone...Alone..."

And the thing was...Tony didn't know if he meant *she* should have left Meridian to her cold, lonely grave.

Or if he meant...

Do you mean that you should have left her alone, you bastard? Because, yes, you should have.

CHAPTER FOUR

If he hadn't given up booze long ago, Aiden could have sure as hell used a drink. As it was, fury and adrenaline still pumped through his body as he sat in the uncomfortable chair at the small police station.

The scene at Tony's place had turned into a circus. She'd called the cops. They'd swarmed. But so had reporters. He'd been filmed leaving Tony's. Getting into a police car with her. Because, of course, the local cops had wanted him riding down to the station for questioning.

That happened when you shot someone.

"I didn't know you even had a gun on you." Tony's voice. Quiet. Measured. That was how she'd been ever since the attack. Too quiet.

Her dog was at her side. Banshee didn't make a sound. Just remained at attention near Tony. Alert and aware. Aiden wasn't much of an animal lover. They'd never been allowed any kind of pets when he'd grown up. And the dogs he'd seen over the years—the dogs that his mother's friends had—those had always been fluffy dogs with high-pitched barks and giant bows pinned in their fur.

Nothing like Banshee.

The German Shephard had saved Tony's life. Aiden knew it with certainty. If the dog hadn't been barking, she would have gone in that house alone. *And the sonofabitch Clayton Duvane had just been waiting for his moment to attack.*

Only Aiden had been the one to shoot him. "Didn't see a point in mentioning it. I can assure you, I'm quite good with a gun."

"Good enough to put Duvane out of commission and save my life." Her hand stroked over Banshee's head. "And I haven't thanked you for that."

They were in a small conference room. Or maybe it was supposed to be an interrogation room. He didn't know for sure. The police chief had questioned him before, and Aiden had answered honestly, though he knew as soon as his lawyer heard that he was talking about a shooting, the woman would probably lose her mind.

But he didn't have anything to hide.

This time.

"Thank you, Aiden. I don't quite know how I'll be able to repay you for tonight."

He didn't want her gratitude. Aiden started to tell Tony just that but stopped. Why? Because he was a cold-hearted bastard at his core. And maybe it would be handy to have a woman like Tony in his debt. But...*fuck it.* "You're taking my case. I consider that repayment enough." Shocker. Perhaps he did have one or two scruples left.

"I haven't done anything yet."

"You will." Absolute certainty. He lifted his hand. They were standing so close that it was easy to reach out and touch her. His hand curled under her chin. His thumb brushed along the curve of her jaw. To him, her skin felt like silk.

"When you dig up the past, the ghosts come for you." Her deep, intense gaze held his. "You saw that tonight. People want their dirty secrets to stay buried."

"That wasn't a dirty secret you dug up. It was a little girl."

Her lower lip trembled. "I could see the breaks in the bones." Whispered. "I knew she'd been hurt. I'd read an old police report where her mother had reported the father for domestic abuse, but everyone—everyone in the family and even the neighbors—went back to swear that Clayton Duvane was a good man. That it was all a mistake." She swallowed. "I knew when I saw her bones, but the cops were taking over. I was just supposed to find the body. I was going to wait and see if they wanted me to consult more. I didn't want to interfere because if you say the wrong thing, you can slant a whole investigation." She blinked quickly. "But I knew. In my gut, I knew."

And the bastard had come after her. Aiden's finger stroked along her jaw. "This kind of thing happen to you a lot?" Rage still burned inside of him. A darker rage than he'd felt in years. Why? Because Tony shouldn't be in danger. She should be safe.

"There's always some danger when you stir up the past. The people I find—someone hurt them. Someone killed them. Those killers don't like what I do."

Because if it wasn't for Tony finding the victims, the killers would get to go right on living their lives. Hiding in plain sight. "Why do you do it?" Face the danger.

"Someone has to."

But did the someone have to be her? *And since when do I care? I wanted to use her to solve the mystery in my own past.* And now...

"Fuck it," he growled.

His lips took hers. Not a planned, carefully calculated move, as he did so often in his life. But instinctive, almost desperate. Emotions and needs churned through him, and all Aiden knew with certainty was that he needed to kiss this woman. To taste her.

To protect her.

To crave her.

To have her.

Her lips parted beneath his almost instantly. Her hands rose to curl around him. To pull him closer. His tongue thrust into her mouth, and Aiden forgot about the police station. He didn't care that they were in a cramped room that smelled of stale coffee. He only cared about her. The way she felt. The way she gave a soft gasp in the back of her throat. The way she kissed him as if she'd never wanted anyone more.

He kissed her the same way because it was the truth. *Never wanted anyone more.* Need burned through him, seemed to electrify him. Her taste made him crave her all the more. Before Tony, kissing had been a means to an end. A seductive technique. A careful skill.

With her, everything was different. He wasn't using careful seduction. Probably not much skill, either. Just desperate hunger. A fierce desire that she'd unleashed, and he knew it could be dangerous for them both. Aiden just didn't care enough to stop.

He wanted more and more. Wanted to take everything from her. His dick shoved against the front of his pants. She had to feel the damn thing thrusting against her, but Tony just dug her short nails into his arms and pulled him even closer.

His hands curved around her hips. It would be so easy to lift her up and put her on the table. To step between her legs. To touch her, everywhere and...

Banshee bumped him.

Hell.

The dog bumped him a second time.

Tony pulled back. "She's letting us know that someone is coming." Her little, pink tongue slid over her lower lip.

His whole body tensed.

"Probably best if we're not caught making out right now."

Making out? That was what teens did. He'd been devouring her.

But he let her go when Tony twisted in his arms. His eyes remained on her because why the hell would he want to look anywhere else? More tendrils of hair had come loose from her braid. One day, he'd get all that hair loose. Loose and flowing over his pillow when he had her in his bed.

Slow the fuck down. It was one kiss.

But her lips were red from his mouth, and her gaze was filled with the same need that pulsed in his blood. Before he even realized what the hell he was going to do, Aiden asked her, "Think you can handle me?"

"I have no idea," she returned with her heart-stopping honesty, voice husky and sensual, and his eager dick jumped. "But I think I want to find out."

Then the door swung open, and his lawyer stomped inside.

"We were supposed to be in town for *business acquisitions,*" Kiara Johnson snapped. "I am not supposed to be dragged out of my lovely hotel suite because my boss *shot* someone." She drew up short. Eyed first Tony, then the dog. "And you're not alone in here. I was told you were alone."

"You were misinformed," he told her as he jerked a hand over the back of his neck.

"Clearly. You are with a woman. And a dog." She frowned at the dog as Banshee advanced on her. "Shouldn't you be on a leash?" She backed up a step. "Nice doggie."

"I didn't have time to grab a leash, but I can assure you," Tony responded as she lightly tapped her thigh, "Banshee is very well-behaved."

Banshee noted the signal and immediately went to Tony's side.

"So glad your dog and all of his—her?—teeth are well-behaved." Kiara drew herself up to her full five-foot-three inches. "But how about you step outside so I can speak privately with my client?"

Tony inclined her head. She took a few steps forward. Banshee moved in perfect sync with her.

Aiden's hand flew out, and his fingers curled around her wrist. "You don't need to go anywhere." He didn't want to let her out of his sight. Too much fear still filled him, and he hadn't been afraid of anything or anyone in a very long time. You only feared when you cared.

And I'll be filing that shit away for analysis later. Because he'd just met Tony. He didn't care about her. He wanted her, yes. But emotions weren't involved.

Tony's gaze dropped to his hand even as a little furrow appeared between her fine brows.

"You don't need to leave," he told her, voice gruff.

"She doesn't?" Kiara repeated. "Sorry, but don't you get the whole client-slash-lawyer confidentiality thing? I'm sure we have talked about it before. Many, many times."

His head turned toward her. Despite the early hour, Kiara's makeup had been fully applied and her dark hair artfully styled. She wore a crisp, light blue suit, and small, silver hoops dangled from her ears. Her expression reflected mild curiosity, but her dark eyes were hard with suspicion as they darted to Tony.

He should probably make introductions. He should also let Tony go. He didn't. But he did say, "Kiara Johnson, this is Dr. Antonia Rossi. Tony, this is my chief legal counsel, Kiara."

"Oh." Kiara edged closer. Her gaze became a little less suspicious. "You're *her*. Now the dog makes much more sense." Her head cocked. "Aiden shot someone at *your* place?"

Before Tony could answer, Kiara waved her hand in the air. "Allegedly shot," she clarified. "Based on what the uniforms outside are saying."

"There is no 'allegedly' about it," he informed her. "I shot him. He'd already fired at us. Nearly hit Banshee with one of his shots."

Banshee let out what sounded like an angry grunt.

"And he'd just fired his gun several times to break the lock on Tony's back door. The guy rushed inside and aimed his weapon at her. He was screaming and threatening her, and I knew he would be pulling that trigger again." His thumb slid along Tony's inner wrist. Her pulse raced so fast. "I fired before he could."

Kiara kicked the door shut. "What is wrong with you?" A low, rushed whisper. "We don't make confessions."

"We do if there is nothing to hide," Aiden returned easily.

She blew out a breath. Nodded determinedly. "We are talking about self-defense. If he was shooting at you, then you had to protect yourself. Clearly."

Tony tugged her wrist free of Aiden's grip. "Aiden protected me. The shooter was aiming at me."

"Why?" Kiara wanted to know. "What are we dealing with here? An angry ex who got jealous when he saw you with Aiden? A robbery gone wrong? A—"

"Try a dad who potentially murdered his eight-year-old daughter and buried her in a shallow grave." Tony's hands fisted.

Banshee rubbed her nose against Tony's thigh.

Her left hand unfisted. Stroked the top of Banshee's head. "Did you see how I used 'potentially' for you?" Tony asked Kiara. "I know how to play the game, too." A soft exhale. "I unearthed a body for the local PD earlier tonight." Her lashes fluttered. "No, that's wrong. It's a new day. I unearthed the body yesterday. The man who came to kill me was her father. As soon as he's patched up at the hospital, I'm sure he will be booked for a slew of charges."

Kiara's eyes had widened. "An eight-year-old?"

"That was twenty years ago, of course, but there is no statute of limitations on murder. As I'm sure you know."

"Of course." Sadness flickered in her gaze.

"I was a witness to everything that happened tonight. So was Smith. Aiden has nothing to worry about."

Kiara's blood-red, index fingernail tapped against her chin. "Oh, I wouldn't be too sure of that. Judging by the swarm of reporters outside, I think he has quite the media maelstrom to face. I blame it on two things. One, that ridiculous ranking that came out saying Aiden was one of most eligible bachelors in the US. God, we did not need that drama. It just has everyone who wants to marry for money throwing themselves in his path. And, two..." Her delicate nostrils flared as she glowered at Aiden. "*I blame it on the fact that you were at her house, in the middle of the night*. That automatically makes it look like the two of you are sleeping together. Sex. Money. Guns. And a billionaire bachelor. The story will sell itself. The clicks online will be insane. Especially when you throw in the dead kid and her crazy dad."

Now Tony stiffened. "Her name was Meridian Duvane."

The mask on Kiara's face wavered, for just an instant. Aiden knew Kiara liked to act tough—actually she *was* tough, she was hell on wheels in a courtroom—but one of her problems was that sometimes, she cared too much.

He wondered if she knew that he was aware of all the pro bono cases she took on the side.

"Meridian Duvane," Kiara repeated. Her gaze turned a little distant. A little sad. Then she shook her head. "Damage control. That's what we need to work on. I need to get Aiden's PR people on the job. They can fire out press releases and work spin so that you look like the upstanding citizen and amazing hero we all know you to be, Aiden. No sense in anyone digging into your past and thinking that oh, if he's so quick to fire this time then maybe he was the one who—" She stopped abruptly, clamping her lips together.

But he knew what she'd nearly said.

He was the one who killed his twin. Like those whispers hadn't followed him plenty of times.

Tony's hand reached out. Curled around his wrist, in a move reminiscent of what he'd done to her just moments before. Frowning, he looked down at her hand. At their hands. Then back up at her face.

"Aiden was a hero," she said clearly. "And as for why he was at my house, it's simple. We're working on a case together."

His case.

"It's not some grand passion," she continued even as her fingers stroked along his inner wrist.

It had felt pretty fucking grand a few minutes ago.

"We're not having some secret relationship. No fodder for the tabloids." Her lips curled down. "I've never been tabloid fodder a day in my life, just so you know."

He leaned toward her. Her lavender scent teased him. "Just so you know, I'm fodder every damn day."

Her head turned toward him. Their gazes caught. "Bet that's a pain in the ass."

God. I love it when she's blunt. "Understatement."

She gave him a wan smile.

He blinked. There was something about her smile. Something that made him... uncomfortable. Off-balance. She wasn't giving him a full smile. Just a weak twist of her lips. He wanted the real deal. A full-blown grin that would light up her eyes.

"So...then we *don't* go with the story that you two are passionately involved?" Kiara asked. "That would help sell things. We could say you two fell fast and hard—"

"I don't do fake relationships," Tony retorted bluntly. "With me, it's the real deal or nothing."

Aiden filed that away for later. His head slowly turned to Kiara. "She doesn't like to lie."

"Why not? Lies can make life far more convenient, but whatever. We'll deal. You're the grieving brother who has sought out the esteemed doctor of the dead."

"I hate that nickname," Tony muttered.

"Then you probably shouldn't spend so much time digging up the dead," Kiara returned without missing a beat. "Try a new career and maybe the name will change."

"That won't happen."

"Because you like the dead?" Kiara pushed, sounding genuinely curious.

"Because someone has to find them."

Banshee walked forward. Sniffed at Kiara's leg.

Kiara frowned at the dog. "Is he about to attack?"

"No, *she* isn't." Tony tapped her leg. Banshee returned to her side.

Kiara's nose scrunched. "A cadaver dog. Never seen one in real-life before."

"We don't call them that any longer." Tony's voice was mild. "Banshee is HRD. Human Remains Detection. If you tell family members you have a cadaver dog, they know you're only looking for the dead. Tends to make them lose it at the scene."

"Like you're looking for something different with a 'Remains' dog?"

"HRD is easier on the family. Let's them deny the truth a little bit longer."

"That's dark."

Aiden had realized that Tony's whole world was dark. More shadows that swirled around her.

"Not like people contact me when their lives are rainbows and sunshine." Tony didn't appear bothered. If anything, she seemed comfortable in the dark. "Certainly not why Aiden contacted me."

No, he'd gone after her to solve the blood-soaked mystery of his past.

Grimacing, Kiara stepped back. "Okay, we need to get this ball rolling. Not like we can hang out in a small police station all day." She pointed at Aiden. "Got big deals to close and businesses to swallow, am I right? So let's go grab the police chief and get you the hell out of here."

"I'm not leaving without Tony."

Kiara rolled her eyes. "Why does that not surprise me? Look, I get that you've been focused like a torpedo on her for the last few months..."

Tony stiffened.

"But she said she's helping you, so take a breath, boss. Not like she's gonna run and leave you high and dry. She called you a hero. You don't run from heroes."

Sometimes, you did. If the hero also happened to be a villain.

"I have to stay here for a while," Tony said before Aiden could speak. "I won't be leaving anytime soon. But you should go with your lawyer. Get things rolling." She glanced around the small room. "I'm surprised you haven't already left. Not like they're doing anything to keep you here."

"There's a cop outside the door," Kiara offered helpfully. "Young but cute. He looked vaguely competent, so he probably would have stopped an attempt to flee. Don't worry, though, he won't stop me." She opened the door. Cleared her throat. "Officer, I want to talk to the chief, immediately. My client is a hero. He shouldn't be held in custody any longer than..."

The door closed behind her.

Aiden knew he was supposed to follow her. He did pay the woman an obscene amount to keep his ass out of an assortment of troubles, after all. But he hesitated.

"Go," Tony urged him. "When I'm clear, I'll call you."

Call him. Right. Because they were working together.

Not good enough.

"When you're done, come to the hotel. *My* hotel. You can crash there." Because she'd had zero sleep that night. "I'll give you a suite. No one will disturb you."

Banshee bumped him.

He reached down, offering his hand for Banshee to sniff. Cautiously, the dog did. And seemed to nod.

"Your dog, too," he said. "Bring Banshee. It will be a pet-friendly suite." He read the hesitation in Tony's eyes and added, "Not like you can go back to a crime scene. There are plenty of rooms in the hotel. Let me help you."

She nodded. "All right. Thank you."

Aiden released the breath that he'd been holding.

"Just for one night, though," she added.

No. It would be for more than one night. A whole lot more. But they'd get to that, later. For now, he had a police chief to handle. He would have handled the chief sooner, but...

I didn't want to leave her.

He still didn't.

But he headed for the door.

"You could have just said for me to drop, you know. You didn't have to tell me to play dead."

He'd wondered when she'd bring that up. "Thought the command might make your dog drop, too."

Silence.

He reached for the doorknob. Stopped. "That won't happen again."

"You yelling for me to play dead? I hope not."

"No, some crazy asshole trying to kill you."

"Oh, I'm afraid I can't make any sort of promises about that sort of thing."

What. The. Fuck?

He swung back to face her.

"Not the first time that's happened." Not even a hint of sadness or fear showed on her face. "And probably not the last, either. But don't worry. Eventually, you get used to it."

The hell he would.

CHAPTER FIVE

"She acts like being nearly killed is *nothing*."

"Oh, no, no, no." Smith shook his head,
adamant. "She doesn't. I stayed with her all day—
just like you asked. Or, I stayed with her when the
cops weren't grilling me." His lips twisted. "You
would have thought I was lying about how you
had to shoot with the way they kept hammering
those questions at me."

Aiden's gaze sharpened on him. They were
back in his hotel suite. The sun was setting,
turning the sky outside of his windows into a dark
and gleaming gold. "I did have to shoot."

"I'm the security chief. You're the—"

"I know what I am. I know I'm the man who
wasn't going to stand there and let that prick hurt
her." Hell, no. That would not happen on his
watch.

But Smith regarded him with a hooded stare.
"You didn't realize I was behind him. And you
were *aiming* for his shoulder, right? Not like you
had bad aim, and the gun slipped a little when
you'd meant, oh, I don't know, to put a bullet in
his heart?"

Aiden didn't take his gaze off Smith. "You know I don't have bad aim."

Smith took a step toward him. "*You* know you need to be careful. Dr. Rossi is smart."

Hardly a big reveal.

"She's going to wonder about you."

He shrugged. "I'll tell her the truth. That you trained me. You wanted me to be able to defend myself. I'll even add that bit about the attempted kidnapping when I was in Mexico." A true story. "There are risks that come my way every day. I have to be prepared to face them."

A low whistle escaped Smith. "You're playing with fire."

"I'm not playing with a damn thing." Smith should know he rarely played. "She's in the hotel?"

Smith glanced toward the door on the right. "Not sure she realizes her suite connects to yours."

He bet that she did. She'd see the door. She knew where his suite was located. It was the same suite they'd used for their first private chat.

I wanted her close.

"No charges are being pressed against you." Smith crossed his arms over his chest. "And you're being hailed as the hero by the media. Guess that's going to make your rock-star, bachelor self even more popular."

"I'm not a rock star."

"Yeah, those are boring. You're just stupid rich, and you have an adrenaline addiction that is going to bite you in the ass one of these days." A shake of Smith's head even as his jaw locked. "If you're not careful, your house of cards will fall. You have enemies."

Like he didn't know that.

"They are looking for a weakness. You give them one, and they will close in on you."

What was that supposed to mean? "Tony isn't a weakness. She's..." He floundered. "An associate?" A question because that response didn't feel right.

"Bullshit. I *saw* you at her house. You lost your shit, man. Your eyes were wild. You've never looked like that, not even when we were kids."

Kids. Because they went way, way back. They'd grown up together. Attended the same, posh-ass schools, until Smith's father had lost everything in a real estate scam. Smith had withdrawn from the school and moved away. Joined the army after he'd turned eighteen. It would only be years later that their paths would cross again.

On a bloody street in Paris.

"I didn't, ah, lose my shit," Aiden replied carefully. "I was concerned for her safety. I acted accordingly."

"Tell me this." Smith sucked in a breath. "If I hadn't appeared behind him, if I hadn't tazed him and taken him down, would you have fired again?"

A soft knock sounded on the door that connected to Tony's suite. The woman truly had perfect timing. Exquisite. "See? Told you she'd realize we were connected."

"The *suites* are connected, you mean."

Was that what he meant? Maybe. Hard to say. "You need to get some rest, too, Smith. I'm good for the night. She's good. Don't worry about us." He turned for the connecting door.

"You've been obsessed with her for months."

He stilled.

"You hired Wilde to dig up every single bit of background intel on her that you could."

Wilde. Normally, the high-end and ever-so-discrete firm excelled at protection. Several of his business associates had used their services over the years when they'd found themselves in dangerous situations. But he hadn't been interested in protection. Instead, he'd wanted information. Luckily, the owner of the firm, Eric Wilde, had owed Aiden a favor or two.

So he'd gotten what he needed.

I know about the demons that haunt my Antonia.

The thought left him with unease. She wasn't his. Just another associate. Wasn't that how he'd just described her? A means to an end. Only she felt like more.

She'd stopped knocking. Fuck, he flipped the lock—he wouldn't be locking it again. She could have access to him anytime she wanted. Aiden swung open the door.

Tony had left her connecting door open. Her back was to him, but she spun quickly, her eyes widening when she saw him. "I just—"

"Obsession is dangerous," Smith rasped from behind him. "You should know. You've been battling an obsession ever since Austin vanished. Maybe you should let the dead stay buried."

Aiden looked back, just in time to see Smith exit. Frowning, he stared after his friend.

"I've been told that more than once, too." Tony's thoughtful voice.

He glanced back at her. *Holy mother of*...Her hair was down. The braid gone. Thick, dark, tousled hair slid over her shoulders. Absolutely stunning.

She gave him that brief, not-big-enough smile. One that just lightly lifted the edges of her full lips. "I've never listened to that advice."

No, he knew she hadn't. "After what happened with Clayton Duvane, do you wish you had?"

"Wish I'd left a little girl in an unmarked grave? Absolutely not." She moved toward him. Stopped at the edge of her room, right near the doorway.

He was on the edge of his room.

She was inches away. "But I am sorry you were put in jeopardy because of me. I knocked to tell you that. To say I hate what happened at my place."

His head tilted. "That really why you knocked?" He freaking loved her hair. He wanted to bury his hands in it while he tipped back her head and kissed her.

Her brown eyes widened. "Why else would I have knocked?"

"Ah, that the strategy you want to employ? Answer a question with a question?" Aiden shook his head. "I thought you were the blunt one. The one who didn't play games."

"I knocked to apologize." She was still in her room.

He was still in his. He wanted to lift up his hands and touch her. To pull her into his room.

"I never expected you to have to shoot someone in order to protect me." She bit her lower lip. "I should have been more aware. Meridian's mother is the one who came to me. She never gave up on her daughter. Brooke—the mom—she was so desperate. She clung to hope for so long." A soft click as Tony swallowed. "Clayton abused her. Six months after Meridian went missing, Brooke left him."

"Do you think she knew what he did to the girl?"

Her gaze turned distant as she seemed to ponder the question. "Sometimes, we know a monster is in front of us, but we deny it because if we face the truth, that truth will break something in us."

He was the one right in front of her. "Is that a yes?" He'd grown used to her being blunt, so this hesitant, vulnerable Tony was...different. He wanted to handle her with extra care.

"I suspect she knew, yes." Her shoulders squared. She wore a blue t-shirt. Faded jeans that clung lovingly to her legs and hips. No shoes. Her feet were bare, the toenails a light blue. "I should have been more on my guard. It was my fault that you had to be dragged into that nightmare."

Aiden hauled his gaze off her cute feet and looked back at her face. "Drag me anywhere. I can handle nightmares."

"Can you?" Her head tilted up as she focused those incredible eyes on him. Deep, dark chocolate.

"Yes." A firm response. Her nightmares would never scare him.

"I lied."

Surprise slid through him.

"I didn't knock so I could apologize. You were right on that. I am usually far more blunt, but this is a different situation for me. You're different."

Aiden could give her the same response. She was very, very different from anyone he'd ever met. But he stayed silent because he wanted to see what Tony would say next.

"I didn't expect the kiss at the police station."

"You want me to apologize for it?" For the best kiss he'd had in ages? Oh, hell, maybe forever? *I could have fucked her on that wobbly table in the interrogation room.* He'd been that far gone. Need had exploded within him. A desire he hadn't quite expected. Yes, of course, he'd known that he was attracted to her. But with that kiss, he'd wanted to devour her.

To own her.

A far too primitive response when he'd never viewed himself as a particularly primitive guy. But, also, deep inside, he'd thought...

If I'm not careful, she'll own me.

Ridiculous.

"I don't want you to apologize, Aiden. No. Not at all. If I hadn't wanted the kiss, I could have stopped you. Saint has taught me plenty of ways to defend myself."

At the name, his eyes narrowed. *Saint* had been mentioned several times in the files that Wilde had prepared on Antonia. Once wanted for murder, Saint had turned his life around. Saint had become one of the toughest bounty hunters in the US, and then he'd decided that just catching the worst of the worst wasn't enough of a thrill for him.

So he'd joined the Ice Breakers.

Saint had also recently become engaged to a woman who had a notorious reputation. Most had thought Alice Shephard was a black widow. Apparently, Saint wasn't scared of being her next victim. He was eager for the job. A volunteer.

But Aiden pushed the matter of Saint to the side, for now. Instead, he stared at what mattered, and asked, "If you don't want me to apologize, then what do you want?"

"I want to know if it will feel the same without all the adrenaline." She wet her lips. "I want to know if I will feel desire pour through me and if I'll want to rip off your clothes and jump you here and now...from just a kiss."

His hands flew up and grabbed the doorframe. It was either grab the doorframe or grab her. His Tony was back to being her blunt self.

He fucking loved it.

"Because that doesn't usually happen to me," she continued, voice serious and determined. As determined as her expression. "I don't get swept away by passion."

His grip hardened on the wood around the door. "You don't say." *Good to know. I don't like the idea of other bastards getting that response from you*. Aiden wanted her reaction to be special. For him alone.

"I do say." Again, her voice was all serious and determined. "I felt different with you." A crinkle appeared between her brows. "I felt *more* with you. Maybe it was the adrenaline. I mean, it was hardly the sexy setting."

Despite the lust pouring through his veins, her words made a smile tug at his lips. "You don't find cramped interrogation rooms sexy? They aren't turn-ons for you?" He would love to have a list of all her turn-ons.

As for him...what turned Aiden on? She did. Her voice like somber music. Her lavender scent. Her blue toenail polish. Her lush curves. The dark, thick mane of her hair. Her deep, gorgeous eyes. And her mouth. Oh, hell yes, her mouth. So lush and full.

She bit her lower lip. Her eyes darkened even more. "To tell you the truth, I hate enclosed spaces. Probably because of my job. Because I can too easily imagine what it's like to be sealed inside and buried."

Fuck.

"That's not sexy." A wince. "See, I have this problem. I don't say sexy things. I don't do sexy things. I don't *do* sexiness. I should probably be saying all these sensual things to seduce you right now, but instead, I'm talking about being buried alive." She flushed. "I can't do sexy. That's not me."

"Oh, I beg to differ." He found her sexy as hell.

"You do. You do sexy and sensual. Like it's as easy as breathing." She waved toward him. A wave that started at his head and jerked down his body. "You ooze this sex appeal that I am sure you're quite aware of projecting."

"Thanks for noticing." He wanted his hands on her. With an effort, he kept them on the doorframe.

Her head tilted to the left, sending her hair tumbling over that shoulder. "It's probably normal for you to get swept away by desire and to make out with a woman the same day you meet her."

"Technically, I think we met yesterday. And, no, despite the incredibly high opinion you seem to have of me, I don't just spend all my time kissing strangers."

"I've offended you."

"No." She hadn't. But it was time to clarify the situation. "You came knocking on my door because you wanted to kiss me again."

A slow exhale. "I came knocking, first, to apologize for bringing you into my nightmare. And second, to say thank you. Oh, but I didn't say that, did I?"

"You said it at the station." He wasn't interested in her thanks. He was interested in her kiss.

"Thank you. I mean it. Though..." Her head gave a quick shake, sending all that luxurious hair sliding once more. Seriously, the woman should be in a shampoo commercial. Why, *why* did she keep that gorgeous mane pulled into a braid?

"Though..." Her voice held curiosity. "I did wonder about how you were so prepared. Most people can't fire without hesitation that way. You didn't seem nervous. You didn't seem like it was your first time to face off against an armed attacker. In fact, you just seemed...quite dangerous."

Smith had been right. She was getting suspicious. "A man in my position has to be prepared for attacks. Sometimes we're targeted by others who want to take advantage of us. One of my associates was kidnapped and ransomed last year when he went on a business trip to the Middle East. I had my own run-in with certain individuals with ill intent in Mexico."

"Ill intent?"

"They wanted to force me into the back of their van and drive off into the night. I wasn't in the mood for a joy ride, so I declined their invitation." Easy words to describe a brutal night. "I've had to be trained to face danger. Smith is good, but he can hardly be at my side twenty-four, seven. I need to be able handle myself."

A nod. "I see. Well, I thought you handled yourself quite well."

Damn, but she fascinated him. "Thanks for noticing." His gaze slid over her once more. A helpless response because he just liked looking at her. All of her. But something—someone—was missing. "Where's the dog?"

"Banshee is sleeping in the den—or whatever the room at the front of the suite is called. She didn't want to leave her post at the door. I think she's guarding me."

Aiden could understand that urge. He wanted to guard her, too. Instead, he was pulling her into the mess of his life. "You don't have to do it." What in the hell? What had he just said?

"Do what?"

"Take my case." He'd researched her, he'd tracked her, he'd been determined to move heaven and hell to get her cooperation. But that had all been before...

Before I had to tell her to play dead so some asshole wouldn't shoot my Antonia.

There he went again. Thinking *my* thoughts when all he'd done so far was kiss her. He wasn't normally possessive about anything or anyone.

She was different.

"You don't want me?" A fast blink. "I mean, you don't want my help on your case any longer?"

"Oh, I want you. Wanting you is not the problem." He was talking about both his physical lust and his desire to have her help him with the hunt for his brother.

"Then what's the problem?" Tony asked.

He didn't want to be the reason she ever got hurt. "Maybe you need to take some time off from finding the missing. You had a big scare tonight. You might want to escape for a bit."

She put her hand on his chest.

His heart thundered beneath her touch.

"I don't scare easily," she told him. "I also don't meet a hero every day."

"Be careful with that label." It was dangerous. She should also... "Be careful touching me."

"Why?" Tony inched closer. "What's so wrong with touching you?"

When she touched him, Tony made him want too much. "You went over the first two reasons for being at my door. The apology and the thanks." His voice was rough. Growling. He cleared his throat. "Ready to focus on reason three?" The throat clearing hadn't helped. If anything, his voice came out even deeper and darker than before.

Her head inclined. "Reason three. To see if the kiss will be as good with the adrenaline gone."

But he shook his head. "You don't need to make excuses with me. You want to kiss me? Then kiss me. Adrenaline has nothing to do with us. I'm not an experiment. I'm a man. You want me. You say you want me."

"Fair enough." She stared straight into his eyes. "I want you."

His hands flew off the doorframe and locked around her.

CHAPTER SIX

She wasn't reckless. Wasn't bold and wild. She never hooked up with strangers because she knew too well about danger. She didn't try to seduce men she'd just met.

There was a whole, long list of things she didn't do. And a list of things she did do.

Tony played it safe.

She was responsible.

Dedicated.

Boring. That was what her social life was. Boring. Because she didn't go on many dates, and when she did, the men weren't exactly charmed by her after-dinner conversation. They didn't want to hear about the dead, and she didn't know how to pretend to be fun and easy going.

But...

She didn't have to pretend anything with Aiden. He knew what she was. He knew what she did. And he still wanted her.

More than that, when she kissed him, the desire she felt overwhelmed her. And, yes, fine, maybe she had thought of this second kiss as an experiment. Because Aiden was wrong. Adrenaline *did* matter. It could confuse you, heighten your emotions, make you think you felt something when you didn't...

But...

But this second kiss...

Fire. That was the only way to describe it. He kissed her, and fire seemed to surge through her body. A desperate, twisting, sensual need that heated her body from the inside out and made her want to rip off his clothes. She was not the ripping-clothes-off type. Yet with him, she wanted to be.

Red flag. Red flag! In her mind, Tony could see the flags waving, but she ignored them. Why?

Because he saved me. It had been a long time since a stranger had rushed in to save her. Actually, one never had.

Until him.

Until the man who'd been so fierce as he stared down her attacker. Did she have a bit of a hero complex going on? Screw it if she did. Tony didn't care. She just wanted more of Aiden.

More of the way he made her feel. More of the consuming need. More of the sensual intensity. He kissed her with passion and hunger, and she responded feverishly, awkwardly. Achingly.

Rawly.

Her hands grabbed for his shoulders as her body pressed to his. His hands had fallen to her hips and curled around her. Through their clothes, she could feel his strength and power. Strength was a turn-on for her.

And when he lifted her up—just lifted her like it was the easiest thing in the world for him—he made her hotter. Her legs curled around him instinctively as they kept kissing. He turned and carried her into his room. Tony didn't open her eyes, but she could feel where they were going. The kiss was so good that she didn't want it to end. If she opened her eyes, if she lifted her head, she'd have to focus on what came next. What *could* come next. Was she ready for that?

No.

But did she want it? Want *him?* Yes.

So maybe...maybe it was time to take a risk.

He was the hero. He'd saved her. What could she have to fear from him?

In the next instant, Aiden pulled his mouth from hers. A cry of protest rang from her, but then his lips were on her throat. He'd lifted her higher so he could reach his goal, and he was kissing and licking his way down her neck, and oh, but his mouth was incredible. She squirmed against him, her hips rocked, and she rode over the long, thick length of his cock.

It felt good—great—so she rode him more. Harder. Faster. Arching and rubbing.

"Fuck me," he growled against her neck.

"That's what I'm trying to do," she muttered back. "But the clothes are in the way."

He stiffened. She felt his muscles turn to stone against her. Well, one particular area had already rather felt like stone. But, if possible, that area got even bigger. And this dick had been plenty big.

Aiden surged forward and dropped her onto the bed. She gave a little bounce before shooting upright.

He stood at the edge of the bed and stared down at her with a gaze that blazed. "You want to fuck me?"

Did she? Yes. She'd said as much, hadn't she?

"You went from a kiss to fucking. That's..." He yanked a hand over his face. "Be *fucking sure.*"

"I assume you have protection." She glanced around his suite. "If not, I can go down to the lobby and get something from the gift shop."

"You don't need to go to the damn gift shop!" He jumped back. Like a good two feet. "You..." He huffed out a breath. "Why?"

"Why what?"

"Why do you want to fuck me?"

He was making this needlessly difficult. "I didn't realize there would be a pop quiz before the event."

His hand fell. His hard gaze pinned her. "I keep feeling like I'm an experiment for you. You wanted to kiss me a second time to see if the kiss would be as good as the first. It was. No, it was even better."

She shoved hair away from her face. "Glad you noticed that, too."

"You want to fuck me to see if the fucking will be as good as the kiss."

"Well, yes." Was that so bad? "Don't you want to know, too?" If her body ignited from a kiss, what would it be like to make love with him?

His hand fisted. "I already know. Sex with you will be fantastic."

Oh. She felt a blush in her cheeks. No man had ever said that to her before. "Setting expectations high." No pressure.

"They should be high. My dick is so eager the damn thing is about to bust out of my pants. I know we'll implode together."

Yet he'd backed away. "It's not an experiment. And it's not about your case. Regardless of what happens between us, I will still help you. You have my word on that."

His eyes squeezed closed. *"Fuck me."*

Again, she'd been trying to do just that. He was the one who'd dropped her like she was hot and jumped back. Hardly a flattering response. Her breath huffed out. Maybe she wasn't explaining things properly. "I like the way you make me feel."

His eyes cracked open. Narrow slits of amber glared at her. "What are you trying to do to me?"

Seduce him? But clearly failing. "Maybe this is a mistake." There was a reason she didn't normally act this way. "I should go back to my room." She scooted to the edge of the bed.

But he moved, too. Moved right to the edge of the bed to block her. A big bed. High up. King size. He put his hands on either side of her and leaned in. "I don't want you going anywhere."

Her heart raced. Fine, it had already been racing. It raced faster. "You are a hard man to read."

"I want you to be *sure*. I don't want to be your mistake when morning comes."

Surprise rolled through her. "I wouldn't think of you that way."

"You don't know all my secrets yet."

"You don't know mine." This wasn't about secrets. It was about need. The kind of desire that if you were lucky—maybe you'd experience once in a lifetime. Because that sweep-you-away madness that was shown all the time in movies? Didn't happen so much, at least not in her life. In her life, this was the first time she'd felt that way. This time. This man.

He leaned in even closer. "What is this? Are you offering me a one-night stand?"

"I told you, I don't do those."

"Right. You don't hook up with strangers." A muscle jerked along his jaw. "But you're here with me."

"You're not a stranger. You're the man who saved my life today."

"*Gratitude.* You're going to fuck me out of gratitude?"

Her hands rose to frame his face. "A gallant effort, but it's not going to work."

His brows shot up. "Gallant? Did you just freaking say *gallant?* When I'm talking about fucking you?"

The stubble on his cheeks teased her palms. She stared into his eyes and saw right through him. "You're trying to scare me off."

"What?"

"You want me. It would be hard to miss that." Because his cock was huge. "But you're trying to be all..." Tony searched for the right word since he hadn't liked gallant and finally settled on... "Noble and get me to leave you."

"I'm not noble, and trust me, the last thing I want is for you to leave."

His mouth was inches away. "What do you want?"

"You. Naked on the bed. Moaning my name."

"A clearly achievable goal," she returned, breathless.

His eyes widened. Then his head turned. His lips brushed over her right palm. His tongue licked against her, and she gasped. Another sensitive spot she hadn't even realized existed. Until now. Until him.

"You undo me." His breath feathered over her palm.

A shiver slid over Tony.

His head turned back to face her. His eyes locked on hers. "You don't want a one-night stand. What do you want?" A pause. "A relationship?"

"I don't do so well at those."

"Maybe you've been with the wrong fucking bastards." His lips thinned. "Know what? I don't want to hear about those bastards now. Don't want to think about some conceited ass computer hacker who should never have touched you. Don't want to—"

Ice. It poured over her. Through her. The delicious haze of desire she'd felt evaporated. "How do you know about Bryan?"

He didn't speak.

"Because you were just very specific." And very right. She'd felt bold and brazen moments before. Now she just felt wrong. "I'd like to get off the bed." This was all...*wrong*.

How did he know about Bryan? About the fact that Bryan worked as a hacker for the government? Such a personal, supposedly classified bit of information. Yet he knew.

How did he know Bryan was my lover? Not like she was the kiss-and-tell type. Her hands slid away from Aiden's face. Moved down to his chest. Instead of pulling him closer, she pushed against him.

Jaw locking, he stepped back.

She jumped from the bed. Took several quick, rushed steps toward the open doorway that connected their suites.

"I researched you."

Tony stopped. She didn't look back. Her gaze remained on the doorway. The news wasn't shocking. After all, his lawyer—Kiara—had said that Aiden had been "locked on her" for several months. She'd been sure he did some digging into her background to make certain that she was the right person for his case.

But there was digging to be sure she was good at her job. And then there was ripping into her life and getting the names of her lovers. Learning about top-secret work that Bryan performed for Uncle Sam.

How the hell did Aiden learn all that?

"I wanted to learn as much as I could about you. I hired a firm, didn't do it in-house with my own people because I wanted strict confidentiality. The firm I hired is the best of the best."

"You didn't trust your own people?" That confused her. And made her glance back at him.

"I wanted you kept secret. I knew that Wilde could give me the assurance that whatever was discovered—that information would be kept in the strictest confidence. And, no, I don't trust my own fucking people. I just had to deal with a bit of corporate espionage. There are always people out to take advantage. Whether you're talking property trespass, cyberattacks, or just straight-up fucking betrayal by employees who get tempted with the promise of big pay days from your competitors...it happens." Grim. "I almost lost a bid on a project because someone in my inner circle sold me out. I have to be careful."

So he'd hired Wilde. Yes, she recognized the name of the company. Wilde just wasn't about protection. The boss, Eric, had even tried to lure Saint into working for him once. Wilde was very, very good. And with some deep ties to the government. *That explains how he learned Bryan's job.* But... "I don't see how learning the names of my lovers is need-to-know info when it comes to whether or not you can trust me." Now she felt anger breaking through her stunned surprise. Anger at him—because she'd been *trusting* him. Been feeling...*something* for him. Something that had made Tony throw her normal caution to the wind. Only to learn that he'd been very much holding back on her.

Just what else does he know? She felt far too exposed. This wasn't some simple background work. Not with Wilde involved. He'd paid big bucks to learn about her. To learn her *secrets*.

Dammit. Why had she lowered her guard with him? Why hadn't she learned yet that when you lower your guard, you just open yourself to pain?

"I wanted to know everything about you." He kept his hands at his sides and his focus on her. "I had tried contacting you. You were ignoring my letters and emails. This might shock you, but people rarely ignore me."

"Oh, forgive me. Didn't mean to hurt your pride. I was a little busy living my own life and finding the dead." She didn't point out that she hadn't seen those notes. That someone else on her team would have read the material. They tried to prioritize based on the cases and the intel. And whether or not they thought they could do something to help.

Instead of getting angry at her response, he smiled at her. A warm, wide smile that made the damn man even more attractive. "I can't get used to you."

What was that supposed to mean?

"You keep saying things that throw me off-balance." He took a gliding step toward her.

Tony stiffened. She didn't want him in her space again. When he was too close, his warmth and strength surrounded her. His scent teased her. She turned her body toward him but threw up her hand. "Just stay where you are."

Immediately, his hands lifted, palms out, toward her. His smile vanished. "I didn't mean that in a bad way. Truth be told, I find you fascinating."

Her stomach twisted. "I don't see why. I'm sure my life story is quite the dull read. Just me taking lots and lots of classes and keeping my head buried in books." *He can't know. He can't know.* Panic flared, but she fought it. Wilde was good, yes. They had ties to the government, *yes*. But they wouldn't know her deepest pain. It had been too long. It had been buried.

Not even her closest friends in the Ice Breakers knew…

"Wilde is very thorough," he said, voice soft. Careful. "Their reach is rather extraordinary. And there is nothing about you that I would call dull."

The drumming of her heartbeat filled Tony's ears. Her breathing hitched.

"I know why you want to help the dead, Tony. I know why you want to find the ones who've been missing. Hidden away."

No, no, no. This couldn't be happening. The scene couldn't have gone from *almost* hot sex to a painful reveal of her darkest time. No.

But he wasn't stopping, and his expression had hardened. "I know why your emotions are all over the place tonight."

They were all over the place because the jerk before her had been throwing his money around and ripping way too deeply into her life.

"I know why you let adrenaline take over."

Let? "Adrenaline spikes when someone shoots at you. It's a thing, I assure you."

A muscle flexed along Aiden's clenched jaw. "When you realized that Meridian's father was the one who'd put her in the ground, it all came back, didn't it?"

She wanted to tell him to stop, but she couldn't say a word.

He kept talking. "It came back when you came face to face with a monster who wanted you dead." Fury flashed, but was quickly concealed, on his face. "That's why your emotions are racing away from you. That's why you wanted to escape with me."

"I wanted to be with you because I'd never wanted a man so badly." Ragged.

"I know about the shit that happened to you when you were a kid."

A dull ringing filled her ears. Not the drumming of her heart. A ringing. And all she could think was...

He can't know. I'm someone new. A different person. My past is buried. I buried it.

"You were kidnapped when you were eight years old. The same age as Meridian, right?"

Meridian hadn't been kidnapped. She'd been killed. "Stop." Tony finally managed to speak.

"The bastard who'd taken you had taken four other girls."

"Stop talking." Soft. Desperate.

But he didn't stop. His stare pierced her. "They didn't get away. *You* did. You got away. You got free of the rope he'd tied around your wrists. You ran through the woods, away from that damn cabin." He took a step toward her, then caught himself. "You were fucking extraordinary even back then."

"No, I was lucky." There had been nothing special to separate her from those other girls. The girls who hadn't been able to go back to their families. The only difference had been...

My necklace. The heart-shaped necklace her mother had given her. She'd used the edge of her necklace to saw through the ropes. And she'd run and run and run.

"You brought the cops back. They found the other bodies. They found him. He fought, and there was a shootout, and they killed him."

She wanted to put her hands over her ears and block out his words because they stirred memories that she'd fought so hard to bury. Memories that would slip into her nightmares and still make her wake up, drenched in sweat. *What if I hadn't gotten away?*

"You were right there. You saw it all. I figured it out even though Wilde couldn't find definitive proof. You *had* to be at the scene when he died. After all, you were the only one who knew how to find him."

"Banshee." Too weak. Too low. "*Banshee.*"

She heard the rush of the dog's footsteps behind her, then Banshee's head bumped into the back of her leg.

A frown pulled at Aiden's features.

Her hand reached back, and her fingers sank into Banshee's fur. Calm spread through Tony. *I'm not a little girl anymore. I'm not lost. I'm okay.*

"That's the real reason you don't like closed spaces, isn't it?" Aiden pressed. "Because you were locked in a closet."

He'd learned everything. Or so he thought. "My name was kept out of the media. Out of all the reports." Because she'd been a minor. Because her family had possessed the right connections. Her father had wanted to surround her with twenty-four, seven protection after that terrible night.

For a while, he had. Until the protection had become more of a prison than anything else. At sixteen, she'd decided she didn't want to live her life in fear any longer. So she hadn't. Or at least, she'd tried not to always be afraid. But late at night, when she was alone, that was when the darkness always tried to close in.

He watched her with his hot amber gaze. "It makes since that you picked forensic anthropology as your specialty. You want to keep bringing the victims home. So you work and you work that ass of yours off on these cases, but you're still haunted."

"I didn't realize I was going to be psychoanalyzed tonight. I'd hoped for something different. Way to crush those dreams." So much for exploring the chemistry between them. She was being psychoanalyzed by a billionaire who thought he knew every secret she possessed. How wonderful. How awful. "I'm at a disadvantage because I haven't hired a professional team to tear into your past. I will have to correct that situation immediately."

"You will." Aiden didn't seem bothered by the possibility. He acted like it was a foregone conclusion. "We both know it. But you don't have to hire others. You'll just get your Ice Breaker friends to rip my world apart, and that's exactly what you should do. Find out everything. Good, bad, and the sorry stuff in the middle. Learn every detail." A jerk of his head. "Because then we'll be even. Then you won't look at me like I'm a stranger again. Then maybe you'll want me close."

Doubtful. She'd almost made a mistake. "Why does it feel like a betrayal?"

Shock flashed on his face.

"There I go again, being all blunt." Oh, well. It was far too late to pull the words back. "But I guess we both know that I'm not blunt about everything." She wrapped herself in secrets when she could. "Why does it feel like a betrayal to know that you learned about my past long before we ever met?" A basic background search would have been one thing. But...hiring Wilde? Digging so deep? And... "My exes? Why them? What else do you know?" Wrong question. Better one... "What *don't* you know?"

His chin lifted. That strong, arrogant chin. "In my world, information is power. I needed you on my side. The more I knew about you, the more likely I would be to get your help."

"To *convince* me to help you...that's what you mean." He'd intended to use the knowledge he learned against her.

"Yes, that's what I mean."

At least he wasn't denying it.

"From the beginning, I was too eager. Too desperate. I sent Smith in at the wrong time. And, apparently, I've just fucked up again."

She would not look at the bed behind him. Her breath shuddered in and out. She would *not* think about just how close they'd come to having sex.

Dammit, I am so thinking about that.

"I don't believe an apology will cut it, huh?" Aiden asked, voice roughening.

"*Are* you sorry?" Because she didn't think he was.

He seemed to ponder the question. Then finally, rolling back his shoulders, Aiden admitted, "No."

"Bastard."

A wince. "I have been called that often by others, though, I was hoping you wouldn't join that particular crowd." He leaned forward but caught himself before he took another step. "Everything I learned about you convinced me that you were the one person I needed."

She blinked.

"Your drive. Determination. You don't give up. If you take a case, you give it everything you have."

"I can't always find the missing." He was looking for a miracle. She wasn't his miracle. She wasn't anyone's miracle.

"You care. You get invested in your cases. I need that. I need someone who cares as much as I do." A hard exhale. He waved his hand in a motion toward her, then toward himself. "But I didn't expect this. I didn't expect to touch you and feel more desire than I've ever felt for anyone in my life. You want to know why I fucked up and said the wrong thing when I was close to touching heaven?"

That was...touching heaven? Was that how he thought of what they'd been doing? Poetic. But maybe that was deliberate. A distraction. A misdirection. She was thinking he could twist words so easily. "Why did you fuck up?"

"Because I'm a jealous bastard. I don't *like* knowing about those other jackasses who got to touch you before I met you. I know that doesn't make a bit of sense but..." A shrug. "It is what it is. I don't react normally to you."

She certainly wasn't reacting in any sort of normal fashion to him. In fact, she'd been ready to break all her precious rules, for him. Only to find out that he'd already been keeping secrets.

"I got possessive. I got primitive. And I...I started thinking things I should not."

Do not ask him. Do not. Just walk into your room and shut the door. "Things like what?"

But he just gave her a slow, sensual smile.

Leave. She crept away from him.

His smile faded. "I will not hurt you."

"I never said you would."

"You're mad because I looked at your past."

A few more steps. "Mad isn't how I feel."

A furrow pulled down his brow. "Then how do you feel?"

She'd already said it once. *Betrayed.* Which probably didn't make much sense considering they'd just met. And in his world, a deep-dive investigation on everyone was probably commonplace. But he hadn't just investigated her. He'd unearthed her darkest secrets. Then talked about them as if they were casual conversation. "I feel raw and exposed. The parts I wanted to bury have just been dragged to the surface."

His jaw locked.

"I look at you," absolute truth, "and I hurt. And so, I can't look at you right now." She spun away from him. "Goodnight, Aiden."

"*Antonia.*" Rough.

"I told you, everyone calls me Tony." A shiver slid over her because in her mind, she remembered someone else calling her...

Antonia, I've been sent to pick you up. Your parents were delayed, and your dad asked me to come by...

Her breath shuddered out. With Banshee, she practically leapt over the threshold that would take her to her room. She kicked the door shut.

Locked it.

And her past slammed into her.

CHAPTER SEVEN

He'd fucked up. A major fuck-up that had cost him something very precious.

Her trust. He'd seen it in Tony's eyes. The pain. The hurt. She'd been kissing him, touching him, acting as if she wanted him as desperately as he wanted her. Then he'd screwed up because he'd opened his dumbass mouth.

"Yeah, so..." An exhale from Smith as he paced in front of the suite's windows. "Your sad-dog expression is telling me you did not spend the night in sensual bliss with the pretty forensic anthropologist."

His hold tightened on the coffee cup that Aiden had just lifted. Steam drifted from the cup. "Do not push me this morning."

"No?" Smith put his hands on his hips. "If I don't push, who the hell will? Everyone else is scared of your crazy ass because they think you'll fire them if they say the wrong word or look too long at you."

Tony wasn't scared of him. Not scared of him. Not impressed by his wealth. Hell, not impressed by *anything* about him. Aiden was pretty sure he currently ranked at the top of her shit list. He'd gone from being her hero...

To the guy she couldn't even look at.

"You messed up with her, didn't you? I told you, that woman is smart. You have to be on your guard with her. Do you really want your whole house of cards falling down?"

He put down the coffee. Watched the steam drift lazily. "It was one slip up."

"Sonofabitch. I knew it!"

Smith needed to calm down. "I...might have revealed that I knew about one of her exes."

"What?" Smith lurched toward him. "What did you do? What did you say?"

Sighing, Aiden focused on his head of security. No, more than that—Smith was pretty much his only real friend. "She knows about the background check I did on her. The very, very thorough check."

"Oh, shit." A look of horror came on Smith's face. "Tell me she didn't *learn about it* when you two were being all hot and heavy."

Aiden didn't speak.

"That's a yes." Absolutely miserable, Smith dropped into the chair across from Aiden. "You were thinking with your dick. You weren't supposed to do that! Hell, you don't *usually* do that. You're like...ice cold and shit, normally. Business and pleasure are separate, isn't that your freaking mantra? Surprised you don't have that crap tattooed on your chest."

His back teeth clenched. "The situation was different," he gritted. "She's just not what I expected."

Smith leaned toward him and peered at him with a questioning gaze. After a moment... "Fuck."

"No, we didn't. Unfortunately." So he'd spent the night thinking about her and how he could not screw up again. "I'm not even sure she's still going to take my case. She felt... betrayed."

"Double fuck."

"I hurt her." He looked down at the table. He'd ordered breakfast for her. Had rapped on her connecting door and called lightly to her once the meal had arrived. She hadn't responded. "I didn't know I could hurt her." He also hadn't known just how shitty he would feel when her dark eyes swam with pain. A pain he'd caused.

It will not happen again.

Hell, who was he kidding? All he did was hurt. And she wasn't the first person he'd betrayed.

"Anyone can be hurt. Even you. The man with no heart."

He *hated* that saying. Not like he hadn't heard plenty of people claim it over the years. Usually it had been competitors, but a few lovers had even tossed the accusation at him. Why? Because he was good at compartmentalizing? Smith was right. He didn't normally mix business and pleasure. He didn't let emotions muddy the waters for him. He liked being in control. Liked things to be ordered. To follow along the path he'd created.

"How do we get your fool self back into her good graces?" Smith reached for the French toast.

Glumly, Aiden eyed the food. "I'd thought to start with French toast."

Smith stilled. "Oh, is this for her? And here I thought you'd ordered the strawberries and mimosas for me because I'm awesome. Knew the mimosa couldn't be for you. Haven't seen you touch a drink in forever."

"She didn't answer when I knocked."

"Because—if I'm getting all this right—in the middle of a hot and heavy make-out scene, she found out you were a crazy stalker. That you were obsessed with her, so she ran the hell to her room, locked the door, and probably had her big German Shephard on guard duty all night." Smith bit into the French toast and chewed for a few moments. Then, "Hate to tell you, but it's probably gonna take a lot more than an ever-so-delicious breakfast to win back her favor. I'd go bigger."

Bigger? "She doesn't exactly strike me as the diamonds and jewelry type." She'd probably toss jewels back at his face. "And I'm not obsessed. I just want her help."

"Her help...or her?"

The guy needed to stop being a dick. "Not like she can help unless she's with me."

"Uh, huh." Smith had finished up the French toast. "How's your grovel? Think you can manage a good enough one to win her back? Oh, and by the way, in case you're not aware, you're on every major gossip site. Trending on social media. All that fun stuff. You and the story of how you saved the lovely doc from her attacker."

"I'm sure she's going to hate that." Because Tony stayed out of the spotlight. Unfortunate, because wherever he went, that light seemed to follow. A side effect of who he had become.

"Yeah, didn't exactly think it would work in your favor." Smith fired a glance toward the connecting door.

The door on Aiden's side was wide open. He'd left it open all night, just in case Tony changed her mind and came back to him.

No such luck.

Her door had remained closed.

"Really quiet in there." Smith scraped a hand over his jaw. "Are you sure she *is* in there? What if she got so pissed, she cut out on you in the middle of the night?"

His fork clattered onto the plate. Aiden had been trying to eat some eggs but—screw that. He shot to his feet and rushed for the connecting door. "I would have heard her."

"Doubtful. Something tells me Tony can be quiet and sneaky when she wants to be."

His fist slammed into the door. "Tony!" Yes, he sounded desperate because he was. What if she had left? Why the fuck hadn't he considered that option?

Because...because I thought I could make things up to her. Sure, he didn't know how, but he hadn't thought she'd cut and run on him.

He pounded again, feeling more desperate. Her dog wasn't even barking. The dog would bark if Tony was inside, right? *Sonofabitch.* He—

Tony wrenched the door open. "Are you always this loud in the morning?"

He grabbed her and hauled her into his arms. Held her tight. "You didn't leave."

Banshee growled.

Tony stiffened.

Hell. He immediately let go. Stepped back. Breathed.

"Why would I have left?" she asked carefully, even as she gave a reassuring pat to Banshee's head. The dog's eyes remained on Aiden, and Banshee did not look happy. "We have a deal, you and I, and I don't plan to back out just because you pissed me off."

"He'll probably piss you off again soon," Smith called. "Get ready for it! And, I just have to say, you look absolutely lovely with your hair down like that. All thick and loose. Why do you pull it back into a braid?"

"Because when I'm digging up bodies, it gets in the way."

"Oh." Smith cleared his throat. "Totally great reason. You keep doing you."

Aiden had turned to glare at his friend because he didn't like the jackass flirting with Tony. But at her cool response, his focus shifted back to her. Aiden realized that her gaze had never left him. Her intense stare seemed to burn through him. "I know I owe you an apology."

"I called Saint."

His shoulders stiffened. Saint. That guy again. Not someone she was sleeping with—Aiden knew Saint was heavily involved with someone else. But he also knew that Tony *was* close to the man, and, clearly, Aiden had some jealousy issues. Surprising, when he'd never been jealous of anyone before. But with her...*fuck, yes, I'm jealous.*

"He's going to get the group started on background work. Just so you know—because I don't tend to keep secrets and spring them on my friends—he will be digging into your past. Not just the shiny parts that are shown on the gossip sites..."

"Saw that stuff already, did you?" Smith released an aggrieved sigh. "They love to talk about him. It's because of the money, you know. And the celebrities he used to date."

He hadn't dated celebrities. He'd been caught at a *few* charity events with them, but only because the women in question had staged the photos.

"Saint and Memphis will unearth every secret you've ever had. When those two work together, they're quite phenomenal."

Memphis. Yes, he recognized the name of another Ice Breaker. "You're telling me that you'll soon know every lover I've ever had, and we'll be even?"

Her long lashes flickered. "There is no even. This is the job you wanted me to do. I never asked *you* to go digging into my life. I didn't come to you for help. You're the one who sought me out."

"*Hit,*" Smith noted. Why was the guy so cheery? "She has a valid point. The woman was minding her own business, having no idea that an aggressive and demanding billionaire was ripping into her world."

Aiden rounded on him. "You are not helping."

His brows rose. "Am I not?"

"Not even a little."

"I told you to grovel. I advised that. I—"

"I don't want him to grovel. Why would I want that?" Tony asked, seeming genuinely curious. "I just need background on the case. I need to know about Aiden's enemies and his friends. And his lovers, too, yes, but that's just to build background. It's nothing personal. I intend to get the same information on his brother. All the secrets that are out there—I need to know them in order to do my job."

In order to find out what happened to Austin.

"I talked to the local police this morning. I need to go to the station here in Biloxi. Tie up a few loose ends. Clayton confessed to everything— the abduction and murder of his daughter, the attack at my house—all of it. Once he started talking, he just wouldn't stop." She brushed by Aiden. Banshee followed in her wake as Tony made her way to the breakfast table. Her hand hovered over the croissants, then she tipped her head toward the chocolate-covered strawberries. "That's not a coincidence, is it?"

If he had information that might work to his advantage, why not use it? "I might have remembered that those were your favorite."

She slanted him an unreadable glance. "Again, I feel I have to ask, is there anything you *didn't* learn about me?"

"Plenty."

"I suspect that's a lie." She picked up a strawberry. Bit into it and let out a sweet, sweet moan.

Every muscle in his body hardened.

"You are so fucked, buddy," Smith muttered as he rose from the table and came toward Aiden. He clapped a hand on Aiden's shoulder. "Fucked."

"Get the hell out," he ordered.

"On my way." Smith let go of Aiden's shoulder and edged around Banshee. "Aren't you a beauty?" He held out his hand. She sniffed. Inclined her head so he could give her a quick scratch. Then Smith double-timed it to the door. *Click*.

Aiden didn't move. "I think your dog likes him more than she likes me."

Tony bit into another strawberry. "She's not your typical HRD."

There *was* such a thing as a "typical" Human Remains Detection dog? But he didn't say those words. He'd already been more than enough of an asshole.

"She was supposed to be a drug detection dog, but Banshee couldn't pass all the tests. She started getting the label of untrainable."

Banshee's head had turned toward Tony as she spoke.

"But you probably know all this, don't you?" She wiped her fingers on a napkin. "So how about we just get down to business?"

"I don't know about Banshee's past."

"No?" Surprise flickered on Tony's face. "Then your investigators are less thorough than I realized. Maybe you should ask for some of your money back because when it comes to my life, Banshee is a very necessary part. She's been with me for eight years now. And without her, I wouldn't be the person I am." Her stare dropped to her dog. "She got kicked out of the program, can you imagine that? But I knew one of the cops who had access to her. He told me about her, and when I met her, I..." Her voice trailed away.

Aiden could figure out the rest. "You knew instantly that she was trainable. That she would be great at the job you needed her to do. And you didn't look back."

Laughter bubbled from her. The first time he'd heard Tony laugh. Rich and warm and her smile curved her full lips and lit her dark eyes, and she was absolutely *stunning*. Nothing could have made him look away from her.

"God, no," Tony said, as she wiped away a tear that had trickled out when she laughed. "Banshee was an absolute terror. That's how she originally got her name. *I* didn't give it to her. The guys at her old station did. When I first got her, she was a mess. She'd terrorize anyone who came close. She loved to steal things from me, from my neighbors. She'd scare the cats on my street. She just..." An exhale. "I didn't give up. Once she realized I wasn't going anywhere and that I wasn't going to throw in the towel with her, she changed." Squaring her shoulders, she angled her body toward Aiden. "Are you getting the moral of this little story?"

He hoped so. "You're not going to walk out on me just because you discovered I'm a bastard."

A tip of her head. "Excellent. I'm not. I said I'd take the case, and I will. I'm not going to get angry and walk after I've given my word. That's not who I am." A long exhale. "I also owe you a debt. You saved my life, and I take things like that very seriously."

He had to close the distance between them.

She stiffened but didn't back up.

"You don't owe me for what happened."

Her eyebrows rose. "It's not every day a man shoots to save me."

"Let me be clear. I would do anything to save you."

Her eyes widened. "Why?"

Because I hate the idea of you being hurt. Because I'm furious at myself for making pain flash in your eyes.

"Do you have one of those knight-in-shining-armor complexes?" she asked with a shake of her head. "Those are dangerous and will get wannabe knights killed."

"I never wanted to be a knight."

"What did you want to be?"

Loaded question. "What I am, of course. A successful businessman."

Her shoulders dipped. "It won't work if you keep lying to me. I will need your full cooperation in this partnership."

He didn't change expression.

"Like I told you before, I need to go to the police station. Then I need to see if I can get the rest of my things from the crime scene that was my rental home. After that, when I get the all-clear that I can leave town, I'll be tying up some loose ends and taking a road trip."

He waited.

"My destination will be your cabin in North Carolina. I want to get started as soon as I can."

"Thank you."

"I haven't done anything yet." She pressed her lips together. "Each of the Ice Breakers has a different skill set. You know I find the dead. You came to me because you believe your brother was murdered all those years ago."

"Yes." He wanted the body. He wanted clues. He wanted to destroy the person who'd taken his brother from him.

"I couldn't sleep last night," Tony confessed.

Neither the hell could I.

"So I did a little digging of my own. Granted, it's not my forte, other Ice Breakers work more on background intel, but I can manage to do an Internet search just fine. I read some articles on you, your family, and your brother's disappearance." A pause. "You were identical twins."

He'd already told her that.

"A lot of research suggests that identical twins have a particularly strong bond. Some think identical twins can read each other's minds. One researcher in particular even believed that they could feel each other's pain."

A lump rose in Aiden's throat. He choked it down. "I just feel like there's a hole in my life. A big, blank space where Austin used to be. I want to know what happened to him."

"You still own the cabin."

Yes. His parents were both dead. The cabin and everything else had gone to him. He'd never thought of selling. How could he? The place was his last tie to Austin. But she already knew that he owned it, so why was she stating that fact again? Where was she going with all this?

"As I indicated before, I'd like to stay there. Banshee and I will study the area. I'll talk to some locals. I'll see what I can discover."

Other investigators had talked to the locals. Others had searched for his brother. Those others weren't her. "I'll be there with you."

"I suspected you would say as much."

"And the dive team will be there, too."

Now she blinked in surprise.

"You said that the killer could have put his body in the lake after the initial search." Just like Clayton Duvane had done with his daughter. Gone back to dump the body in a place that no one would ever think to search again. No one but Tony. "I called in a team last night. They'll be at the cabin in a few days."

"Don't expect a miracle," she told him.

"I don't believe in those." He believed in pain and death and retribution. But he didn't mention that info to Tony. She believed that he wanted to find his brother.

He did.

But he'd long ago given up any hope that his brother would be found alive, so, yes, that was why he'd focused his attention on Tony and not any of the other Ice Breakers.

Perhaps the divers would find Austin's body, and with his body, with his remains, there would be evidence that Aiden could use.

Because this wasn't about putting the past to rest.

This was about punishing the sonofabitch who'd killed his brother. A punishment that was long overdue.

But he didn't say any of that to Tony. Why would he? She'd probably balk at the idea of him committing murder. *Balk?* She'd flip the hell out.

And that's why she can't ever learn all my secrets. He reached around her. Picked up a chocolate-covered strawberry, and holding her gaze, he took a bite.

He savored the sweet taste.

But she tastes better.

"Delicious," he murmured.

Almost as sweet as revenge.

CHAPTER EIGHT

There were plenty of places to dump a body in the woods. The thick forest seemed to stretch for miles and miles. The cabin—more of a mini-mansion, in Tony's opinion—sat nestled right in the middle of that wilderness. The lake was to the right. The water dark and still. So deep that the surface almost looked black. She could imagine that the water would be ice cold.

Tony didn't intend to find out.

Her hands shoved into the back pockets of her jeans as she took in the sights around her. "Perfect place to dump a body."

"Excuse me?" The woman who'd met her outside the cabin—just moments before—gave a nervous laugh. "I don't think I heard you correctly." Melanie Rodgers worked for a real estate company in town. The small, somewhat sleepy town of Eagle's Ridge, North Carolina. She'd been waiting at the cabin when Tony arrived. Apparently, her company watched over the property for Aiden, and she'd come out to make sure everything was running smoothly.

Or, in Tony's mind...she'd come running to the property because she'd expected Aiden to be there.

But instead, you got me.

"When Aiden called to say that he needed the cabin opened up and prepared for a stay, I didn't realize he was allowing a...friend to visit."

Tony turned away from the lake and the woods and focused on Melanie. In her experience, real estate agents always had their fingers on the pulse of gossip, especially in small towns like this one. "I'm not really a friend."

Melanie's hair—cut in a bob that angled around her slightly pointed jaw—blew lightly in the breeze. A very bright blond, a color that made her green eyes sparkle a bit brighter. Those green eyes took in Tony's braid, her sweatshirt, her battered jeans, and her scuffed, black boots. And her dog. "You're involved with Aiden?"

"Not in the way you're thinking. I'm working a case for him."

Curiosity appeared in the depths of her eyes. "So you're *not* dating him?"

"Despite what you may see on social media sites, no, I am not." There had been plenty of stories circulating. Stories that said Aiden had been at her house because he'd been in her bed.

Melanie sniffed. "I don't bother reading tabloid stories on BS social media."

Fair enough. "I'm trying to find his brother, Austin."

Melanie jerked back a step. "What?"

"That's what I do. I look for the missing."

"And you're looking *here?*" Her mouth sagged opened, then snapped closed. "Austin isn't here!"

"You sound very certain of that fact."

"It's been *years*. He's long gone. Probably living on some Mexican beach somewhere. He used to talk about going down there all the time. The guy sure did love the water." Her expression tightened with what could have been a hint of anger. "So like him to cut out and not care about the chaos that was left behind. He never looked back. One and done, that was Austin."

Okay, so, clearly, they'd been involved. Didn't take a psychologist to figure that out. "Ah, one and done?"

Melanie flushed. "You've seen Aiden. Austin looked the same only..." A roll of her shoulders. "He had this sexy, bad-boy edge that would melt your panties."

Melanie was definitely the type to chat. And overshare.

"Everyone knew he was trouble, and every girl wanted him."

Tony cut to the chase before she had to hear more about Melanie's panties. "You slept with him."

Another roll of her shoulders. "That was so long ago, I can hardly remember."

I think you remember plenty. One and done.

"Everyone always raised such a fuss about him being abducted or being dead." A shake of her head. "He just ran off. Austin *hated* the whole Warner world. Thought it was stuffy and boring and a pain in the ass. He would have done anything to get away. *Anything.*"

"Even fake his own death?" Tony asked because the question had to be voiced.

Before Melanie could answer, a black SUV pulled into the driveway. Melanie's head whipped toward the vehicle. "Aiden," she said. She smoothed down her pencil skirt and tugged at the bottom of her blouse before her heels raced toward him.

Tony didn't move. She'd already gotten some preliminary reports from her team. Nothing she'd found had indicated that Austin had faked his own death. But it was curious that, immediately after meeting her, Melanie would start spinning that story.

The SUV braked. Tony expected Smith to hop out of the driver's side, but instead, the door opened, and Aiden emerged. Aiden, wearing jeans and a sweatshirt, with stubble coating his jaw and his thick, slightly wavy hair tousled. His head turned, but he didn't look at Melanie.

Instead, his stare locked straight on Tony.

He had this sexy, bad-boy edge that would melt your panties.

"Aiden!" Melanie announced as if greeting a long-lost lover. She threw out her arms and ran toward him. "It's been far too long." She collided with him, embracing him fiercely.

Tony's brows rose. *Well, all right.* Only, it wasn't all right. She didn't like the sight of Melanie hugging Aiden. Not one bit.

Oh, hell, jealousy. Great. Now it was a real party. All sorts of fun emotions were plaguing her.

As if sensing her unrest, Banshee pressed closer.

"Totally fine," she muttered to her friend. "Really." Her steps shuffled forward.

Melanie finally released Aiden and sent him a sugary smile. "I was just telling your associate how happy I am to look after your property. Though instead of just paying us a fee for upkeep, you really should let my company rent out the house when you're not using it. People would pay top dollar to stay at a place like this."

Tony ambled a bit closer. She noticed that Aiden stepped back from Melanie. "She's right," Tony felt duty bound to say as she considered the sprawling property. "People would pay top dollar. There's a segment of the population that loves to stay at murder sites."

"Yes, see, even your associate agrees—" Melanie stopped. Gasped. Seemed to finally have let all of Tony's words sink in. "What are you—" She spun on Tony. "That's a terrible thing to say!"

Was it? "It's true."

"And this isn't a *murder* spot!" Melanie rushed to say. "I told you, Austin probably went down to Mexico. He's sunning himself near the water, working on his tan." A frantic shake of her head. "I can't believe you're dragging this all up again," she told Aiden as she angled back toward him. "Don't you want to just move on?"

He eased past her and toward Tony. "You beat me here."

"Only by a few minutes."

Surprising her, Banshee bounded toward Aiden. The dog lowered her head, and Aiden gave her a quick pat.

"Have you already gone in the house?" Aiden stopped right beside Tony.

It had been two days since she'd last seen him. Two days since she'd left Biloxi and gone home. She'd wanted to prepare. Wanted to get fresh clothing. *Wanted to put some emotional space between us.*

But the whole emotional-space idea hadn't worked so well. Because seeing him again hit her with the force of a punch. Melanie had been right about one thing...

The Warner men were quite unforgettable.

But...

One and done.

Was that how their world worked? The preliminary reports she'd gotten on Aiden hadn't linked him to any serious relationships. He dated plenty, yes, but, nothing serious. Nothing that ever lasted.

Tony cleared her throat because he'd asked her a question, and she wasn't supposed to be obsessing over his past lovers. *But isn't that only fair, since he knows everything about me?* "I haven't gone in yet." No time. Melanie had been waiting to pounce when Tony exited her small rental car. "I would love to start surveying the area while there is still good light."

"Surveying the area?" A nervous laugh came from Melanie. "What exactly is it that you think you'll find? That *others* overlooked?"

"*Dr.* Antonia Rossi is the best when it comes to finding the dead," Aiden informed her.

Tony hadn't gotten to introduce herself to the other woman. Melanie had introduced herself, then started talking about her rental company. She hadn't seemed interested in learning Tony's name, so Tony hadn't given it. "Just call me Tony."

A faint smirk curled Melanie's carefully painted lips. "Let me guess. Toni with an I?"

"No. It's a Y." A deliberate choice from long ago. When she'd first started her investigative career, all of her paperwork had just listed her as Tony Rossi. When they saw the name on paper, most people had assumed she was a man, and, in a field often dominated *by* men, she'd been called again and again to some of the most gruesome and challenging scenes out there. Of course, when she'd arrived, law enforcement personnel had realized that *Tony* was, in fact, a woman. But it hadn't taken her long at all to prove herself to them.

Her name didn't matter these days. All that mattered was that she had a reputation for getting the job done.

Aiden's stare lingered on Tony's face as he told Melanie, "She often notices what others don't."

Sometimes, she did. If there was something to be found. But, sometimes, there was nothing there. "I want to look at the terrain first." Tony glanced toward the trees. She'd need to do grid work as she tried to keep track of the areas she searched and those she hadn't. "If the killer was in a hurry, you might see a small hill where the body wasn't buried deeply enough. Depressions in the ground from the soil settling after all this time. A heavy growth of vegetation that would come from the body decomposing—"

"My God, that's morbid," Melanie cut in with a shudder. "Just what kind of doctor are you?" She stared at Tony with horror on her pretty face.

Like she hadn't seen that look before. "The kind that finds dead bodies." She tapped her thigh. Banshee hurried back to her. "She'll be my best weapon. She can sniff for any remains as I go through the woods." But there was *so* much territory to cover. The property backed up to a state park. Miles and miles and miles... "Eventually, we can try ground penetrating radar, if we find potential hotspots. And, of course, once the divers arrive, we'll make sure that they check every inch of the lake."

Melanie swallowed and backed away. "I'll just...leave you to all of that." A weak smile curved her lips. She sent that smile to Aiden. "Aiden, if you need me, you have my number." With that, she rushed for her red sports car. And tossed one last, horrified glance at Tony.

Aiden watched her go. "I think you scared her off."

"I think she slept with your brother."

The sports car *vroomed* before it sped away.

Aiden coughed. "She...ah. Yes, yes, I think she did."

Tony stared straight at him. "Did you sleep with her, too?" That hadn't been in the file.

A wide grin curved his lips. "God, I missed your bluntness. The past two days seemed very, very long."

Was he teasing her? Uncertain, she said, "Don't make fun of me." She'd asked a legitimate question.

"Never." He positioned his body right in front of hers. "I did miss you." The grin slowly faded. "Is there any chance at all that you missed me?"

The wind sent tendrils of her hair sliding over her cheeks. "You didn't answer my question."

He caught those tendrils. Tucked them behind her ear. His fingers lingered against her cheek. "If I answer your question, will you answer mine?"

"Yes."

"No."

Her brow furrowed.

"No, I have never slept with Melanie, though she has certainly indicated that she's interested. I have this rule, though, you see. I prefer not to sleep with women who also slept with my brother."

Her brows rose. "That's a good rule."

"Um. Don't exactly want her pretending I'm Austin. That would be weird. Because back in the day, I think she loved my brother."

Pretending I'm Austin.

"Your turn." He smiled at her once more. His smile was killer. Seductive. Charming. Dangerous. "Did you miss me? Even a little bit? Or are you back to your only-business mode?"

She gave him the truth. "I missed you. I have no idea why, but I did."

His smile flickered. Died. "Shit." His gaze heated. "Really thought you'd lie and say you didn't feel a thing. How the hell am I supposed to react when you're this honest?"

"You could try being honest with me. You might be surprised at the results you get."

His amber gaze glinted. "The last time I was honest, you left me with blue balls and a sleepless night."

Well...*ahem.* "That was your fault. If you'd been *honest* before that moment..." But she stopped.

"I never would have gotten to kiss you, if I'd been honest before then." His fingers slid down. Eased under her chin. "And the kiss was worth the blue balls, just so you know."

She thought he was going to kiss her again.

Instead...

He let her go. Stepped back. "I don't like this place." His shoulders straightened. "I don't like who I become when I'm here."

What a curious thing to say. "Who do you become?"

His gaze slid to the dark, still water of the lake. "An even bigger bastard than I normally am."

***

Melanie pulled off the side of the road. A cloud of dirt and dust filled the air around her car as she hauled up her phone and dialed quickly.

Answer. Answer. Pick up the freaking phone!

"Hello?" His rumbling voice slid over the line.

Her breath shuddered out. "We have a problem."

"Hey, sweetheart," he murmured. "You missing me again?"

"Aiden is at the cabin."

"So?" Complete unconcern. "He goes out there sometimes."

"He brought a *woman* with him."

Laughter. "Good for him."

He wasn't listening to her. "She's some kind of doctor—she's there to search and try to find a body. She's got a dog with her, and she was talking about shallow graves, and she mentioned getting divers in the lake. This is a *nightmare*."

He wasn't laughing any longer.

"What in the hell are we going to do?" she whispered.

"Simple. We're going to stop her."

"Yeah? Well, we better do it fast. She's out there right now!"

"Take a breath, darling. No sense in getting so stressed."

There was *every* sense in getting stressed. "It's easy for you to say, but you can damn well believe I will not go down alone. If anything happens, you'll be dragged down with me."

Silence. Then, "Thanks for the warning."

This wasn't the first warning she'd given him. When she'd learned Aiden was coming back, Melanie had called him then, too. Why couldn't he understand her worry? "Listen—"

He hung up.

Her breath shuddered in and out. *Take a breath, darling*—my ass. He'd better take a breath. He'd better get a handle on this situation.

She was not about to be fucked over and left to twist in the wind.

***

Tony had walked for hours, and, no particular surprise to her, she'd turned up nothing. Aiden had trailed her, a silent shadow for each step that she took, and she'd felt his disappointment.

"Warned you not to expect a miracle," she said as they headed into the cabin later that afternoon. The hinges squeaked as the door opened wide.

"No, I think what you said was that *you* weren't my miracle." He shut the door behind them. Locked it. Her luggage sat in the entranceway. So did his. He'd been eager to start the search with her, so they'd gone right out after dumping the bags inside.

"I'm not. I'm not anyone's miracle." Aware that her words sounded stiff, she huffed out a breath and tried to explain. "I just don't want you getting disappointed. You have to realize there's a chance I won't find anything." She stroked Banshee's head. "I need to get her some water."

"Got things set up in the kitchen. Figured you had your own food for her, but I gave instructions for bowls to be put out in there."

Instructions...to Melanie. "You trust Melanie to have open access to your home?" After grabbing Banshee's food from one of her bags, Tony followed Aiden into the kitchen. A bowl of water was, indeed, waiting for the dog. Tony filled the food bowl.

"Melanie runs the *only* property management company in the area. And we go back a long time, so, no, I don't trust her at all."

Her eyes widened because that response had not gone at all how she'd anticipated.

A soft laugh rumbled from him. "Antonia, I trust very few people in this world."

Goose bumps rose on her arms. "I told you to call me Tony." Abruptly, she turned away, leaving Banshee to her dinner as Tony stalked back into the den.

Aiden followed her with slow but steady steps.

She went toward the fireplace. No fire crackled inside the massive structure. *Massive.* That was a good word for everything in the cabin. Larger than life. Expensive.

Cold?

"What did I say that made you angry?" he asked, voice curious.

"Nothing." Her arms wrapped around her stomach. "I will need a full list of people who have access to this cabin. Both now and back at the time of your brother's disappearance."

"Not gonna be easy. The now part, sure, I can get you that info. It's me, Smith, and Melanie. Perhaps an assistant or two at her company. The person Melanie sends to keep the place tidy before I arrive. As for who had access when my brother vanished, that's harder. My parents. Me. Austin. And pretty much every person he met in town and invited to the party."

Her head angled toward him.

He shrugged. "Not like you needed some magic word to get in the party. Austin wanted the word spread that he was celebrating for summer, so word spread. I have a vague memory of the house being packed. Bodies jumping in here..." He motioned to the pristine den. "As music blasted. I have no idea who all was here. Don't think the local cops ever figured it out completely, either." His gaze watched her. "Why don't you like your name?"

"I love my name. It was my grandmother's name. Beautiful." An exhale. "Let's focus on your case, shall we? Not my name."

"You tense whenever I say it."

"Then don't say it. Call me Tony. *That's* my name preference."

"Why—"

"Because *he* said it, all right? Because he kept calling me Antonia over and over again, and when the police shot him, he stared straight at me, and the last thing he said was my name."

Shock rippled across Aiden's handsome face.

And shock filled her because she had never, ever told anyone why she didn't like to use *Antonia* any longer. Not the shrinks her father had insisted she see as a child. Not even her close friends on the Ice Breakers. But she'd told Aiden.

"*Tony...*"

Wonderful. *Now* he called her Tony. "You already knew this, remember? You have your file. You figured me all out."

"There was nothing in the file about him saying your name at the end. I realized you had to be on the scene when he was killed, but...*that close?* Close enough to hear his last word? What the fuck?"

What the fuck, indeed. "Some memories last a lifetime." Because they were branded into your mind. Your soul. She would never forget that moment.

He stalked toward her. Tight, angry movements. "What happened in those hours with Timothy Brandon?"

She flinched at the name. Because saying his name made him appear in her head. She hated that the bastard was still in her head. "We aren't working on my case. My case is dead and buried." She knew. She'd gone to the asshole's grave. "I want you to walk me through the morning you woke up and you realized your brother was gone. Take me to the room you were in. Show me the steps you took."

"What happened in those hours?" he pushed.

This isn't the way home. Her voice. Her memory. Whispering through her mind. "Stop it. Right now."

A muscle jerked in Aiden's jaw. "Sorry."

She hadn't meant those words for him. *For me.* Because she wanted the memories to stop flashing through her mind. "Digging up painful memories from my past *isn't* my idea of a thrilling adventure. I get that's what we're doing here for you—I get that I'm asking *you* to dig up your pain, too. And it sucks. But you don't get to turn it around on me so that I have to suffer, too. That isn't how it works."

A hard, negative shake of Aiden's dark head. "That's not what I was doing."

"No? It felt like it to me."

"I *want* to know about you. I want to know what I do that upsets you—so I can stop it. Like when I said your name, I wanted to know why it looked like I hurt you." Gruff. Rasping. "Because I don't want to hurt you, not ever again. I want to do everything in my power to make sure that pain is the last thing you feel."

"Why?" Genuinely curious, she waited for his response.

"Because I don't like it when you hurt." Simple. "It pisses me off. I want to stand between you and every threat, but the only threats, the only pain—it seems to come from me." He inhaled. Stepped back. "I'll change that, Tony."

Tony.

He turned around. "I was in the bedroom at the end of the hallway on the second floor."

She didn't move.

His hand curved around the banister. "You coming?"

Of course. She'd been the one to ask for this tour, hadn't she? Her feet stumbled over the floor as she hurried to catch him. He waved for her to pass him and go up the stairs first. But as she passed, he whispered, "If he were still alive, I'd kill the sonofabitch."

She froze. Her body whipped around, and she would have slipped on the stair if he hadn't caught her. His hands locked around her waist, and he held her securely in place. Because he was on the stairs below her, they were perfectly positioned on eye level. Automatically, to balance herself, her hands flew out and clamped around his shoulders.

"Why would you say that?" she asked.

"Because he was a bastard who hurt kids. Murdered them. Because he hurt *you*."

"You're not a killer." He shouldn't just—just say things like that.

But a cold smile tilted his lips. "How do you know what I am?"

She remembered the way he'd fired the gun in her rental house. No hesitation at all. Just cold calculation. Determined fury.

Saint had talked to her last night about Aiden. "*Some kind of business whiz. Took his father's failing business—the guy had driven the hotel chain into the ground—and Aiden turned things around. Seems to have a golden touch. Can make money wherever he goes. Got his MBA from Harvard. I know, shocker, am I right? Like you didn't see that shit coming. But he's also one of those annoying do-gooder types. At least on paper. Always donating to charities. Building youth centers. Digging wells. You know, the stuff that makes me look like a total asshole and him look like a shining star.*"

Because Saint had never, ever been accused of being a do-gooder.

Except, the man before her, the man with the cold, glittering eyes and the touch that seemed to singe her through her clothes, the man who'd just casually said he would kill for her—that man didn't seem to be at all like the one Saint had described to her.

He seemed completely opposite of that guy.

"Be careful," he murmured, "I'd hate for you to fall."

"Aiden—"

He kissed her. His mouth took hers. Not softly. Not hesitantly. But frantically. Desperately. The same way that her mouth was suddenly taking his. Because maybe he'd kissed her. Or maybe she'd been the one to close that distance and kiss him. Tony wasn't sure. All she knew was that he tasted incredible. That the lust roared through her body as she kissed him. That she'd never, ever had this reaction to anyone else before. And that...

He scared her.

Correction, her reaction to him scared her.

Because she wasn't being cautious. Wasn't following all her careful rules. In fact, she didn't want to follow any rules at all when it came to Aiden.

"Fucking missed you," he growled against her mouth. "Just met you and I missed you."

She'd missed him, too. More than she'd expected.

He kissed her again as he pulled her even closer against him. Her short nails sank into his shoulders. They were both going to be staying at this cabin. And, yes, she'd already wondered what would happen between them when they were alone in this place.

Then he abruptly pulled back. He kept his hands on her waist, but he put some space between them. "Should I apologize for that?"

"For threatening to kill a man?" She considered it even as her heart raced. Tony was pretty amazed her voice came out so steady. "No, he's already dead, so I don't see how it matters."

His gaze held hers. "I meant apologize for the kiss."

"I know."

"Tony..."

"Don't apologize for something we both wanted." She let him go. Her hands moved to cover his. To—unfortunately—pull them away from her. "Show me the room." Her voice was still steady, but her knees weren't. So when she turned and made her way up the stairs, she made sure to hold the banister. Not like she wanted to take a fall.

He didn't speak as they climbed the stairs. At the landing, he eased past her and turned to the right. As they walked down the hallway, she noticed that they passed three other rooms. All bedrooms with the doors wide open.

Hardly some small mountain retreat. This cabin was easily three times the size of her place.

They reached the last room. "I woke up in here," Aiden said.

The door was closed for this room. The others had all been open.

"Was this your bedroom? When you stayed here, I mean?"

His jaw tensed. "No. It was Austin's. He was the one who always used this room. I don't know why I was in there that night."

Her gaze darted back down the hallway. "It would have been the quietest one. If you were looking to get away from the noise downstairs, maybe this was the best place for you. You came up here and you crashed."

"Maybe." He reached for the doorknob. Turned it. "Maybe that's exactly what I was—*sonofabitch*."

She stopped. Stared. The room had been trashed. The bed overturned. The drawers yanked from the dresser and tossed onto the floor. The chest looked as if a hammer had been taken to it. Smashed. Destroyed. Even large chunks of the hardwood floor had been ripped up.

Delicately, Tony cleared her throat.

His stunned gaze flew to her.

"If I were you," she told him, "I'd get a new property management firm. STAT."

CHAPTER NINE

"I get that it looks bad, Aiden. I get it," the police chief told him. "But it was probably just some kids messing around. The cabin is usually empty, and you know there's practically a legend circulating about this place. Likely was the result of some damn dare...teens got challenged to sneak into the place and—"

"Destroy property?" Tony inserted carefully as she stood on the porch beside Aiden. "Challenged to vandalize a home *after* they'd done a wee bit of breaking and entering?"

The police chief—Barrett Montgomery—focused his attention on her. His blue eyes narrowed as his stare swept over her.

Aiden had known Barrett for years. Only back in the day, Barrett had been tight with Austin. They'd loved raising some hell during the summer days. Only the hell-raising teenager had now turned into the town's quiet and steady police chief.

"Dr. Rossi." Barrett tipped his head toward her. "Your reputation definitely precedes you." His head cocked. "So you're here to find Austin, huh?"

"At the moment, I'm here to give my statement about a breaking and entering. But you don't seem too concerned about the crime." Her shoulder brushed against Aiden's arm. "Why is that?"

Sighing, Barrett suggested, "Because I remember—too well—what it was like to be a dumbass kid? Because there are no security cameras at this place, and we have no idea when the intruders were even here? Because I can take statements, but there isn't much else I can do?"

"Really?" Her doubt was clear. "How about dusting for some fingerprints?"

He sent her a smile. "We're a small town, Dr. Rossi, and this crime—"

"Don't give me the small-town BS." Flat.

His smile died.

"I've been in plenty of small towns," Tony continued. "And the police still do their jobs. If you won't check for prints, then I can get in a crew who will."

He stiffened. "Now, hold on..."

"No, you hold on. Because you might think this is some harmless prank, but I don't. I don't think we should just overlook an attack in the room of a missing man. A man who could quite probably have been killed in this house years ago. You can say it's kids. Fine, say it. But you don't have proof of that. And in *my* experience, I find that killers truly do like to go back to the scene of their crimes."

Aiden stiffened.

"They like to return. They like to relive the attack. And sometimes, sometimes they like to destroy. Rage builds inside of them until it has to explode. Know what I saw in that room?" Her chin lifted. "Rage. So get a crime scene team here. Check it out. And if you can't do it, then I will make a phone call and have my own people here in an hour." Her head turned toward Aiden. "Or Mr. Big Bucks will do the job, and Aiden will have his people here in—"

"Thirty minutes?" he finished for her. "Maybe even faster. Money is a great motivator."

She nodded. "Great. Perfect. Motivate away."

"*Hold on!*"

They both looked at Barrett.

He had his hands in the air. "My team will check for prints. They'll collect evidence. Just— calm down, will you?"

"I am perfectly calm," Tony responded. "Aiden, do you feel calm?"

"Feeling a little pissed honestly." More than a little. And, rattled, dammit. He'd been rattled when he opened that door and saw the destruction. He'd tried calling Melanie while they waited on the police chief to arrive, but she hadn't answered him. How the hell had this mess even happened?

Barrett's hands went to his hips. The movement pushed back his coat to reveal his holstered weapon. "It's gonna take my people some time, all right? Why don't you two go to town for a bit? Give us some space. I'll let you know when we're done here."

"That's it?" Tony gaped. Obviously, this was not the way she was used to working with law enforcement personnel. "You just want us to go on our merry way?"

Barrett nodded. "If you want me to be thorough, yeah, I do. I want you away from my crime scene for a while. I'll call Aiden when the house is clear." He exhaled. "I'll also talk to Melanie and find out exactly when she was in that room last. Maybe we can pinpoint a date to figure out when our intruder was here."

"*Maybe* you can," Tony responded tightly. "Because that would certainly be helpful."

Jaw locking, Barrett turned and strode back into the house.

"Was the previous police chief like him?" Tony wanted to know. "So...I don't know, unwilling to do much of an investigation?"

"The previous chief was his stepdad. And, yes, I remember his response being pretty similar." Unfortunately. "When I reported Austin's disappearance, he said that my brother had probably run off."

"Even with the blood? That was the chief's response?"

"At first, the chief said the blood could have been anybody's. Took a few days to get the labs back." More than a few days. More like two weeks. Everything had been slow then. And... "My dad was on damage-control mode." Aiden climbed down the porch steps, wanting to put distance between himself and that place.

He fucking hated the cabin.

Banshee had been sitting on the edge of the porch, calmly watching all the activity. But when Aiden moved, she rose to her feet.

"I don't understand." Tony quickly followed him. So did Banshee. "Damage control—why?" She reached out and curled her hand around his arm. "Because your father thought that you had been involved?"

"No, dammit," a low, rough growl. *"Everyone said Aiden was the good twin. The good twin doesn't do shit like that."*

Her expression tightened.

Fuck. Watch yourself. He put his hand over hers. Lowered his head toward her. Near her ear, he whispered, "My father was on damage control because he thought my brother had hurt someone, okay? He thought Austin had hurt someone and run away after the attack. My father wasn't convinced that my brother was the victim. He thought Austin was the assailant. He didn't change his opinion, not until the lab results came back. By then, my father had spent so much time and money covering up that there wasn't much we could do to actually *find* Austin." His head lifted.

"Why was he so quick to believe that your brother had hurt someone?" Like him, her voice was low, carrying only to the two of them.

"Because Austin had done it before." He let her hand go. "Let's go for a drive, all right? We'll talk when we're away from here."

Without another word, she turned and marched for his SUV. He didn't immediately follow. Instead, he looked back at the cabin. Looked upstairs at the last bedroom, and he saw the curtains twitch in that room. The room that had been trashed. *Austin's* room. The room he'd woken up in that terrible morning.

Aiden realized that someone had been watching them. One of the cops?

Some days, he felt like someone was always watching him.

Banshee's head bumped against him.

"Yeah, I'm ready. Let's get the hell out of here, girl."

***

"What do you mean, the room was trashed?" Melanie's voice rose, and she gave a nervous laugh. "I can assure you, everything should be perfectly fine at the cabin."

"It's not perfectly fine," Barrett responded. Barrett, in his full-on, police chief voice. No-nonsense, as if he hadn't spent plenty of summers drunk off his ass with her. "I'm standing in Austin Warner's old bedroom right now, and the place looks like someone took a sledgehammer to it."

Oh, shit.

"When were you in this room last?"

Her mind scrambled. Barrett was a pretty good police chief, he'd probably follow up with her assistant, so she had to be honest. "Two days ago." When Aiden had called to say he was coming back. "I checked the whole house, and everything was in perfect condition."

Silence.

"Was...anything taken?" she asked carefully.

"I have no idea. I'll have to get Aiden to look through everything. Right now, it's fucking chaos. And I have to get fingerprints."

Fingerprints. "It was probably just some kids messing around." Her nails tapped on her desk. "I told Aiden that we should get security cameras out there, but he didn't really like to talk about the cabin. Just wanted me to keep it locked up, then, on the rare occasions when he did come to town, he'd want me to stock the fridge. Make sure the power was still running, all that boring stuff that I'm sure you don't care about." Did her voice sound normal? She hoped it did. Damn, it was hot in her office.

"When was Aiden's last visit?"

She didn't like these questions. "He always comes back on the anniversary."

"That would have been the summer? He hasn't been back since then?"

Tread carefully. "Not that I'm aware of."

"I need to know who all has keys to the cabin."

Fuck. "I do. My assistant has access. And, of course, anyone that Aiden has given keys. I'm sure his buddy Smith has some. Smith was with him last time."

Silence.

Right. Because Smith and Barrett weren't exactly tight.

There was a murmur of voices in the background. Then, voice lowering, Barrett asked her, "Do you know who's with him?"

"A woman. He said she was there to help, ah, find Austin." She injected sympathy into her voice. "Poor Aiden. I guess he will just let any scammer trick him into thinking that she'll magically find his brother even though I've said multiple times that Austin is probably on a beach, enjoying the water and cheap margaritas—"

"Dr. Rossi isn't a scammer." Impatience bit into his words. "She's the real deal. I saw a lecture she did about five months ago when I was down in Savannah. Guys in law enforcement say she can find just about anyone. Her dog picks up the dead like you wouldn't believe."

Her stomach twisted. "I see." The dog was a problem. *No, Dr. Rossi is the problem.*

"If she's here with him, if she's taken his case...hell, I saw the stupid social media posts about them, but I just thought it was BS. Didn't realize he'd actually be bringing her here."

She'd never heard Barrett sound quite this way. "What? What is it?"

"If she's here, then she thinks Austin is, too. The woman is gonna find his body, and this whole town is about to be turned into freaking crime central. Aiden isn't like Austin. You don't see his emotions blaring on the outside. With Austin, you always knew how he felt. If he was pissed, he'd punch you in the face. If he liked you, he'd tell the world you were his best friend." A long exhale. "Aiden was the opposite. You *never* knew what he thought. He's cold and calculating, and, after all these years, he still hasn't gotten over what happened."

Her stomach didn't just twist. It knotted. "I see."

"Aiden is gonna make sure that he gets his revenge. Count on it. Dr. Rossi is going to be his ticket to finding the truth, and he will use her and not stop. He will never stop." A low exhale. "My town is about to be lit on fire." He hung up.

She gripped her phone too tightly. Wonderful. The town would be on fire. Just the reassuring words she'd hoped to hear from the police chief.

That fire can't touch me. I won't let it.

Melanie jumped to her feet. She shoved her phone into her bag and grabbed her purse.

The last thing she intended to do was burn.

***

"I expected you to throw your name around," Tony said. "Or maybe your money. Or both." The trees were a blur as they passed the woods on the long, winding road. "Instead, you just—"

"Let you do all the talking and threatening?" Aiden interjected, voice mild. "You seemed to be getting the job done, so why stop you? Besides, throwing my money around is a real dick move." A brief pause before he added, "One that I try to reserve for very special circumstances."

"Your home getting trashed isn't special enough?" She thought it qualified as a very special circumstance.

"My home getting trashed is...unusual."

Such careful words. She could read between the lines. "So you're not buying that some kids broke in for shits and giggles?" Had the chief really bought that? If so, the man would be useless to them. And if he hadn't bought that story, then why the hell had he lied?

Aiden pulled into the parking lot of a small diner. Killed the engine and glanced over at her. "Are you buying it?"

"No." Not even for a second and she had a whole list of reasons why. "Because those mysterious *kids* managed to get in the house without damaging either the front door or the back door. And none of the windows on the lower level showed any sign of forced entry, either."

His brows rose.

"I looked while you were chatting it up with the chief." Of course, she'd made herself busy and useful. Investigating was what she did. Speaking of investigating... "I'm assuming Barrett was also at the party the night Austin vanished?"

"Yes."

A nod as Tony filed away that bit of info. At this point, she'd started to wonder who in this small town hadn't been at the party. "From my experience, teenagers looking to cause trouble are sloppy. They don't get into ever-so-expensive homes without leaving even scratch marks on the door. And until we stepped foot into that bedroom, there were no signs of an intruder. Nothing at all appeared out of place in the cabin. At the very least, teens looking for trouble would have left dirty footprints or beer cans. They would have smashed more shit." She shrugged. "And I don't think they would have ripped up the flooring. That seemed too deliberate."

Aiden jerked off his seatbelt and turned to face her. "What do you mean?"

Banshee continued to sprawl in the backseat, paying them no attention.

"I mean someone was clearly looking for something in that room. They tossed the drawers, but really, I think that was for show. Not like you're still going to have the same things in those drawers that you did all those years ago." She waited for him to respond.

His expression tightened. "My mom emptied everything out of his drawers. She donated all the clothes years ago. The stuff in there now—hell, it was just things like sheets. Extra towels. Random crap."

"That's what I thought. And that's why the intruder came equipped with both a crowbar and a sledgehammer. The intruder believed something important was hidden in that room. Perhaps under a loose bit of the hardwood floor that was ripped out. *Not* in the drawers." The destruction of the drawers had probably just been for show. To distract from the real search area. *My money is on the flooring. The intruder thought something was hidden beneath the floor.* "The real question we need to be asking..." Actually, there were several main questions. "What was the intruder looking for?"

Aiden stared back at her. "Something that belonged to Austin."

Because it had been Austin's room.

"That leads us to our next bit of curiosity." She licked her lower lip. "Did the intruder find what he was looking for? And, why, after all this time, did he finally decide to search for this mysterious item?"

Aiden's phone rang, the chime shrilling in the small space. He pulled it from his pocket, glanced at the screen, and said, "It's Barrett." He swiped his fingers over the phone, answering the call and putting it on speaker. "What did you find out?" No greeting. Just the flat question.

"Talked to Melanie." Barrett's tone was grim. "She went through every room two days ago when you called her. She swears that everything was fine then."

Two days ago. Now they had a timeline. Provided that Melanie was telling them the truth.

She could very well be the one who trashed the room.

"We'll need a few more hours out here," Barrett added. "Then I'll give you the all-clear to come back."

Aiden ended the call.

"The room was trashed *after* you told Melanie you were coming back to town." Again, provided that Melanie was telling the truth. But to determine that, there was only one option. "I think we should go have another chat with your property manager."

"So the hell do I."

***

But Melanie wasn't at her office. The business was shut down for the day. Not surprising, really, considering the hour. A trip to her house revealed that her car wasn't in the drive, and the place appeared shuttered. Aiden drove them through town—the small strip that constituted the downtown area—but they didn't see any sign of Melanie.

Barrett called again, told them that his people had finished up. The house was clear. So when they returned to the cabin, the drive was empty. The setting sun cast heavy shadows around the house, and the trees seemed to twist and stretch. An ominous feeling seemed to cling to the place, and Tony didn't know why, but dread settled around her.

Something bad happened here.

But she'd known that already, hadn't she?

Aiden braked. "You have to be starving. Bet you're wishing we'd had more than some quick fast food while we hunted for Melanie, huh? Come inside, and I'll make you some dinner."

"You cook? I'm impressed already." She tried to lighten some of the tension she felt.

"Clearly, you have not tasted my cooking. Amateur hour at best." He opened his door and slid out.

She followed, aware that her stomach was giving a little growl. Tony's fingers curled around the back door. "Maybe I can help." She swung open the SUV's rear door. "I'm not too bad in the kit—*Banshee!*" Her words ended in a cry of dismay because Banshee had just blasted out of the vehicle and past her, barking and snarling, and heading straight for the dark and twisting trees. "Banshee, stop!"

But her German Shephard, the dog she'd painstaking trained, ignored her. Still barking louder and more furiously than Tony had ever heard before, Banshee charged for the woods.

Fear chilled Tony's blood. "Something is wrong." She lunged after her dog.

Aiden grabbed her. His arm curled around her stomach, and he hauled her back. "What's happening?"

She squirmed in his hold. "I need to get to Banshee. Now. Something is—"

A howl. A long, desperate howl. Tony stiffened.

That howl...

"Oh, God," Tony whispered.

The howling changed. Her eyes strained, and she could just make out the pitiful sounds coming from Banshee. The sad cries that drifted on the wind...

She stopped struggling in Aiden's arms.

"What's happening?" he demanded.

Her head turned toward him. "Banshee always cries...when she finds the dead."

CHAPTER TEN

Tony's low words turned Aiden's blood to ice. *Banshee found my brother?* Tony wasn't fighting him any longer, so he eased his hold on her.

Apparently, that was exactly what Tony had been waiting for him to do. She bounded forward even as she yelled, "Banshee, to me, *now!*" Her feet thudded as she rushed toward the twisting trees.

Swearing, Aiden flew after her. No way was he going to let Tony run off into the dark, into the woods, without him. She seemed to have trouble understanding that they were in a partnership. She didn't get to take risks while he waited on the sidelines. No fucking way.

Just as he reached her, a dark shadow raced out of the woods and came straight at Tony. She bent her knees and reached out to the dog, pulling Banshee in close.

"Do not do that again," Aiden heard Tony order as he shuddered to a stop beside them. "You scared me to death and—" Tony broke off. Slowly, she lifted her right hand. The hand that she'd just been using to stroke Banshee's head. "It's wet."

He could see darkness on Banshee's head.
The wetness just appeared dark on the dog, but
when Tony lifted her fingers a bit higher and the
light from the setting sun hit her hand, he saw that
the color wasn't black but was actually red. Red
because it was—

"Blood." Tony straightened instantly. "That's
blood on her. She was crying. Oh, God. It's not an
old kill. She found a fresh body. Banshee, show
me!"

Banshee barked, spun around, and ran back
to the woods.

Tony started to follow, but he grabbed her
wrist. "That's not how it works." Time for her to
get this in her head. "You don't rush into danger.
You don't risk yourself."

"This is my job! This is what you wanted me
to do!"

Putting her in danger had never been part of
the plan. "You got a gun on you?"

A quick negative shake of her head even as
Tony said, "We need to follow Banshee!"

"I have a gun." He had it gripped in his left
hand. He'd been carrying the concealed weapon
the whole time he'd been in North Carolina. "So
that means I go first. If there's a fresh kill out
there, then the sonofabitch who did the killing has
to be close." He would not risk Tony. "*Stay behind
me.*"

"Fine, whatever, let's just go!"

They went. He made sure to stay in front of
Tony and to keep his gun at the ready. She didn't
understand that he'd been trained for this shit.
Didn't understand because he'd been keeping

plenty of secrets from her. But that was the way he worked. Secrecy was a part of Aiden's life. He kept secrets from everyone.

Aiden and Tony twisted and turned as they snaked through the woods after the dog. Banshee paused just a moment for them to catch up, but when the German Shephard caught sight of them, she instantly turned and jumped forward again.

Branches scraped and tugged at him, but Aiden shoved them out of his way. The dog moved unerringly, and admiration filled him because Banshee sure as hell knew her business. The dog was pretty damn amazing.

They broke into a small clearing. Banshee rushed forward, but then jerked to a stop. At full attention, she stared down at her goal.

The sun had fallen even lower in the sky, but there was enough light for him to see the woman's sprawled body. The tangle of her blond hair spread around her. Slowly, he and Tony crept closer.

"That's your property manager," Tony said.

She was right. Melanie Rodgers had been left on the ground, with her body twisted to the right and her face aimed toward the woods. Blood pooled beneath her. Blood—from the knife wounds in her body. From the *knife* that had been left in her chest.

Tony crouched next to her. Tony's fingers went to Melanie's throat.

He knew she wasn't going to find a pulse. After all, hadn't Banshee cried?

Banshee always cries...when she finds the dead.

"She's still warm," Tony whispered.

What the fuck? Still warm meant her killer had to be extremely close. Aiden hadn't heard the sound of any motors, so it was unlikely the killer had come in the woods on an ATV. *That means he is here on foot.* Aiden grabbed Tony's wrist to haul her back up and beside him just as he heard a twig snap.

Banshee growled.

Aiden shoved Tony behind him and rounded on the threat.

Barrett burst out of the woods and came at him with a gun drawn.

"Freeze!" Barrett snarled.

Did it look like they were running?

Barrett's head whipped toward the body on the ground. "Fuck me, Austin...*what did you do now?*"

Shock held him immobile. So the police chief *had* made him freeze, but only for a moment. Jaw locking, he gritted back, "My name is *Aiden*, and I didn't do anything to her. The dog just found Melanie. She's freaking *warm,* and her killer is close."

So close that maybe...am I staring at him?

"Call for backup," Aiden ordered him when the police chief just kept staring at Melanie's sprawled body with wide eyes even as his trembling fingers made his gun shake. "We need to search the woods, *now.*"

***

"So you were with Aiden the entire time?" Barrett swiped a weary hand over his forehead. The swirl of lights from the patrol cars lit up the scene in front of Aiden's cabin.

The body had been removed. The woods had been searched. The killer had not been found.

Tony's arms curled around her stomach. "Every moment. There's no way he did this." But Barrett's words kept playing through her mind. *Fuck me, Austin. What did you do now?* The way he'd phrased that question, as if...

As if something bad like this had happened before. As if Austin had done something terrible before.

And hadn't Aiden told her that his father had feared Austin had hurt someone on that long ago day?

Because he'd done it before.

"If she'd *just* been killed..." Barrett's hands curled around his hips. "And if the perp was still in the woods, why the hell didn't your dog give chase? Why did she let the killer go?" He tossed a glare down at the dog.

Banshee whined and pressed closer to Tony. "Easy," she comforted. The blood had been removed from her dog, but Banshee was nervous. Not because of the lights and all the noise. Banshee knew how to stay focused. But because...

"She's not used to finding such a fresh kill." Flat. "Banshee finds the dead." That was her job. Not to rush after killers. "She leapt out of the car and went straight to the body. She didn't chase after the killer—if the killer was still here at the time." *And I think the killer was. I think the killer was in the woods while we were out there.* "She found the body, then she found me. That's Banshee's job. That's what she was trained to do. There was a whole lot of blood out there." So much that the ground had been soaked with it. "The blood was all Banshee could smell. Blood and death."

Swearing, Barrett looked away from her and her dog. His stare focused to the right, where Aiden was talking to two uniformed cops.

"Why were you in those woods?" Tony asked him.

Barrett's head whipped back toward her.

"I thought you'd cleared the scene. I thought you'd gone." She hadn't seen his vehicle when she and Aiden arrived. "Just what were you doing out there?"

He stalked toward her. Stopped when he was just inches away, and he ignored Banshee's soft growls. "You accusing me of something?"

Did he think he was going to intimidate her? She almost laughed. Instead, Tony kept her control and even managed to keep her voice civil as she pointed out, "Well, you pretty much just accused Aiden of something, but he has an airtight alibi. Me. So I'm asking the next natural question. Why were you running around in these woods?"

"You think I'm a killer?" he demanded. "I'm the police chief. I protect people. I wear the badge to keep people safe."

"You haven't answered my question."

Aiden appeared behind him. "I'd like that answer, too."

Barrett didn't look back. "I'm the one who gets to ask the questions in this town." His stare remained on Tony. "You may find the dead, but I'm the law here."

"Most people I know in law enforcement keep multiple weapons on their bodies." Tony continued to keep her voice calm and cool. "They have backup guns that they strap to their ankles, and typically, they have knives on them, too." A pause. "Where is *your* knife?"

"I didn't leave it in Melanie's chest, if that's what you're asking," he snapped.

Yes, she had been asking that question.

Before she could ask anything else, he whirled on Aiden. "Do you see what shit you've stirred? Death follows you. You and your brother were always trouble. Not even back in town one full day, and Melanie is *dead*."

"You think this is my fault?" Aiden's hands fisted.

"You can't stir up the past without waking all the demons. We both know you and your brother had plenty of demons." One of the officers called out to him. Barrett jerked his head in acknowledgement, but his hand rose, and he pointed his index finger at Aiden. "You need to pack up and go back to your mansion in Miami or go sail out on one of your yachts. Leave us the hell alone here." With that, he stalked toward the officers.

Frowning, Tony watched him stomp away. "Odd." Her head tilted. "Usually in situations like this, the police tell the suspect *not* to leave town."

"You think I'm a suspect?" Low. Growled.

"No." She kept her eyes on the police chief. The search for the killer had been going on for over five hours now. Five long, excruciating hours since they'd found Melanie. The police chief would be calling it off soon, she knew that. Probably telling them that his crew would be back at first light to look for more clues.

If there were more clues to be found.

With a crime like that, there should be clues.

But, back to Aiden's question. "You were with me. No way could you be in two places at once. Not unless you know..." Her head angled toward him. "You had an identical twin or something."

He surged toward her. "That supposed to be funny?"

A shrug. "I have been told that, on occasion, I can be freaking hilarious."

"Sweetheart, this is not one of those occasions."

Probably not. Especially since there was a murder involved. But she was very, very tired of being kept in the dark, and her temper was short. It always got short when there was fresh blood nearby. "Barrett wants you gone, not hanging around here, so he doesn't think you're guilty, either." If the chief *had* thought Aiden was guilty, she knew Barrett would never have told him to haul ass out of town.

"Wonderful. So glad you both agree I'm not a knife-wielding killer. Because, for the record, I'm *not*. Why the hell would I hurt Melanie?"

Great question. Why had someone else killed her? "We need her phone records." Low. Just for him. "She was in the woods near your cabin, and my gut says it is because she was there meeting someone. The killer lured her to this spot. Hell, maybe her attacker expected us to find her when we went on our search for Austin. This is very deliberate, very calculated." *Very scary.* "But we are going to catch him." Hell, yes, they would. *You have screwed with the wrong people.*

"How do you think I'm going to access her phone records? That's for law enforcement."

Really? Adorable. Her hand rose to stroke his cheek.

Aiden tensed.

She pressed onto her tiptoes even as he bent toward her. With her mouth near his ear, she whispered, "You have money to burn. You're actually going to tell me that someone with your resources can't access that info? Because I will be disappointed in you."

"Didn't realize you were so comfortable with me breaking the law." A rasp from him. "I'll remember that for future reference." He began to pull back.

"We're packing it in!" Barrett announced. "Coming back at first light." He paced toward them. "I need to...I have to go call her family." A huffed breath as his gaze raked Aiden. "When the media gets wind of this...with *your* name, *your* fame, it will be a cluster. Dammit, I told her you'd burn down my town."

Tony's hand slid back to her side. "You told the victim this information? Did you often share info like that with her?"

"I talked to Melanie when I called about the break-in at Aiden's place." He motioned toward the dark cabin. "And I was right, wasn't I? Right to tell her that my town would burn." A long exhale as his shoulders slumped. "Be damn careful out here tonight. My advice is to go to town and get a room there. Or, even better, get the hell out of the area. But you're not going to take my advice, are you?"

"I came here for a reason," Aiden replied, no emotion in his voice. "And I'm not running."

"No, but people are dying, aren't they?" Barrett walked away.

Tony, Aiden, and Banshee watched until all the patrol cars had left. The authorities took the bright lights with them, and as soon as the rumbles from their engines died away, a shiver chased over Tony's body. "We should go inside." Because when she looked at the heavy darkness around her, she wondered...

Just where did the killer go?

Without another word, Aiden turned and strode for the house. He climbed the porch steps, and she followed behind him. "I'm sure your lawyer will need to know about this development."

"Because people are going to think I killed Melanie?" He opened the door for her. Stood back so she could go in first. "Good thing I have you as my alibi, right? Can't be cast as the bad guy in this story."

That wasn't what she'd meant at all.

He shut the door behind them. Banshee trotted off for the kitchen and food, and Tony stood in the entranceway, aware that her own emotions were barely contained.

She could still feel the warmth of Melanie's skin beneath her fingers. Tony's hands pressed to the tops of her thighs, as if trying to wipe away that memory. "I counted at least seven stab wounds." She hadn't been able to investigate thoroughly because Tony hadn't wanted to disturb the crime scene more than had been necessary. "That many wounds suggests a lot of rage to me."

"Fuck." He paced into the den. Turned on the gas fireplace and the flames flashed.

"I didn't see any defensive wounds. No broken nails, no cuts on her forearms." She'd shone the light from her phone onto the body. "The killer got close to her. So it was probably someone she knew. We need those phone records to see who called her. Who asked her to meet near your place. Who lured her out here so—"

"So that she could be killed on my property? So that we could find her body?" Rage simmered beneath his words. "So that she could be left as a sick message for me?"

Tony blinked. "I hadn't thought of that."

He spun toward her. "No? You don't think she was killed because of me? That's sure as shit what Barrett thinks. It's what the town will think."

Tony took a cautious step toward him. "I think she was killed because she knew something." And the killer hadn't wanted her talking. "The chief just very calculatingly reminded us that he had a reason to talk to the victim. So he'll be on her phone records when we get them. We have no idea what all he said to her." Aiden needed to understand the full picture, so she didn't sugarcoat. "For all we know, he was the one who staged the meeting."

"Barrett?" he asked in disbelief.

Yes, absolutely, Barrett. "He never said why he was in those woods."

His eye lashes flickered. "You think the police chief just murdered a woman outside of my home."

"I think someone in this sleepy little town is a killer, and right now, you're the only one not on my suspect list."

Aiden raked a hand over his face. "Well, that's certainly good to know. You don't think I'm a killer."

Someone needed to not get carried away. "I don't think you killed *her*."

His hand dropped. Aiden rocked back, his shoulder brushing against the mantel. "That's some careful wording." His gaze raked her. "What are you saying? That you think I *have* killed someone else?"

If he was going to put the question out there... "Have you?"

He laughed.

Not an answer, but a very good deflection mechanism. Too bad she wasn't in the mood to be deflected. "I should tell you that Saint is very thorough when it comes to digging, and when he finds blank spots in someone's life, he gets curious." A pause. "You looked great on paper to him. He called you a do-gooder."

"Yep, that's me. A real do-gooder."

"But he sent me a text this morning saying there were some dark spots. Some periods when you went off-grid. Want to tell me about those spots?"

"Sure." A mocking smile curved his lips. "That's when I went rogue. Decided to go off on my own and hunt down bastards who've pissed me off over the years. I mean, seriously? Is that what you expect? For me to say that I'm some kind of—of what? What is it that you think I do?" He didn't rock back again. Instead, he surged forward. Closed in on her with slow, deliberate steps.

She'd told him before that adrenaline could heighten emotions. It could put you on edge. Make you do things you wouldn't normally do. Adrenaline and attraction—especially a consuming, primitive attraction like they had—would make a dangerous brew. She needed to step back. To stay the hell away from him.

So she did. A strategic retreat. "They found Melanie's car. I heard the uniforms talking. Her vehicle was about a mile from here, parked on some dirt road that cut through the property. They had it towed."

He watched her with his intense stare. "Now who isn't answering, hmm? You didn't respond to *my* question."

"It's late. We should get some sleep."

As if on cue, Banshee padded out of the kitchen. She headed for the front door. After a quick circle, Banshee lowered herself onto the rug there. Her head tilted toward Tony.

"Good girl," Tony praised. *And haven't you had one hell of a night?* "Banshee will be on guard duty. If she hears anyone outside, we'll know."

Tony looked toward the stairs. "Which room should I take?"

"The one at the top. First door on the left."

She went for her bags. They were still near the door. After everything, still there. But before she could get them, Aiden beat her to it. He scooped them up and carried them up the stairs.

Tony didn't follow him, not immediately. She went to Banshee. Stroked her dog's head. "Good job tonight."

Banshee licked her.

"I know it's hard. You did great." Another careful stroke. "Try not to dream about the dead, would you?"

Then she climbed the stairs.

Aiden was waiting in her designated bedroom. The bags were already placed near the foot of the bed. A big, wooden four-poster bed. Looked like antique furniture in the room—a chest of drawers, a dresser, nightstand, and a bookcase. Expensive, to match the rest of the cabin.

"Bathroom is that way." He motioned to the left. "And if you should need me, I'll be right next door."

Good to know.

His stare lingered on her.

"Is this the first time you've found a dead body?" she asked him. "Because I know it can be hard. If you want to talk—"

"It's not my first time."

Okay. She stepped to the side, clearing his path for the door. "Certainly not mine, either. I can't remember the number of bodies I've found."

That was a lie. She remembered exactly how many she'd found. They were all burned into her memory. Every single one. But especially the first ones. Those first, tiny bodies...

He advanced. Tony thought for sure he was going to brush right by her but he—

Kissed her.

Wrapped an arm around her body, pulled her against him, and took her mouth. Hotly. Fiercely. With a hunger that seemed to call to her very soul. A passionate intensity that was pure Aiden. Reaching out to her. Promising to wreck her. Promising oblivion and heaven and the release that she needed so desperately to stop the darkness that was closing in.

Because the moment he left her, the moment that bedroom door shut and she was alone, the dark would come. Tony knew it with utter certainty.

How could it not? The body in the woods. The blood. All so much like...

Stop it.

She stiffened. Pulled back.

His head slowly raised. "Do you think I'm a monster?"

"No." Why would he ask that? "I've seen monsters." Up close and personal. "You're not one."

His arm was still around her. "Not a monster. Fair enough. But I'm not good enough to be touching you." He let her go. "Remember that. The next time I try, tell me to keep my hands to myself." With that, he marched past her.

Didn't look back.

The door shut behind him.

"I wanted your hands on me," she whispered.

Silence.

Her gaze darted around the room. The darkness began to slowly creep in...

CHAPTER ELEVEN

"Where the hell are you?" Aiden demanded of Smith. He kicked the door to his bedroom shut. "You were supposed to arrive this evening!"

"Sorry! I got held up with those new hires, but I'll be there by dawn. Just relax, okay and—"

"We found a body."

"*What?*" Shock. Then an admiring whistle. "Already? She is that fast? Damn, man. I had no idea she'd be that good. But how are you? You sure it's your brother—"

"No, it's not my brother. It was Melanie Rodgers. She was murdered in the woods near my cabin."

"You are fucking kidding me."

Like he'd kid about murder. "Stabbed to death. The knife was left in her chest. Tony said she counted seven wounds." His left hand raked through his hair. "Not even here twenty-four hours, and someone is dead. First Austin's old room is ransacked, and now this." No wonder Barrett wanted Aiden to get his ass out of town. Aiden could hardly blame the guy. *I feel like the freaking Grim Reaper.*

"Wait, wait, wait. *His* room was ransacked? When? Dammit, why am I not in the loop? You understand you can text me when shit happens, right?"

"Your ass would have been in the loop if you were here." He paced to the window. Glared out at the darkness below. A darkness that he could feel inside of himself. This place always did that to him. Put him on edge. Pushed him. Pulled up the worst parts of himself.

Don't you get tired of following rules? Fuck them. Fuck them all. His brother's voice whispered through his mind. A temptation. He'd been so good at tempting. *We can do whatever we want. No one will ever be able to touch us. Together, we are unstoppable.*

"Are you okay?" Smith asked him.

His chest wasn't the one littered with stab wounds. "Fine. I wasn't the target."

"And your doc? She's good?"

His grip tightened on the phone. "She wasn't the target, either."

"You got eyes on her?"

"She's in the room next door. She's safe." *I've got her.*

"Fuck." An exhale.

Yes, indeed. Fuck. "I want you to get me Melanie's phone records."

"What else?"

No questions about legality because, yeah, this wasn't the first time he'd asked Smith to break rules. "I want her email exchanges. Every message she's sent across every social media platform. I want her bank info. I want to know why the hell someone killed her on my property."

"You think it's linked to your brother."

"It has to be." The day she discovered he was digging up the past again, Melanie died. "She was involved with him back then, and she was the one who kept telling everyone that he'd just run away, even when the evidence clearly said otherwise."

"Like she was trying to cover something up?"

"Yes." His suspicion, but he'd never been able to get proof.

"On it. And I *will* be there at dawn." A pause. "But, maybe you need to get out of the cabin? I mean, what if the killer is watching you?"

Let him watch. Let him come for me. Wasn't that what he wanted? To get the bastard in front of him? *Payback.* "Then maybe I'll give him a show."

"Aiden." A rumbled warning. "Look, I know how much you like to live on the edge, but it's not just your life we're talking about here. Your doc is vulnerable."

I will protect her. Always.

"Is it safe for her out there?" Smith pushed.

A soft knock sounded at his door. He hadn't locked the door, so the soft knock was followed by the faint groan of the door's hinges as it swung open.

As if their discussion had summoned her, Tony stood on the threshold. She'd changed clothes. Put on an oversize t-shirt. Black. One that fell to mid-thigh.

Was she wearing anything beneath that t-shirt?

Fuck. "Got to go. Going to keep my eyes on her for the rest of the night." His eyes. His hands. His mouth.

"Wait, Aiden—"

He hung up on Smith. Tossed the phone onto his nightstand. Tried like hell not to pounce on Tony. His nostrils flared as he pulled in her scent. The lavender did zero to calm him down. "There something you need?" He was looking at what he needed. But this wasn't the time. Kissing her moments ago had been a colossal mistake. His control was too raw. His need too savage. He'd tried to pull the fuck back and leave.

He'd gone to his room, dammit. He'd done the good-guy BS.

Only now she'd followed. But maybe...maybe he could get her out of there.

Before it's too late for us both.

Waiting, body tense, Aiden expected she'd tell him that she needed extra blankets. That she was thirsty. That the water in her shower was too cold. She'd give him some problem he could handle, and she would be on her way. "Tony?" Aiden prompted when she stared back at him with her deep, dark eyes. "Is there something you need?"

"Yes." A brisk nod. Her hair was loose and tumbled over her shoulders in thick and gorgeous disarray.

He loved her hair. His hands wanted to sink into it while he sank into her. Over and over, he'd thrust into her. Endlessly. He'd make her come. Make her scream for him. Get her to go crazy with her orgasm. "What do you want?" Rough. Gritted.

Her steps shuffled forward. Those painted toenails of hers were still so freaking cute, and the blue color disarmed him. Unexpected for her because Tony always seemed so serious.

I want to stop that. I want to make her smile. I want her to laugh. I want all the shadows around her to vanish.

But he wasn't the man to do that. He was just the opposite of that guy. He was the man to bring more darkness. *So don't touch her. Get her out of here. Try doing one thing right even if it guts you.*

"I want you," she said.

His hands fisted. "Death turns you on, huh? Wondered if that might be the case." A dick thing to say. But it would make her leave his room. She had to leave. He was too close to losing all control. She couldn't see him that way.

Hadn't he warned her that he was a bastard?

Her lips parted as she sucked in a deep breath. She'd leave now. *Leave.* Any second, Tony would turn and storm away from him. Maybe she'd run back to her room. Probably better for her. *Just go.* Because if she didn't go...

"Not a turn-on. Quite the opposite." She took a step toward him. "It chills me to the bone. And seeing that scene earlier, running through the woods..." Her gaze darted around the cabin, taking in the gleaming walls. "Even this place...it reminds me too much of my past. Sure, the cabin I was held in was an eighth of this size, but it was near the water, too. A tiny lake. And the twisting trees were everywhere, and when I ran away, I slipped in some leaves as I rushed through the woods. It was so dark. The leaves felt wet against my skin, and I didn't even realize that it wasn't water on those leaves. It was blood. He'd killed the last girl just hours before. He killed her while I was there. *In the cabin.* He did that, you see. Only killed another when he had a new girl, and he had me. I ran, and I fell in her blood, and I didn't know until a woman in a sedan picked me up when I finally reached the road. I got into her car, and the interior light was on, and I remember she asked me if I'd cut myself—"

He broke. There was no way Aiden could listen to her voice quivering with pain without breaking. Hadn't he suspected it from the first moment? That Tony would be his undoing? And she was.

She was.

His arms grabbed her, and he pulled her against him. "Block it out. Forget it. Forget him. He can't touch you. Not ever again." *If I could, I would kill him all over again for you.* He'd told her those words before. Did she understand just how serious he'd been?

"That's why I came to you." Her head lifted. Her hair slid over her shoulders. "I tell you things that I have never told anyone else. I hide from everyone else, but I don't do it with you."

He could not look away from the darkness of her eyes.

"I don't think you'll judge me when I tell you about my past. Even if you do give me bullshit comments about death turning me on."

The words sliced into his heart. "I was trying to make you leave."

"I know." Soft.

She did. He was starting to think she knew him better than anyone else ever could.

No, you're lying to her. She doesn't know your secrets. You have to keep it that way. "I want you more than I have ever wanted anyone in my life." A stark truth. "But you should not want me. You shouldn't let me touch you. You should probably go back to that hacker asshole you dated before. He was a fairly decent man." But just thinking about the prick made Aiden want to drive his fist into the guy's jaw.

Because the sonofabitch had her. She should be mine, but he had her.

"I'm not the kind of guy who comforts in the middle of the night. I'm not going to hold you and tell you that everything will be all right." Because so few things were in this world. And dammit, he did not comfort. That wasn't him. "That's what your prick ex is for."

"I don't want you to tell me everything is all right."

She wasn't leaving. He was holding onto her so tightly that she couldn't go. His hands had clamped around her hips. He didn't feel panties beneath the shirt. Was she not wearing panties?

Fucking hell. The woman was about to bring him to his knees. He was trying to send her away, but she wasn't going.

"I don't want pretty promises and lies, that's not why I came to you."

"Tony..."

"I came to you because when you touch me, I forget everything else."

Nothing else mattered to him when he touched her. Not even his long overdue plans of vengeance.

"You kissed me before you left my room. You started this. You didn't have to kiss me and walk away."

Yes, he had. It had either been walk or toss her onto the bed.

"Kiss me and stay," she whispered. Tempted. "Stay with me all night. Keep the dark away because I don't want it tonight. I want to think of something other than death. I don't want to think of the killers that wait just outside the doors. They wait when you believe you're safe, but you're not. Not really. Because they are always there." Her hands rose to grip his shoulders. Her breasts brushed against his chest. He could feel her nipples. *No bra.* She was naked beneath that shirt.

He was losing his fight to hold onto control. Losing his one effort to be good. Because he knew in his very core that if he took her, he wasn't ever going to let Tony go.

The problem was that she was coming to him because she was afraid of the darkness.

When all he did was carry darkness inside.

"I want to think of you," she told him. "And I want you thinking of me." Her mouth pressed to his neck. Right over his racing pulse. She kissed him there, then she licked.

Fuck. "That's the problem," he forced out the words. "I think about you too much already."

She kissed his neck again.

His eyes squeezed shut. "I won't fuck you at night and act like nothing happened in the morning."

"Good." Her breath teased his skin.

She didn't get it. His fingers dug into her waist. His fingers—those treacherous bastards dug in even as they pulled *up* her t-shirt. "If I fuck you, you're mine."

"Promises, promises..."

She didn't believe him. She should. "Yeah, it's a vow." He hauled up the shirt more. Definitely no panties.

And no *way* was he turning back now. He'd tried to be good, in his own way. He'd tried to get her to walk even though he wanted her so badly he was already about to come. But she'd stayed. She'd touched him. She'd kissed his neck.

She'd come to him without panties, and what kind of a fool was supposed to be able to turn her away?

His right hand slid down. Moved between her legs. Touched her core. Her heat.

He was done.

A savage snarl broke from him because once you touched what you wanted most, you damn well didn't give it up. You didn't keep trying to play the tortured hero who did the *good* thing. You took and you took, and you destroyed anyone who tried to keep you from getting what you wanted.

I will destroy anyone who ever tries to take her from me.

He wasn't civilized with Tony. Wasn't the controlled *do-gooder*. That bullshit image he'd painted for the world.

He was basic. He was savage. He was hers.

She is mine.

His hand was between her legs. He was stroking her. She was wet and hot for him, and nothing in the world could have stopped him from taking her then. Nothing. No one. He was way past the point of no return.

He pulled his hand back. Dropped to his knees before her.

"Aiden? What—*ah!*"

He parted her thighs more. Dragged her toward him. Put his mouth on her. He didn't just want her wet. He wanted her aching and hungry. Desperate. He wanted her begging for his cock.

And he wanted her taste on his tongue. He wanted to learn every single inch of her. To mark her. To own her.

She trembled against him, so he gripped her legs tighter. Licked his way over her clit and felt her jolt. He did it again, and she sagged forward.

"No, I-I can't stand..."

She didn't have to stand up. He'd hold her. He kept licking as he angled her so that he could taste and explore her, and when the position wasn't good enough, when he couldn't thrust his tongue into her deep enough, he growled and rose, carrying her with him even as she gasped again, and her nails dug into his arms.

He took her to his bed. Spread her out and shoved that shirt up to her neck. For a moment, he just looked at her.

Stunning. So sexy. Tight, hard nipples. Thrusting toward him. Her lush hips. The little tattoo along her abdomen.

A dark, crescent moon.

And her legs. Those long, golden legs. Open for him. So he could see her sex. So he could put his mouth on her again and lick and suck and kiss and taste. Her hips arched up against him as she called his name.

His body tensed. His hands flew to hold her hips as he licked her over and over again. Until she came. Until her body shuddered and thrashed with her release beneath him. Then he just rose. Put his mouth on one tight nipple. Laved it. Loved the ragged moan that came from her.

"You have...on way too many clothes," she said, voice husky and so sensual.

He did. He should strip. The second time, he would. No way could he wait that long now.

His fingers yanked open his pants. Shoved the underwear out of his way. His dick was so swollen the thing hurt as it bobbed eagerly toward her. He snatched a condom from his wallet. Shoved it on.

And was in her two seconds later. He drove all the way inside and lost his mind. She gripped him greedily. All hot, wet silk around him, and when she gave a little moan in the back of her throat, when her legs wrapped around him and her head tipped back, a savage snarl broke from him. In and out, he pounded. Withdrew. Thrust. As deep as he could go. She clamped so tightly around him. Perfectly. Sex had never been this good. This consuming.

He knew he was being too rough. He'd gotten her ready for him, yes, but he should slow down. Be easier. Use some restraint.

I have none.

All he had was need. Desperate desire for her. He caught her legs and pushed them over his shoulders so he could open her even more to him. His fingers pressed to her clit. Rubbed her feverishly and this time when she came, he felt the ripples of her release around his cock.

He went over the edge with her. The orgasm ripped through his whole body, a surge of pleasure so powerful that he lost his breath even as his heart thundered in his ears. On and on, the release consumed him until all he could feel...was her.

All he could taste...her.

All he knew...*her.*

Everything he'd ever wanted...*her.*

***

Her own choked scream woke Tony. She jerked upright, or tried to, but a strong, masculine arm covered her upper body. She pushed at the arm, the scream building.

"Tony."

Her head turned.

The lights were off, but tendrils of moonlight drifted through the curtains so she could see Aiden staring straight at her.

"Darkness closing in again?" he asked her.

"Yes."

"Told you, I'm not really the type to comfort."

She wasn't looking for comfort. "I'm fine." She didn't need someone to hold her hand in the dark.

He kissed her. A deep, drugging kiss. "Baby, you are one hell of a lot better than fine." A rasp against her mouth before his tongue dipped past her lips again. She met him immediately, sucking his tongue lightly. Eagerly kissing him back.

Passion was better than pain any day of the week. Who needed comfort when he gave her such beautiful chaos?

She was naked. Her shirt long gone. So was his. He'd stripped off his clothes earlier. The second time they'd had sex. A time that had been just as bone-meltingly wonderful as the first. What she liked most? He didn't treat her like she was some fragile thing that was going to break.

Others had. The hacker that Aiden mentioned so much? He'd learned about her past, too. And had acted like she was some porcelain doll that had to be cradled and shielded from all harm.

She didn't want to be cradled.

She wanted passion strong enough to rip her world apart into a thousand brilliant, glittering pieces. In other words, *chaos*. When nothing had to make sense. When she didn't have to solve puzzles or hunt for facts.

When she could just be.

Her hands pushed against Aiden's broad shoulders, and she rolled with him across the mattress. The covers slid down her body, and she didn't care about modesty. Why bother? He'd already stroked and kissed every inch of her. Tony climbed on top of him, straddling his hips and pushing her knees down into the mattress on either side of him. Her hands splayed over his powerful chest as she gazed at him in the darkness. His cock—thick, full, so wonderfully hard—pressed against her sex. It would be so easy to rock forward and take him inside.

"Need protection," he growled even as his hands rose to curl around her hips. "Get a condom out of the nightstand drawer."

She would, in just a moment. Her hips rocked against him, but she didn't take the head of his cock inside of her. Instead, she just enjoyed the slick glide as her body became wetter and more eager for him. Again and again, she rocked.

"Baby, you are torturing me."

Not her intent. "I thought I was turning you on."

His fingers slid from her right hip to move down, down...He eased his wicked fingers between them and stroked her. "I am plenty turned on. You breathe, and I'm turned on," Aiden confessed in a voice dark with lust.

Her breath choked out because he knew how to touch her in *just* the right spot.

Okay, yes, condom. STAT. She angled her body and stretched out her arm to reach into the drawer and snag a condom. Her fingers were shaking because he kept strumming her clit, and it took her two tries to open the condom packet.

Then she had to ease away from him, but only long enough to slide the condom down his dick. To take a moment to tease and stroke him.

"Tony."

She pushed his cock between her legs. Pressed up higher on her knees so she could get him in at just the right angle. As she drove down, he thrust up, sinking into her fully. Her head tipped back as pleasure surged through her. He filled her completely. Stretched her deliciously. His fingers kept working her clit as she rocked against him. As she lifted her body up and down, finding the rhythm that would take them back to that beautiful chaos.

Over and over again. Faster. The bed squeaked beneath them, but she didn't care. Her movements became jerkier. Harder as she fought for that chaos.

"You are so fucking gorgeous." A sensual rumble. "Come, baby. Let me see the pleasure hit."

She wanted that pleasure to hit. So badly. It built and built and then it exploded—shattering her world. A million pieces.

Her breath sawed in and out, and he tumbled her back onto the mattress. He loomed over her. "Mine."

His...his turn to come? Or did he mean that *she* was his? No, no, he wouldn't think in those terms. Not so basic and primitive, and she couldn't think clearly herself. She didn't want to think clearly. She wanted to hold tight to her chaos.

He slammed into her. A rhythm far faster and harder than her own had been, and her climax didn't seem to stop. His thrusts made it compound. Made the pleasure shake through her again and again, and he was kissing her, and she held as tightly to him as she could. Her short nails scraped against him. She was too rough, suddenly a wild thing that she didn't even recognize, and Tony did not care.

The pleasure overwhelmed her. It took everything else away. Everything but him.

His hips jerked as he came. *"Tony!"*

This time, she was the one to say... "Mine."

She didn't know if she meant the pleasure—it was hers. Or if she meant...he was.

***

Someone was knocking at the door. At the *bedroom* door.

Aiden's eyelids flew open, and he jumped out of bed.

"What's happening?" Tony's sleepy voice.

He bounded for the door just as it opened.

"You're so desperate for me to get here," Smith began, voice sounding both annoyed and long suffering. "And everyone in this house is sleeping like the dead—" He broke off. Noted Aiden's nudity. Then his gaze jumped to the bed.

"Shut the fucking door," Aiden snarled.

"Shutting the door," Smith agreed in an instant. He yanked the door closed.

Aiden whirled back toward Tony. The covers were over her body. Thank Christ.

"What time is it?" Tony glanced toward the window, where thin beams of sunlight slid through the curtains. "Dawn already?"

"Probably a little past dawn. Punctuality is not one of Smith's strong suits." He grabbed a pair of sweats from the dresser drawer and hauled them on.

Tony had climbed out of bed. He paused to just admire the sight. *Absolutely stunning.* His dick totally agreed because it was giving her a morning salute.

But she'd just snagged her t-shirt. She dragged it over her head. Covered up the perfect view he'd been enjoying. A forlorn sigh slid from him.

She tugged down the hem of the shirt. "How did Smith get all the way up here without us hearing him enter the cabin?"

"He has a key. Getting inside wouldn't be hard for him. Trust me, the man can be silent as hell when he wants to be." Aiden raked his fingers through his hair. "I need to go find out what he's dug up on Melanie's phone records."

"*We* need to find out." Determinedly, she strode forward, even as a faint furrow remained between her brows.

Aiden stepped into her path. She seemed to be forgetting one thing. Clearing his throat, he said, "You need to get dressed."

"Excuse me?"

Maybe that had been too much of an order. He'd rephrase. "For the sake of my sanity, will you please put on underwear and preferably pants before you get around Smith again? Because he's my friend, but I will deck him in an instant." They were about equal when it came to fighting skills, but Aiden knew his right hook was a bit better than Smith's.

"You'll deck him." She frowned. "Because I don't have pants on?"

"Because I don't want him lusting after you more than he already does." He whirled for the door.

She laughed.

The sound stopped him cold.

The sound was light and sweet and so different from her somber tones. He glanced back, hungry for more of that sweet sound from her. A smile lingered on Tony's lips and made her dark eyes shine. "Your head of security does not lust after me," she told him.

It was cute the way she missed the obvious. "Yes, he does."

"Why in the world would you think that?"

Oh, let me count the reasons. "You're fucking unforgettable. You've got legs for days. Fuck me, dark and deep eyes, and lips that make me fantasize about—"

Another knock at the door. "Ahem." Smith cleared his throat. Loudly. "I do vote for pants. Makes conversations easier. And I'll just take myself on down to the kitchen. I'll hang out with the sleeping dog while you two finish your lovely conversation."

Wonderful. Great. Smith had lingered. Jaw locking, Aiden started to haul open that door.

"Banshee shouldn't be sleeping. Not with a stranger in the house." Tony shoved past Aiden and yanked open the door before he could.

Smith gaped at her. "Pants. You forgot the pants—"

"Banshee should have reacted to a stranger!" Her quick yell as she rushed down the stairs. "She should have still been guarding the front door and not sleeping in the kitchen!"

Frowning, Smith peered at Aiden. "I'm not a stranger. Thought the dog liked me."

Aiden ignored him and gave chase. "Tony?" What was happening? He hurried down the stairs after her, aware that Smith had given chase, too.

"Banshee?" Tony called when she reached the first floor. "*Banshee?* To me! To me!"

But Banshee didn't come running from the kitchen. What had Smith said? That the dog was sleeping?

Tony shoved open the door to the kitchen. "*Banshee!*" Her horror-filled cry seemed to echo through the cabin.

Aiden grabbed the door and rushed in after her. With a quick glance, he took in the scene. Tony had dropped to the floor beside her dog. Banshee lay sprawled near her bowl of her food, with small pellets on the tile near her. The dog's body was dangerously still, her chest seeming to barely rise and fall.

"Banshee?" Terror clawed in the dog's name as Tony stroked the German Shephard's head.

But the dog didn't respond. Didn't so much as bat an eye.

Tony ran her hands over Banshee's body. He could see the quiver in her fingertips. "Tony..." Aiden began, feeling utterly helpless in the face of her fear.

Her gaze whipped to the bowl of food. Her eyes widened. "That's not..." A jerky breath.

"That's not the food I give Banshee." Her stare jumped to him. Tears swam in her eyes.

He took a step back, sure someone had just punched him in the chest. Because that was what it felt like. Her tears hit him with that much force.

"Help me," she begged.

He surged forward and grabbed the dog, hauling Banshee into his arms. Lifting the dog, he whirled for the door. "Levi Russell has a vet clinic on the edge of town."

Smith blinked at him from the doorway.

"Get him on the phone. Tell him I'm coming. Tell him I'll pay anything to have his ass meet us there." The clinic wouldn't be open yet. Screw that. *My money will open it.* The dog didn't even whine in his grip. *Fuck, fuck, fuck.*

"Poison," Tony breathed from behind him. "We need to get the food and take it with us. Some sonofabitch poisoned my dog!" Tears thickened her voice.

He held the dog tighter. If there was one thing Tony loved in this world, it was the dog. "Get the vet," he snapped to Smith. "*Any price.*"

Smith's worried eyes fell to the dog. "Money can't buy everything." A warning.

Screw that. "It can sure as hell try." Without another word, Aiden carried the dog out of the cabin.

CHAPTER TWELVE

Aiden lowered the dog onto the exam table. His hands lingered near Banshee's side.

Rising. Falling.

Tony watched Banshee through a haze of tears. Her dog's side was rising and falling. She was still breathing. Still alive. During that terrible car ride to the vet, Tony had sat with Banshee's head in her lap. Every moment had been hell. She'd been so afraid that Banshee would stop breathing.

No. Don't do this to me!

"You say you found her like this?" The question came from the vet, a guy around Aiden's age, with reddish blond hair that stuck up at odd angles. Glasses perched on his nose. He wasn't wearing a white lab coat. Just jogging shorts, a sweatshirt, and tennis shoes.

She knew Smith's call must have pulled him out of bed. It wasn't even six thirty in the morning yet, but Levi Russell had met them at the vet clinic.

Not like she could complain about the vet's attire. *I'm wearing a t-shirt.* She hadn't stopped to change. There had been no time to waste.

Aiden was just wearing sweatpants. Not even shoes.

Hardly the polished billionaire.

He's doing this for me. Racing out like this, carrying my dog. Taking care of Banshee...for me.

"I think poison was in her food," Tony said as the vet began to examine the dog.

The door to the right squeaked open, and a pretty, petite brunette walked inside. Her eyes were wide as the woman took in the scene. Her stare lingered a bit on Aiden's bare chest.

Then his bare feet.

Tony's toes curled against the floor as she lifted the bowl of food she'd brought with her. The vet was busy examining the dog. Pulling up Banshee's eyelids and shining a little light at her.

Tony glared at the food. Those soft, dark pellets weren't what she fed Banshee. And...

Wait, could she see a bit of white peeking out from one of those pellets? She took a quick step away from the exam table, put the bowl down, and grabbed one of the pellets. It was soft and squishy in her fingers, malleable, and she pushed the material away because inside... "Bastard." A white pill was inside the pellet. She grabbed another pellet. Searched it. Found...*another pill.* "Pills are inside each one." Whirling, she shoved her palm— and the two pills she'd found—toward the vet.

Frowning, he looked up at her. No, at the pills. He took them from her and headed toward a round light that shone on the counter.

"Do you know what it is?" Something had been written on the pills. She just hadn't been able to quite make it out, but the vet was nodding as he held the pills near that bright light.

"Looks like..." His eyebrows scrunched as he peered at the pills. "Acepromazine."

"What the hell is that?" Aiden barked.

The vet turned back to him. "Tranquilizer. For dogs and cats." A pause. "Normally, it would be fairly harmless."

Her hands were clenched so tightly that Tony's nails bit into her palms. "It doesn't look harmless." She rushed back to Banshee. Stroked her fur. "She's barely breathing!"

"It depends on how many she ingested," the vet said, voice muffled as if he'd been mostly talking to himself. "Got to check her heart rate. Blood pressure. Make sure she's stable."

"You need to get the damn pills out of her!" Aiden ordered. "Now! We found her on the floor less than twenty minutes ago!"

But Banshee could have taken the pills during the night. They'd come in so late after finding the body...

The pills must have been in the kitchen before we found the body. They were in there before we returned to the cabin.

Cold slithered through her.

"Can't you pump her stomach?" Aiden's voice roughened more. "Get the pills out of her! Get her *fixed!*"

Levi's shoulders squared. "I can take care of her. Now that I know what she was given, I know what to do." A quick nod. "Give me time with her. I'll treat her. I'll give her the best care, you have my word."

He was kicking them out. "No." Tony shook her head. "I need to be here, I need—"

"You need to wait outside," Levi told her as his stare flickered her way. A steady blue gaze behind the lenses of his glasses. "Go so that my assistant Sharon and I can get to work."

"Just get to fucking work!" Aiden demanded.

Levi frowned at him. "Not with you shouting at me. Wait outside, Aiden. And maybe get some clothes?" But he glanced toward Tony, and his expression softened. "I will take care of her."

"You'd better," Aiden growled before Tony could respond. "Because that dog is extremely important. Do *everything* to make her better, you understand? Whatever it costs, whatever you need, do it." He let go of Banshee. Held out his hand to Tony. "Come on."

She leaned down. Whispered to Banshee, "I love you." Because she did. Banshee wasn't just some training companion. Banshee was family. She was a friend. She was the safety and warmth that Tony needed when the bad things in the world closed in.

Sympathy softened Levi's face when Tony straightened. "I'll take care of her."

She blinked away tears again and reached for Aiden's hand. He pulled her toward the door. Out of that small room. Away from Banshee and down a narrow, white hallway. Framed pictures of dogs and cats hung on the walls. Some drawings with bright colors that had obviously been made by small hands.

Bright. Happy. Jolting because the dark swirled around her.

"Got some clothes for you both." Smith's voice. "Figured you, ah, didn't exactly have backups in the vehicle when you sped away. Followed you as soon as I could."

Her head lifted. He stood in the nearby lobby area with a duffel bag held in each hand.

"One for you," he said to her. "And one for Aiden."

Aiden pulled one bag from him. "Thanks."

Smith kept extending the other bag toward Tony. "How's your dog?"

"Poisoned." Was that even the right word? *Drugged.* And someone would pay.

"Levi is working on him," Aiden added.

Tony forced herself to move forward. With fingers that trembled, she reached for the bag. "Thank you."

"I'm sorry about Banshee," he told her.

A lump rose in her throat. She choked it down. "Be sorry for the bastard who did that to her. Because he's going to pay." Her hand tugged the bag from him. She headed for the bathroom to change, and with every step, more rage built inside of her.

He's going to pay.

***

Aiden hauled on a t-shirt and tennis shoes. There were other clothes in the bag, but he didn't bother with them.

"Sure, okay, get dressed right here. Check."

Aiden glared at Smith. "I am not in the mood for your shit right now."

"Because it's been one hell of a morning. Got you." His head craned as Smith tried to look down the hallway and back toward the exam room. "Your doc was plenty pissed."

"Someone tried to kill Banshee." Of course, she was pissed. More than that, she was scared. Hurting. *No one makes her afraid.* "It will be the last mistake the bastard makes."

Smith spun to face him. "So, okay, it's just me and you, right now. I'm going to talk straight with you."

Like he had been doing anything else?

"Can't help but notice that you seem more upset about the dog than you did about Melanie's death."

His hold tightened on the bag. "That's an asshole thing to say."

"Look, I get it, I do."

"I don't think you get me at all." After all this time, Smith should have, though.

"You need the dog. The dog is the key, right? The dog is the one who finds the bodies. The dog is the one who finds the dead. It's not Tony. It's the dog, and with the dog out of the picture, you're worried you are shit out of luck."

A door clicked closed just a few feet away. The door to the women's restroom. Because, sure, Tony would have to be there so she could catch those damning words. When he tilted his head, Aiden saw her standing behind Smith. She'd ditched the black t-shirt. Put on gray sweatpants, a form fitting, white shirt that hugged her breasts. Tennis shoes. She'd twined her hair into a quick braid, one that was looser than her normal style.

Smith winced. "That came out way harsh, but, hey, we all need to face facts." He glanced over his shoulder at a statue-still Tony. "Without the dog, the investigation ends. The person who poisoned Banshee knows that. Even if the vet gets her to live—"

Jesus, the man had no tact.

"She's gonna be out of commission for a while. Who knows what the poison did to her? She can't be at the top of her game after this attack." He took a step back. His head swung between Tony and Aiden. "I get that was why you lost your shit back at the cabin, Aiden. You knew the big plan was going up in smoke. All the money in the world can't fix this situation. We have to come up with a new tactic or maybe just put this whole investigation on hold before anyone else gets hurt."

He hadn't lost his shit because of the case or because Banshee might not be able to help him. Yes, absolutely, he liked the freaking dog. But he'd been *enraged* because Tony had been hurt. Tony *loved* her dog. And he didn't let things Tony loved get hurt.

And if they did get hurt...*I'll get vengeance for you, baby.*

He opened his mouth—

"I am the new plan," Tony announced flatly. "I found bodies before Banshee came into my life. I can find them without her. If the prick that did this to her thought the investigation would end, he is sorely mistaken. All this has done is make me even more determined. I will not stop."

"Uh, maybe we should all take a breath..." Smith said uncertainly. He wasn't normally uncertain. "A woman was murdered yesterday. The dog was poisoned. What the hell is gonna be next?"

"Next we find the bastard," Tony responded without missing a beat. "The poison—the pills Banshee was given, they are a lead. We call the police chief. We get Barrett to search Melanie's car and home. We see if she had any Acepromazine in her possession. We get those phone records—"

"Uh, already did," he interjected with a little wince. "Didn't exactly have time to update you, but, ah, yeah, I can tell you exactly who she texted or called in the last few days. And, honestly, there aren't any big red flags." He shoved his hands into the back pockets of his jeans. "She had several calls with clients—the mayor, the lady who owns the bakery, the elementary school counselor. Hardly dangerous thugs. She talked to you, Aiden. She talked to the police chief the day you arrived."

"We already know that." Frustration pulsed inside of Aiden. "Did she talk to anyone *after* her call with Barrett? Or anyone else before him?"

"The mayor," Smith replied. "Tom Lassiter." He scratched his chin. "I think he was another townie that was tight with you back in the day."

"Who wasn't?" Tony wanted to know. "Was there one person in this town who wasn't tight with Aiden and Austin all those years ago? Anyone who didn't attend that infamous last party?"

"Yeah." Smith rocked back on his heels. "Interesting little coincidence there, but Aiden was adamant earlier, so I didn't see the point in mentioning it at the time..."

The exam room door opened. They all jerked to attention as Levi stepped out of the room. He blew out a hard breath.

"Levi wasn't tight, isn't that so, Aiden?" Smith inquired softly. "Seem to remember that he never liked Austin. Oh, and you both might want to know, the last text Melanie received was from him. He told her, 'It's over.'"

Levi strode down the hallway toward them. A broad smile curved his lips. "I think your dog is going to be just fine."

Acepromazine. A tranquilizer for dogs and cats. And they were staring at a vet. A person who would have the best access to that drug. The single person in town who probably had a giant supply of it. The man who'd been Melanie's last contact before her murder.

Levi's smile faltered. "That's not good news?" He pulled off his glasses and polished the lenses on his shirt. "Banshee will need to stay under observation for several days. I'll have to monitor her here at the clinic, but with the right care, there is no reason to suspect that she won't make a full recovery."

Silence.

Levi pushed the glasses back onto his nose. Looking uncertain, he asked, "Is there a problem?"

"You rushed in so fast this morning," Smith said, clearing his throat. "That I bet you missed the local news."

Sharon appeared behind him, hovering nervously.

"I—yes." Levi seemed confused. "I should get back to my patient."

"The news was important," Smith continued, tone careful. "I suspect they led with the story of the woman who was murdered last night."

Levi had turned away. But at those words, he whipped back around to face Smith. "What murder?"

"Melanie Rodgers," Aiden said. "She was killed on my property last night."

All the color bled from Levi's face as his attention flew to Aiden. "No."

"Yes." Aiden nodded. "I found her body. Actually, Banshee found her."

Now Banshee was lying on an exam table.

"No!" Levi said again, voice closer to a shout. "That's not possible! Melanie isn't dead!" He hauled his phone from his pocket. Pressed the screen frantically before shoving the phone to his ear.

"Levi?" Sharon lightly touched his shoulder.

He shoved her hand away. "Stop it!" His wide eyes locked on Aiden. "She's not answering."

"Yeah." Aiden's voice was quiet. Grim. "Hard to do that when you're dead."

The phone slipped from Levi's fingers. It slammed into the floor. Even as it bounced and hit the tile again, cracks spiraled along the screen.

CHAPTER THIRTEEN

The police chief found an empty bottle of Acepromazine in the back of Melanie's car. A bottle that was traced back to Levi's vet clinic. So, surprise, surprise—*not*—the vet was pulled in for questioning.

Aiden made sure that Banshee was transferred to a different facility. A veterinary hospital over in the next town. Tony went with Banshee to get her dog settled safely, and Aiden stayed to shadow Barrett and to figure out what the hell was happening.

What's happening...well, the vet looks guilty as hell. A man I've known since I was a punk kid looks like he might have killed my brother.

"This is crazy!" Levi paced inside the police station. Not some interrogation room. They were in the chief's office. Aiden, Levi, and Barrett. Friends once upon a time. A million years ago. But they were all different people now.

And one of them might just be a killer.

Aiden was damn grateful that Barrett had let him in for this scene. If Levi was guilty, if he was the one who'd caused all of this misery...

I want to hear every word that Levi has to say. The vet sure was sweating a whole lot. And twitching nervously. Not exactly appearing calm and collected. More like seeming guilty as hell.

"I didn't give Melanie the pills!" Levi's hair still jutted out at odd angles. "I didn't! She must have taken them! Sh-she had a key to my house and the clinic."

"Because you were romantically involved with her," Barrett noted with a nod.

"Because she was my property manager!" Levi fired back. "She could have gotten inside whenever she wanted. She *must* have taken the pills! Stolen them!" His head swung toward Aiden. "I didn't do this! I help animals. I don't kill them!"

"What about people?" Barrett's voice was smooth. "Do you kill them?"

Levi blanched. "No!" He shot to his feet.

Aiden remained seated in the chair across from Barrett's desk.

"No, I would never kill anyone, especially not Melanie!"

"Because you were involved with her." Once more, Barrett went back to that point.

"Was. As in, past tense. We broke up. A while back. I-I'm seeing someone else now."

Barrett pursed his lips. "I got Melanie's phone records. I saw the text you sent her. If you broke up a while back, why did you tell her it was over just hours before her body was found?"

A shudder ran over Levi. "Because she wanted to get back together. She'd come to me. Told me I was the one good thing she had and that she wanted another chance. That she was changing." A ragged exhale. "But I'd moved on. So I sent her the text, and I told her it was over." He swallowed. "I didn't kill her. Look I—" Once more, he dragged his hand through his hair, making chunks jut up even more. "I have an alibi."

"Interesting." Aiden considered the other man. He could feel rage building. Twisting up inside of him. *Did you kill my brother?* "I don't remember anyone telling you Melanie's time of death." He directed a questioning look at Barrett. "Unless that info was released to the local media and I missed it? But...Levi supposedly missed the news this morning so..."

"It wasn't released." A fast response from Barrett. "So Levi doesn't know, not unless he was there."

"I *wasn't!* I *was* with Sharon all day and all night yesterday. We closed the clinic, then—then we went to her place. I was there the whole night." Levi's cheeks flushed a dark red. "When Smith called me this morning, I was still with her. With her every moment, and I know Melanie was killed sometime late last night—"

"Technically in the evening," Barrett clarified, watching him closely. "That was when she was stabbed seven times."

"Jesus." Levi's shoulders hunched. "*Jesus Christ.*"

"But you have an alibi." Now the chief rose. "Your new girlfriend...who also happens to be your assistant, Sharon McIntrye."

A bob of Levi's head.

Barrett scratched his chin. "It's been a long, long time...but don't I remember that Austin dated her briefly, way back in the day?"

Levi didn't answer.

"In fact, didn't you fight him once, because you were pissed at him for taking her away from you?"

Yes, you did. I remember the fight. It hadn't been the only time that Levi and the Warner brothers had come to blows.

In fact, the summer that Austin had gone missing, there had been another fight. *The day of the party.* A group had been hanging out, and Levi had been arguing with Sharon. When she'd started to walk away, he'd tried to grab her.

And he got a fast punch for that move. Levi had run away to lick his wounds, but he'd come back. Apologized to everyone. They'd moved on. Hadn't they? *Hadn't they?*

Levi's head leaned forward. He seemed to be staring down at his feet. Instead of answering Barrett's question, he muttered, "Do I need a lawyer?"

Barrett crossed his arms over his chest and seemed to ponder the matter. "I don't know," he finally said.

Levi's head lifted.

"I guess it would depend..." Barrett continued. "On whether or not you killed Melanie Rodgers..."

"And Austin Warner," Aiden rumbled as he, too, rose. The past and the present swirled in his mind.

"Did you kill them?" Barrett demanded. Just flat out asked.

Levi's breath came faster. "I want a lawyer."

To Aiden, those words sounded like an admission of guilt. He remembered the blood he'd found in the cabin so long ago. His brother's blood. Had a flash of Melanie's body in the woods. All the blood around her.

The dog. So still. Pills that traced back to Levi's clinic.

"I want a lawyer," Levi repeated. "I'm done playing nice."

I'll show you nice. "You sonofabitch." Aiden grabbed Levi and threw the bastard against the wall. He drew back his right hand and plowed it into Levi's jaw.

"Fuck," Barrett growled.

***

"I hate paperwork. It's a pain in my ass." Barrett glared at Aiden through the bars.

Actual freaking bars. Because Aiden was in the small cell at the back of the station. He had no idea where Levi had gone. Maybe to get his face patched up. "So sorry for you." Aiden sent him a cold smile. "You'll have even more when my lawyer gets done with you."

Barrett curled his hands around the bars. "Right. My wet dream. More paperwork. Because this is what I wanted, clearly? For you to *assault a man* right in front of me. Not like, as police chief, I can pretend to look the other way when a situation like that occurs. Can't very well act like I didn't see it when the jerk is bleeding all over my office! Dammit, I was letting you listen in as a courtesy! I knew I shouldn't have done that shit, I knew I was bending my own rules, but I didn't expect you to lose your mind and attack!"

Aiden flexed his right hand. He might have bruised his knuckles on Levi's face. "You heard him. It was a confession."

"No, it wasn't! It was a man asking for a lawyer! Then it was *you* assaulting the guy." Barrett huffed out a breath but didn't release the bars. "Austin was the one who thought he didn't have to answer to anyone. You were the responsible one, so I thought you could handle that scene. Apparently, I was very wrong." Another huff of breath. "I always *liked* you! What the hell happened to you?"

Oh, just the usual. "I woke up to discover that someone had murdered my brother and hidden his body. I watched my mother fall apart because her son never came home. Watched my dad turn to alcohol and a dozen other women because he couldn't handle what had happened. Because while trying to help Austin, my father covered up the crime even though I *begged* him to stop." A swallow. "Sorry I'm not the same easy-going asshole that I was when I was a teenager, but life happened. Life and death and everything in between."

"Fuck." Barrett's brows raised. "You're as screwed up as the rest of us, aren't you?"

You have no idea. "You weren't always wearing the badge. You partied with my brother.

You raised your share of hell. Don't act like you've never thrown a punch."

"Not these days, I don't raise hell. I don't take swings. I have a reputation to maintain. People in this town look up to me. I'm not going to betray their trust. I won't lose what I have." He pulled his hands away from the bars. "God, you reminded me of him. When you took that swing at Levi...that right hook..."

"I want my lawyer here. I want my phone call." Like he didn't know he'd lost control. He did. Not something that usually happened. *What is going on with me?* But to have Levi right in front of him, to have the evidence pointing at him. After all these years, to be so close...

"*I'm trying to get your ass out before you need a lawyer!*" Barrett's eyes widened at his own outburst, and the chief quickly looked over his shoulder. No one else was in the holding area. Exhaling slowly, he turned his attention back to Aiden and lowered his voice as he said, "I'm going to talk to Levi some more. See if his alibi holds, but so far, Sharon has sworn that it does. And maybe—*maybe*—the guy won't press charges. Maybe he'll realize that pressing charges against one of the richest assholes in the nation is a bad idea for him. Because we both know you will just make his life miserable." He took a step back. "Or maybe he'll decide you're his big pay day and he'll go on every news channel talking about how you hurt him after he saved your girlfriend's precious dog."

Was he supposed to be worried? "Not like it will be the first time someone has gone after me for a financial shakedown."

"I'm sure it's not. But he has an actual witness. Me. If I have to get up on a stand, I'll damn well say you swung first but...I get it, I do. The way he talked, the fact that he was involved with Melanie, that he has a past with Austin—*it all makes him look guilty*. But you can look guilty and still be innocent."

Only for so long. "I'm going to find my brother's remains."

"How?" Barrett's hands lifted, then fell in a helpless gesture. "The dog is out of commission. What are you going to do? Go sniff in the woods by yourself?"

Was that crap supposed to be funny? It wasn't. "I have Tony. She can find the dead with or without the dog."

"So she can smell them, too? I don't think so." A doubting shake of his head.

"She's a forensic anthropologist," he snapped. "Have you seen her list of degrees? She's been tracking the dead for a long time. She told me that she can do it, and I believe her." Tony had his faith, one hundred percent.

Now Barrett appeared interested. "You really think she's gonna find him?" He scratched his jaw. "Because evidence of Levi's guilt would change everything. *If* he killed your brother. I mean real, hard evidence. Not circumstantial BS that he can explain away."

He was going to get enough evidence to nail the bastard to the wall. "I want my lawyer. I'm not staying in this cage."

"Where is Dr. Rossi?" Barrett looked at his watch. "Shouldn't she be back from dropping off her dog in Fairley by now? I expected her to roll up here, but she didn't show." Fairley, the town closest to Eagle's Ridge. The town with a vet not tied in any way to Levi.

"She texted me a bit ago," Aiden revealed. "*Before* you locked me up."

"You mean before you took that swing at a man in my custody and caused a major clusterfuck?"

Before that. Yes. His control had shattered. *Dammit.* He couldn't allow that to ever happen again. "She's on her way back. Will be here before nightfall. She's going to the cabin to meet me." Only he wasn't there because he was in a cell. *Smith is there. Smith is at the cabin.* Tony wouldn't be alone.

"If she's waiting on you, then I need to hurry my ass up and convince Levi *not* to press charges against you. Just work a miracle, no big deal." Barrett swung for the door. "Maybe after that, I'll turn some water into wine, and we can all have drinks."

"I want out of here," Aiden called after him. "*Now.*"

"Working on it. Why don't you just sit the hell down and cool off?"

The door closed behind Barrett. Aiden stalked to the window and glared at the bars.

***

Tony braked the rental car in front of the cabin. She felt drained, emotionally and physically, and all she wanted to do was go inside and collapse.

But you don't have that option. You never do.

Banshee was going to be all right. Judy Gillroy, the vet in Fairley, had promised that Banshee would survive. The German Shephard would get plenty of fluids, be monitored carefully for the next few days, but she would make it.

Tony pushed open the SUV's door. *You'll make it, Banshee. You will make it.* The sun had already dipped low behind the tree line. It had taken her far longer to get back to the cabin than she'd realized. She tried to text Aiden again, as she'd done several times before to let him know she was running late. He hadn't responded to those texts.

Maybe he'd respond this time. The text went through. She saw the little delivered note. For a moment, she paused by the rental car.

No response.

He'd been at the police station earlier. The last update she'd gotten from him had been about Levi.

Gravel crunched beneath her feet as she headed toward the cabin. A black pickup truck—one with a rental sticker on the back—waited to the right of the cabin. Smith's ride. He had to be close by. Aiden had told her he would be at the cabin, too.

She started to go inside and talk to Smith, but she hesitated. Her gaze slid around the area, sweeping over the trees. So many miles and miles of trees. Too many places to bury a body.

But hikers are often out there. Aiden's property butts up against a state park. If you're burying a body, you run the risk of discovery. If you don't put him down deep enough, an animal will come and dig him up. So even if you did manage to bury the body without someone seeing you or without someone stumbling onto the disturbed dirt, you have to worry about the animals pulling up his remains.

Her attention shifted to the lake. The water was so still and looked even darker with the sun riding so low in the sky. The lake had been searched. Such a deep lake. Deep and wide. She'd read the reports on the search. In her mind, she could see the schematics and grids. The divers had sunk down to the very deepest area.

They'd turned up nothing.

The new dive team would arrive tomorrow. Or at least, that was the plan. They'd search the lake again. What would they turn up this time?

She didn't head for the house. Instead, her footsteps took her toward the long, wooden pier that stretched over the lake. She passed by an old fishing pole and saw names carved into the worn wood of the pier.

Aiden.

Austin.

***

The cell doors seemed to shriek as they were opened. "Your lucky day," the young cop told Aiden.

"No, it isn't." His grim response.

"No charges. Chief Montgomery talked to the guy, and you're clear. If that's not lucky, I don't know what is, Mr. Warner."

Aiden stepped out of the cell. "Where is Levi?"

The cop eyed him nervously. "Already gone."

Hell.

"Chief didn't have enough to hold him. Warned me you were gonna be pissed."

Yes, I am.

"I'm supposed to take you back to your cabin. Make sure that, ah, you don't do anything crazy."

He was getting babysitting services from a junior cop? The kid barely looked legal. But Tony had taken his rental car to Fairley, so, unfortunately, he did need a ride. And the ride would give him the chance to grill the cop. "What's your name?"

"Deion. Deion Thomas." His thin shoulders straightened.

Aiden held out his hand. "I'd appreciate the ride."

Deion frowned at his hand. "Chief told me you were gonna be a dick about things."

His brows rose. "I like honesty. And just so you know, I'm often a dick." The chief had not been wrong on that count.

Deion slowly took his hand. "Thanks for the warning."

"Get me the hell out of here, Deion." He didn't know where Levi had gone and that made him nervous. Tension rode him, and all Aiden wanted to do was get to Tony. To get to her and make sure she was safe.

***

The wood had been warped by time and weather. It twisted and creaked beneath her steps as Tony carefully crept onto the pier. She could imagine a younger Aiden on that pier. Running with his twin. Maybe jumping into the water once they reached the edge. They would have spent so many summers having fun in that lake.

Her sneaker-clad shoe hit the top of a nail that jutted loosely from a board. Frowning, she glanced down. Some of the boards were so old. Deep cracks ran through them.

Aiden doesn't come here much any longer. He can't stand the memories. Because the bad memories had overshadowed the good ones. But...

But he'd hired a real estate management company to keep up the property. Everything else seemed to be in pristine condition. Everything but the pier. Why hadn't Melanie had it repaired?

Not like I can ask her now. Tony gingerly moved her foot away from the nail. She took a few steps forward even as something began to nag at her mind. She pictured the search images of the lake once more. All of the grid lines and—

A board broke beneath her left foot. Her foot—and her leg—shot straight through the broken chunk. Her jogging pant leg shot up, and she felt the wood slice across her skin. Tony cried

out in pain as she fell, and her hands scraped over
the pier.

CHAPTER FOURTEEN

"Sonofabitch," Tony huffed as she grabbed tightly for the wood of the pier and hauled herself up. Her foot had gone into the water, icy cold water, just as she'd feared, and she could feel the throbbing burn where the broken pieces of wood had sliced into her leg.

The jogging pants had offered no protection.

Wincing, she jerked free of the broken section and then scooted back a bit to take stock of her injuries. One particularly long, vicious cut went from the top of her ankle all the way up to her knee. Not like it needed stitches, but it was oozing blood. Fabulous.

Why hadn't the pier been repaired? That question kept hammering at her. Melanie had kept everything else up to date at this property, but not the pier.

Being extra careful, Tony inched forward. The slat of wood she'd been standing on had given way, cracking right in the middle. When she looked down through that gaping hole, she saw the dark water staring back at her. Except...

She could have sworn something glinted in that darkness. With a frown, she leaned forward even more, staring down below.

It glinted again. Glinted because it wasn't too deep in the water. She lowered her body flat against the pier and put her hand through the gaping hole, stretching as far as she could. Her fingers dipped into the icy water, but she couldn't reach her goal.

The grid lines from the old dive search slid through her mind once more. "Sonofabitch," she cursed again. "They didn't search under the pier." The lines had all been *out* in the lake. With the team focusing most on the deepest parts.

There had been no indication that they searched *under* the pier.

And even if something hadn't been under the pier all those years ago...

Something—someone—could be there now. Because the easiest way to keep a body from rising to the surface? Sure, yes, of course, you could weigh it down. That always worked. Or...

Or you could tie a body to a pier piling. Strap it tightly to the wood. No way would it rise then. Especially if no one ever did any repair work on the pier. Especially if no one looked too closely at it.

Her fingers stretched out again, and, for just a moment, she could have sworn she touched something. Something strong. Hard.

Not wood.

Bone.

Because when you'd touched as many bones as she had over the years, you knew exactly how one felt.

She rose on legs that weren't quite steady. Her breath sawed in and out as Tony looked toward the sky. Not much light. Dammit. If she didn't move now, the search would have to wait until tomorrow. And the way things had been going...

What will happen by tomorrow? Another murder? The killer was closing in, circling around them because he didn't want the truth found. Every instinct she had screamed that she was literally standing right on top of the truth. But there was only one way to know for certain.

Tony glanced toward the house. She'd get Smith to watch her back. She'd get her waterproof flashlight, and she'd get him to watch her, and she'd find out what was glinting in the water.

And I'll find out if I really did touch bone.

She ran for the cabin.

***

"There are a lot of stories that circulate about you," Deion said as he gripped the steering wheel and drove like an old man through the downtown area of Eagle's Ridge.

"I don't think you're even going the speed limit," Aiden noted from the backseat. From behind the freaking perp wall in the officer's car.

Deion glanced toward the rearview mirror. "I'm obeying the law."

"I should have gotten another ride." He'd just been lucky no reporters—not even the local ones—

had seen him getting into the back of the car. Like that image wouldn't have been splashed everywhere.

"I'm sorry about your brother."

His head jerked. "Don't be. You didn't kill him."

"No, no, of course, I—"

"I'm being an asshole," Aiden said. "Ignore me. It's what I do." *Who I am.* An odd sense of urgency rode him. He pulled out his phone and realized that he'd missed multiple texts from Tony. The clerk at the station had handed Aiden his phone right before he and Deion had left, and it had been turned off.

Should have turned it back on sooner.

Quickly, Aiden scanned her messages. She'd been running late. She asked if everything was all right on his end.

Not quite. Got tossed in a cell because I assaulted our chief suspect. Lost my shit and reacted like I was a crazy teen again. Not a man who should've had more control.

He didn't text her that news. Some things were better delivered in person. But he did fire off...*I'm on my way.*

If the cop in front of him could just *hurry.* "I'll give you a thousand dollars if you actually hit the speed limit."

"You trying to bribe an officer?" Deion asked.

Aiden rolled his eyes. Someone save him from the upright, law abiders. "I'm trying to contribute to your vacation fund."

"Oh, that's really generous of you."

No, it wasn't. *Speed the hell up.* Because he needed to see Tony. The odd desperation he felt seemed to deepen with every moment that passed.

***

No sign of Smith. His truck was still near the cabin, but Tony figured he had to be out scouting somewhere in the woods. Like her, he probably didn't want to waste the little bit of good lighting they had left.

And since she didn't see Smith...

She gazed at the dark water of the lake. *Screw it. I'm just going in.* Gripping the flashlight tightly, she waded off the shore and headed for the side of the pier. The water pushed against her ankles. Rose to her knees. Chilled her at her thighs. Such cold, cold water. The closer she got to the area of the pier where the wood had broken, the deeper that water became. It dropped suddenly, and the water was at her chest. Her breath came a little faster. Harder.

She was so close to her destination. Almost there.

Another quick drop off. Her feet stopped being able to touch the bottom. She hit the button to turn on the flashlight. Maybe she was wrong. Maybe it hadn't been bone. Maybe she was just going to wind up soaking wet, cold, and wrong.

But maybe she wasn't. Maybe she was finally going to be able to give Aiden what he wanted most.

Sucking in a deep breath, she slid under the water. She used her light to slide between the pilings of the pier. She swam forward, forward and...

The rope appeared first. A loose piece floating before her eyes. Then she saw the glint she'd caught before. Carefully, Tony propelled herself closer to that glint.

A ring. Still on a finger. No, what *had* been a finger. *Just a bone now.* The ring hadn't floated loose because the fingers were bound to the piling. Fingers. Arms. Legs. Tied so tightly. Rope bound over and over again.

No way were you going to break free.

Her light hit the front of the skull.

He stared sightlessly back at her. Eyes long gone. Skin, muscle, tissue, all gone.

Gone.

No, no, he wasn't gone. She'd found him. Her light skimmed over the bones—what bones were still there. The ropes had kept most of them in place, but some were missing. She backed away, and her shoulder bumped into a piling. *You found him. Go call Aiden. Go call the police.*

She twisted her body, turning away from the man who'd been held captive beneath the water for far too long.

Not a man. He was a boy when this happened. Seventeen. If she'd found Austin Warner.

Who else would be trapped down there?

Her head broke the surface, and Tony sucked in a deep breath. She reached out for the pier.

And someone grabbed her shoulder. One strong hand on Tony's shoulder. One on the top of her head.

"What—" Tony began.

She didn't get to say more. Those hands shoved her beneath the water. Her lips were still parted, and water poured into her mouth. She twisted and heaved, but those hands didn't let go.

Tony kicked out with her feet. The water was so deep that she couldn't reach the bottom. The flashlight fell from her fingers as Tony fought. She reached upward, her hands and nails frantically going for her attacker. Her nails scraped over—

Gloves?

The punishing grip kept her beneath the surface. The frantic drumming of her heartbeat filled Tony's ears, sounding like a drum. Frantic, her eyes locked...

On him.

The flashlight was floating away, but in the darkness, it had hit the skull one more time. The skull stared back at her, as if waiting.

No, no, no.

Her attacker was on the edge of the pier. She just had to get out of his range. Or she had to get *him* to fall into the water, to let her go.

She kicked out with her legs, trying to get away from him. And, yes, his grip eased. It was working. It was working. It was—

Crash. Water bubbled all around her.

Her attacker had fallen into the water. Tony tried to surge away. But both of his arms wrapped around her. He shoved her deep. Held her with a strength that terrified her. She kicked and punched. She twisted. The light was gone. She couldn't see her attacker.

And her lungs *burned*.

Burned and burned and burned. She needed a breath. She had to open her mouth. She needed—

"Aiden!"

But the cry never broke the surface of the water.

***

The patrol car pulled to a stop. "That is one beautiful house." Deion whistled as he turned off the vehicle. "Bet it was heaven growing up here, huh?"

"Until my brother was murdered." Then it had become hell.

"Right. Yeah. Sorry." Deion climbed out of the car. Opened the back door. He had to open the damn thing since there wasn't a way for Aiden to get out on his own.

"Thanks for the ride," Aiden said. His gaze fell on the black SUV that was parked about ten feet away. Tony was back. And Smith was there, too. Aiden saw his truck. In fact, Smith was coming out of the woods right then. He threw up his hand in a wave.

"Hope you find out what happened to your brother," Deion told him. "Oh, and...the chief said you shouldn't punch anyone else. That's really good advice. Maybe you should try an anger management class. My uncle did one of those." Deion turned away, heading back to the front of his vehicle. "That is one incredible lake. Bet the fishing is insane."

Automatically, Aiden's gaze dipped toward the lake.

Something bobbed near the surface of the water. There one moment...gone the next.

He took a step forward as his eyes narrowed. Only the faintest glimmer of sunlight touched the lake.

What's in the water?

It bobbed again. A...a light color. White. White against the dark lake. White like...

Fuck. Like the shirt Tony had been wearing earlier! When she'd changed at the vet clinic, she'd come out and had on a tight, white shirt. One of those exercise compression shirts with long sleeves. "Tony!" Aiden roared as he ran toward the lake.

"What?" Deion's confused voice. "Where are you going? What's—"

She was in the water. Face down. Face fucking down near the far edge of the pier. He rushed across the wood, hearing it creak and groan beneath him. She kept floating in the water. *Face down.*

"No!" A bellow from his soul as rage and fear twisted through him. Then Aiden dove into the water. Swam for her. Grabbed her and flipped her over.

Water streamed down her face. Her gorgeous, still face. Her eyes were closed. Her lips barely parted. She was a dead weight in his arms.

Dead. Dead. Dead.

No, no, no, no, no, no, no.

Someone splashed into the water beside him. Smith. He barreled closer. "What the hell?" Smith seemed stunned. *"Tony!"*

Aiden's arms tightened around her. "Baby? *Baby?*" No response. "Help me get her on the pier!"

He and Smith grabbed for the pier. Smith climbed onto the wooden surface, reaching back down as water streamed across his body. Aiden lifted Tony. Her head hung limply, her dark hair trailing over her face.

Smith took her. Put her down on the pier. Aiden heaved onto the pier and immediately crawled to her.

Smith crouched at her side. "How long was she in the water?"

"I called for help!" Deion yelled as he raced toward them.

Aiden slid the wet hair away from Tony's cheek and mouth. He turned her head to the side, and water drained from her mouth and nose. *Baby, no. No.* This couldn't be happening.

"She's got a weak pulse," Smith said. "But she is *not* breathing."

Aiden fucking knew she wasn't. He turned her head back toward him. Parted her lips. Breathed four deep breaths into her mouth as he held her nose pinched shut. *Please, please. Breathe for me. Come back. Do not do this. Do not do this!*

Aiden put his ear near her mouth. His gaze locked on her chest. He needed her chest to rise. He needed her to breathe.

She wasn't.

Smith kept hold of her wrist, with his fingers over her pulse.

Aiden covered her nose once more. He put his mouth over hers. Breathed for her. *Once. Twice.*

She jerked.

His mouth flew off hers. Desperate, terrified, he watched as she coughed and shuddered and came *back* to him.

"Thank Christ," Smith muttered. "Thank—"

Aiden pulled Tony into his arms. Held her as she shuddered. Chills skated down his body. The worst terror he'd ever felt in his life tried to choke him.

She's back. She's back.

He would never let her go again. "Baby?"

She grabbed his arm. Her fingers dug into him. "A-Aiden?" Raspy. Rusty. Too weak.

Rising, he held her tightly. He had to get Tony to a hospital. Aiden began to run down the old pier with her cradled against his chest and held carefully in his arms. One of the boards cracked beneath him—

"No!" Her weak cry. "Don't...don't leave..."

"I will never leave you again."

Her head shook against him. A small *no* gesture. "No...don't l-leave...him..."

He'd already jumped off the pier. Deion tried to take Tony from him, but Aiden just tightened his grip. "Who?" Who was she talking about? Wait...had Tony killed her attacker? Was he somewhere in the water?

He'd better be. And if he's not, I will be killing him soon.

"Y-your brother...F-found him..."

Stunned, he looked down at her.

"B-beneath the p-pier..." Shudders wracked her body. "Found...him."

CHAPTER FIFTEEN

"I'm not leaving!" Tony shoved aside the oxygen mask that the EMT had been trying to put on her yet again. She was breathing fine. She didn't need the damn thing any longer. What she needed was to get out of that ambulance and get back to her crime scene. She pushed past the glaring EMT and started to climb out of the ambulance—

Only to find Aiden blocking her path. He stood on the ground, his body nearly touching the back of the ambulance with its wide-open back doors, and his arms were crossed over his chest. "You weren't breathing," he snarled.

She stilled.

"You're going to the hospital. You're getting checked out by a doctor. You are *staying* there."

"I don't do so well when I'm told what to do." Her hair was wet, and her clothes stuck to her and she couldn't seem to stop trembling.

"Not. Breathing," he said again, his voice even harder and more grating. "You weren't moving in my arms. I had to breathe for you."

When she swallowed, Tony could taste the lake water. Her throat felt raw and savage.

Knowing her own voice still sounded slightly off, she nevertheless told him, "I'm fine now."

His head tipped back as he glared up at her. "Liar."

Enough of this. The EMT was being all grabby, putting his hands on her shoulders and trying to pull her back inside.

A hard hand on my shoulder. One on my head. Shoving me down. Down. Down. "Stop!" she cried.

The EMT froze.

Her breath shuddered in and out. Fear snaked through her, but Tony still jumped out of the ambulance. She pretty much jumped onto Aiden because he didn't back up.

He did immediately lock his arms around her, and unlike the EMT's touch, he didn't make her afraid. Didn't bring terrible memories crashing back on her. Instead, she felt safe.

"I found him," she whispered. Whispering was easier than talking at full volume.

"I know." He turned his head toward the lake. The scene was packed. Patrol cars. Bright lights. A black van that she knew would belong to the medical examiner. A diver was in the water because, yep, even the promised dive team had somehow gotten to the scene.

After she'd done their job for them.

A light rain had begun to fall on the scene. Some of the cops had on ponchos. Splashes of yellow.

"You were *never* supposed to get hurt," Aiden added. He pulled her closer. Brushed back some of her still wet hair from her forehead. "That wasn't part of the agenda."

"I—"

"You shouldn't have gone in the water alone," Barrett said as he marched toward them. Like a few of his deputies, he, too, wore a poncho. The hood had been pulled over his head. "Should have waited for backup. You must have gotten scared down there and hit your head." He stopped right beside Aiden. "You're very lucky Aiden and Smith dragged you out of the water."

Smith. He was there, too. Slinking closer. Eying her with the same concern everyone else showed.

Her hand was on Aiden's chest. She didn't even remember touching him, but her hand pressed over his heart. His shirt was wet. His slick hair shoved back. Smith was the same. Wet clothes. Wet hair. They were all wet.

She barely felt the rain drops falling onto her.

But, wait, what had the chief just said? That she'd hit her head? Where had he gotten that bullshit idea? "I didn't hurt myself down there."

Barrett's attention shifted to the EMT. "Does she have a concussion?"

The EMT began, "I—"

"I don't have a concussion because I didn't hit my head!" Okay, she sounded like she was a croaking frog. That happened when you swallowed a lake. "Some asshole grabbed me after I found the remains. I was coming up for air, and he locked one hand on my shoulder and one on my head and he shoved me back down."

She felt fury tighten Aiden's body. "The sonofabitch came after you."

"Hold on, hold on!" Barrett edged even closer. "Look, everyone, take a breath."

There was no breath to take. There was just the water. All around her. Slipping past her lips.

She started to wheeze.

"*Tony.*" Aiden's sharp voice. "Baby? Baby, look at me!"

Her gaze jumped to his face. So many lights around them. She could see him so clearly. The hard, locked jaw. The glinting, amber eyes. The stony, promising hell-on-earth expression.

"I have you," he told her. The words sounded like a vow. "I have you."

"Aiden, did you or Smith see anyone near the pier? Because I talked to Deion, and he swears no one else was here. That he dropped you off and you immediately went running for the water like you knew she was out there."

"I *saw* her." His hand slipped to her shoulder. Feathered lightly over the fabric. "Her white shirt in the dark water." His brows furrowed as he gazed at her shoulder, then he caught the wet material of her shirt. Eased it to the side. "Fucking dead bastard!"

She stumbled back. Hit the rear of the ambulance. The bright light from the back of the vehicle spilled down onto her, and her head turned so she could gaze down at her shoulder.

At the vivid red marks still on her skin. The angry impression from fingers.

"Doesn't look like she hit her head down there, after all," Smith stated, voice grim. "Looks like you need to reevaluate that shit, Barrett. Maybe get some of your officers to, oh, I don't know, fan out and *search* the woods."

Her head lifted. She stared at Aiden. His eyes were still locked on her shoulder. "Dead man," he stated. She knew he was making a vow.

Tony swallowed. "I didn't see his face."

Aiden's gaze lifted to pin her.

"He was strong. He was waiting for me on the pier."

Barrett swore.

"He must have been watching me. When I came up for air, he was there, right in the spot where h-he knew I would be." The weak sound of her voice made her angry. She was angry because *he* had made her weak. "He knew where the remains were. The bones still tied to the old piling. He knew. He waited for me to come up." Her hand rose to her head. She could feel the pressure. "He pushed me down. Down, down..."

"*Look at me.*"

Aiden's voice.

She realized her gaze had jerked to the lake.

"I have you," he told her again.

Swallowing, she kept going. Tony knew she had to give a statement. The police chief was right there, body tense, and she needed to get this all out now. "He fell into the water." Or had she pulled him in? Tony couldn't quite remember. "He kept holding me down. I tried to claw at him. To p-punch. He was so strong."

"You're sure it was a man? Did you see his face?"

She remembered hitting his chest. Kicking at his legs. "A man." Definitely. But his face? "I never saw him...and he...he had on gloves." She looked at her own hands. She turned over her palms. Saw the skin that was still prunish. "Didn't scratch him. Don't have any DNA. And the water...the water washes away so much..."

"*Tony.*" Aiden's voice. Soft. Careful.

Once more, her gaze found him.

"I want you to get in the ambulance. I want you to go to the hospital for me." His throat moved as he swallowed. "Please."

She shook her head. "The remains." This was important. "I s-saw his ring. Silver. Round. Still on him."

Aiden jerked. "My father's ring. If it *is*...there'll be an inscription inside. He gave it to my brother on our sixteenth birthday. Gave it to him because he was born first."

"The killer tied him to a piling." With such thick, heavy rope. "He could have been there wh-when the first dive team went down. I saw their report." She licked dry lips. How could her lips be dry when she felt so wet and cold? "Didn't go under the pier." They should have. *Why hadn't they?* But she suspected. She'd seen the name of the original dive team in the files. A group that had long ago disbanded after reports of shoddy work. Unprofessionalism.

You didn't check under the pier, and you let the killer get away with his crime. You rushed to search the scene, going for the deepest spots without realizing the body was right under your nose. Of course, the body could have been moved there after the initial search. Two possibilities.

"You're shaking, baby. I want you to go to the hospital. I need you to get checked out."

But she didn't want to leave him. "Stay with...you." Her stomach churned. She'd spat out so much water earlier, was more coming?

"Hell, yes, I'm staying with you." And he picked her up. He did that so much. Just lifted her up and carried her and she would have complained but she was cold, and the shaking was getting worse. He tucked her into the back of the ambulance. Perched beside her. "Every moment, I'll be with you." His head turned toward the EMT. "Can we get this thing moving?"

"Your brother," she said, pushing up because he'd put her back down on the gurney. "You've been looking for him. All this time—"

Aiden put one hand on either side of her and leaned in close. "I'm staying with you," he spoke flatly. "Every single minute. Understand? *You matter.* You are my priority." His head turned to the right. "Now someone get this ambulance moving!"

Smith slammed one of the rear doors shut. "I'll handle things here."

"Good. Fabulous." Aiden's gaze had returned to her. "Never again," he vowed.

Her brow furrowed. What was he talking about?

"I will never be that scared again. I will never lose you again. *Never again.*"

Smith slammed the second door. The ambulance's siren screamed.

***

Smith watched the ambulance drive away. Aiden had been wrecked, so close to the edge of his control. The guy had needed to get away from the scene.

"I had more questions," Barrett blustered. "I wanted to know more about her attacker."

Such a prick. Never liked this jackass. Because he had known Barrett for a very, very long time. When he'd been a teen, he'd come up here a few summers with the Warner brothers. Wherever they went, they always included him. He'd wondered if they'd realized, even back then, before all the drama with his dad hit, that his family was just living on fumes. Keeping up appearances. Because Austin and Aiden had always invited him to everything. Always footed the bill.

Until that last summer...

Putting on his game face, Smith spun to face the chief. "When she's cleared by the hospital, I'm sure she'll tell you everything. I think the priority now is making sure she's safe."

"She was talking just fine. Aiden didn't need to whisk her away!"

"Yes, he did." The chief should know this shit. "The time *after* a drowning can still be extremely dangerous." She'd need to be carefully watched over the next few days. Lots of complications could follow—infection, heart failure. Smith knew Aiden would be keeping her chained to his side.

He shouldered past the chief. He wanted to get closer to the lake and see what was happening.

He knew some of the cops were divers—like that young kid, Deion. He'd suited up and was going in for retrieval with the team that Aiden had hired. A team that had finally arrived. They'd been checking in at the hotel when he'd called them to tell the team leader about the discovery and ask him to haul ass to the cabin.

To bring up my friend.

"Did you see anything?" Barrett pushed him.

Voice grim, he replied, "I saw Aiden jumping into the water and yelling. I immediately ran to help him."

"Where were you? When you saw Aiden, I mean."

He pointed to the right. "In the woods. Doing some searching of my own."

"And you didn't see *anything* suspicious during that search?"

"No."

One of the divers had come up. He was holding...

Fuck.

"This is going to be bad," Barrett said.

It wasn't *going* to be bad. "It already is."

They'd just brought up a skull.

***

"This is absolutely absurd." She swung her legs to the side of the hospital bed, and the thin, paper gown she wore hiked up to the top of Tony's thighs. "I'm not staying here. I need to get back to *my* crime scene. Those local guys are not going to know a thing about proper recovery techniques. They'll screw up all my evidence." She rose.

Aiden immediately stepped in front of her. "You heard the doctor. She wants you here for twenty-four hours."

Tony glared up at him. Her eyes gleamed with her fury and determination. With *life*. There had been no life earlier, not when she'd hung limply in his arms and his whole world had stopped.

"I'm perfectly fine."

"Sweetheart, you were perfectly dead."

She sucked in a breath. "I wasn't."

"It sure as hell felt that way to me. You were sagging my arms. Your eyes were closed while water poured from your mouth. It's a nightmare that I will replay for the rest of my life." He leaned in closer. "So get that sweet ass of yours back in bed."

She didn't. She did tilt up her chin. "I'm going back to the crime scene."

"No. You're getting back in bed. If you don't do it in the next five seconds, I'll be putting you back there."

A gasp slid from her. "What is wrong with you?" Tony demanded. "You don't get to boss me around like this! I'm not one of your employees, you don't get to—"

He hadn't been bluffing. "Five seconds are up." He picked her up. Put her back in the bed.

"*Aiden.*"

He sat down beside her. Trapped her there when he put his hands down on either side of her body. "You were dead."

"Stop—"

"I couldn't get you out of the water fast enough. I had to pass you up to Smith. When I crawled onto the pier, you were still and cold, and I breathed for you."

Her gaze searched his.

"Never again. You will never go through that again. I fucking won't let it happen. Because I can't do that." Didn't she get it? "I can't see you die. I can't lose you. I won't."

Her lips parted.

He kissed her. Soft. Desperate. Frantic but careful because…she was too delicate. Too easily destroyed. Fucking fuck—he'd planned to use her at the beginning. He'd done this. Brought her into the nightmare. *His* nightmare. And she'd nearly lost her life.

And I nearly lost my mind.

He forced his head to lift. "It's my fault."

"You weren't the one holding me beneath the water."

His fingers grabbed the sheets. Fisted them. "I said you were the key. Told everyone. *You* were the one who was going to help me find him."

"And I did."

She didn't get it. "*I* put the target on you. You were the key, so the killer came after *you*. You're the one who finds the dead." The dog had been targeted first. Maybe as a warning to her? But she hadn't backed off. So the SOB had gone straight for her. "I wasn't with you. You were alone. You needed me. I *failed*."

Her hand rose to press against his cheek. "I'm pretty sure you saved me."

He turned his head. Hungrily, desperately, he kissed her palm.

"You pulled me from the water. You breathed for me. You saved me. Don't think that's a failure at all. Some people would say that you saving me means that I'm now supposed to owe you my life."

"You don't owe me a damn thing." He owed her. A debt that could never be repaid. *You found my brother.* She'd almost died trying to help him.

He kissed her palm again.

"Something is different," Tony murmured.

His head turned so that he stared into her eyes again.

"I'm okay." A furrow appeared between her eyebrows. "But something is different."

Yes, something was different. He'd realized some hard truths in those terrible moments when he'd seen her floating in the water. "The past isn't worth the present."

"Aiden?"

"*I won't lose you.*" Maybe if he said those words enough times, they'd be true. Because he couldn't lose. Would not.

I love her.

He hadn't loved anything, not in years. Not anyone. His parents were gone. His brother—his brother was his obsession. The fury and pain had twisted him up inside until he'd only been living for vengeance. A powder keg, ready to explode.

Until her.

"Whatever I have to do in order to keep you safe, I will." A vow. "Even if it means I have to tie you to this bed because the doctor said you needed to stay here for observation."

"Tying me up, huh? Are you sure that's not just some kinky fetish you have?"

She was trying to joke? Now? After everything? He leaned closer. Wanted her mouth. Wanted her. "Oh, tying you up is definitely on the sexual agenda."

Her tongue snaked out and licked her lower lip.

"When you've recovered from *drowning*. When rage isn't still flooding through every cell of my body. When the doctor gives me the all-clear that you're good, I plan to fuck you long and hard until I am sure that you are back with me, one hundred percent."

Her eyes widened. "Thank you for the...warning?"

"Promise. It was more of a promise." Since he was sharing promises... "I'm going to kill him."

Her head shook. "The police chief—"

"Maybe he'll find the bastard first. Maybe he'll put bars between us so I can't get to him." Not like the bars would slow him down. With his money, he would still be able to get to the piece of shit. "We both know the person who killed my brother came after you. He doesn't get to target two people I love and walk away."

Stunned silence.

Oh, hell. He'd overshared. Too late now. So he waited. And he watched.

"You...don't mean that."

"I always planned to kill him. Just didn't tell you. Thought you might frown on it."

"I meant you don't—you don't love me."

Now he had to kiss her. Nothing could have stopped him from brushing his lips over hers. "How could I not?"

Her hand still lingered along his cheek. "You just met me."

"I knew a million things about you before we ever met," Aiden confessed against her lips. "Then I got face to face with you, and I learned so much more."

"You don't love me."

Why did she keep saying that? "You are the only one I do love. You marked me every time we touched. And when we had sex, I knew there would never be anyone else for me." He caught her hand. Pulled it slowly down. Pressed it over his chest. "You own my heart. When you weren't moving, it felt like someone had cut the thing out of my chest." A ragged breath. "I'm not good. I can keep up appearances with the best of them." Usually. Unless he broke and took a swing at a police station... "I know how to play the game, and, sure, on paper, I can look like an angel, but deep down, you should know I'm the devil."

"That's not true."

It was. "I've lied to you."

Her long lashes flickered.

"Kept secrets. Twisted things. That's what I do. I warned you, I am a bastard." She was so lovely that it hurt. "But I am *your* bastard. I will tear the world apart for you. You are what matters. You will always be what matters."

She seemed stunned. Probably because he'd told her he planned to murder her attacker and Aiden had said that he loved her, all in the same breath. A whole lot to take in. He eased back from her. Put some space between them. "I don't expect you to love me back." He rose from the bed. Turned away.

"Why not?"

Easy. "Because I'm not a man you should love." He was the man she should run from. *But what would I do if she fled?*

"I've never been good at doing what I *should*."

He spun back toward her.

"Thank you for pulling me out of the water, Aiden."

Like he would have left the water without her.

"I called for you."

Not understanding, he shook his head.

"A lot of the attack is sort of blurry, but I remember the end. I could hear my heartbeat pounding in my ears. It was blasting over and over, like a striking drum. My lungs burned, and every part of my body felt tight and hard. I needed a breath so badly, but I'd already swallowed some water, and I was afraid to swallow more. I-I knew what would happen if I opened my mouth."

His hands fisted. Released. Fisted. Released. *He is dead. I will find him. I will kill him. Slowly. He will beg me before the end comes for him.*

"At the last moment, I couldn't hold out any longer. I opened my mouth, and I screamed. Silly, huh? Screaming under water, but I wasn't rational then. The only thing I could do was scream for you."

Once more, his hands fisted.

"Because I knew you would come for me."

He shook his head. His chest burned, as if he was the one under the water, struggling so desperately to hold on until he could take a desperate breath.

"No one ever came for me before." Soft. "I got away myself. I saved myself, and that's what I've always done."

"Because you're strong." The strongest person he'd ever met.

"Then you were there for me in Biloxi."

Another scene that would give him nightmares forever. Danger stalked Tony, and that crap had to stop.

"I couldn't get away this time. I needed help."

I wasn't there.

Her dark, deep eyes held his gaze. "I needed you, and even as I opened my mouth, and I knew the water would sweep in...I *knew* you were going to find me."

I found you floating. I found you cold.

"I've never counted on anyone that way before, but deep inside, I knew you were going to save me."

And again, he shook his head. His hands clenched so tightly they ached.

"I knew it...because I trust you."

You shouldn't.

"I knew it...because I love you, Aiden."

She loved the wrong man. He was so wrong. A thousand times *wrong*. But he surged back toward the bed. Bent low and curled his hands under her delicate jaw. He kissed her as if his very sanity depended on her.

Because he feared it did.

CHAPTER SIXTEEN

Her eyes opened. Tony turned her head and saw Aiden sitting in the chair beside her bed. She'd agreed—grudgingly—to stay in the hospital until dawn. He'd insisted on staying with her. Even though his brother's remains had finally been found, even though divers had been bringing them up, he'd chosen to stay with her.

Because he loved her.

His fingers were still twined with hers. He'd held her hand all through the night. She'd been able to drift off to sleep only because she'd felt the reassurance of his touch.

It had been easy to act tough. Strong. But the truth of the matter was that she was shaken to her absolute core. She kept feeling pressure in her chest. Kept fearing that she wouldn't be able to breathe.

Once upon a time, she'd thought the darkness in that terrible closet—the closet that had haunted her since she was a child—she'd thought that was hell. She'd been trapped in that closet. Tied up and thrown away into the dark. A nightmare that never ended. To her, hell.

But her hell had changed. Now hell was a watery grave. Darkness all around and her lungs burning and burning and when she tried to breathe—

Ice.

The water had felt just like ice sliding into her mouth and down her throat. Filling her lungs. Not slowly. But so fast. Horrifyingly fast.

Her fingers squeezed his.

Instantly, Aiden's eyes opened. His penetrating gaze locked right on hers. "What's wrong?"

She could lie. Say nothing. But that wasn't who she was with him. "Drowning isn't an easy way to die."

He leaned toward her. "Baby..."

"I want to get out of this hospital." It felt cold. She was plenty cold enough. "The doctor will be by on rounds soon. If she gives me the all-clear, we're leaving." Even if she didn't give them the all-clear, Tony still planned to get out of there.

"She wanted you to stay twenty-four hours."

Not going to happen. "You can tell her that you'll be at my side every moment until that twenty-four hours is up. I'll have a constant watch."

He brought their joined hands to his lips. Kissed her knuckles. "Yes, you will."

She knew he was going to give in even before Aiden's head moved in a jerky nod. But she wasn't done. "I need to call my team. I want backup down here." Her people. A team she trusted to have her back.

"I already called them."

Surprise rolled through her.

His lips twisted in a humorless smile. "Figured they would want to know what happened. I sure as hell would if I'd been in their place."

"Who did you talk to?"

"Saint. Memphis. Called your friend Lila, too."

The core members of her team. Her best friends.

"They're all coming. So you'll have the full team at your command."

"That's not how it works. No one commands. We all work together. We're not billionaires giving orders, you know." She didn't pull her hand free of his grip because she liked it when he held her. But...

"My mistake," he murmured. "That would be me."

Tony pushed up. She frowned at their hands. "What happened to your knuckles?" She could see faint bruises on them.

"They ran into Levi's face."

Her gaze flew up. "What?"

"That's why I was late meeting you at the cabin." The faint lines near his mouth deepened. "Barrett tossed me in a cell when I lost control and plowed my fist into Levi's face. Barrett had to talk Levi down and get him to not press assault charges against me."

"Why did you hit him?"

"Because he wanted a lawyer."

Tony blinked. Maybe she was missing something? "That...doesn't seem like a punching offense."

His lashes flickered. "I punched him because I think he killed my brother. The man seemed guilty as hell, and I know he's hiding something." A pause. "But he has an alibi, at least for Melanie's murder. Turns out, Levi had broken up with Melanie and started a fling with his assistant, Sharon. Sharon is his alibi."

Tony swallowed. "Melanie knew your brother was beneath that pier." It was the only explanation that made sense to her. *Melanie must have known.* "She didn't repair it, even though the wood was rotting away. So either she was just really bad as a property manager or..."

"Or she knew that if someone started pulling up the wood and repairing the pier, they'd find him."

Yes. "Maybe she planned to eventually move the body, but it's..." She stopped. This was the tricky part. "There were an awful lot of ropes down there."

Once more, his lashes flickered.

"He was bound tightly. So tightly that his hands were still in place. Whoever put him there didn't want him to move. It seemed to me..." This was going to hurt him. She hated hurting him. "It was a job that took two people."

His hand jerked in her hold. "*What?*"

"Melanie wouldn't have been able to move that body alone. She knew he was under the pier, so I think she helped someone put your brother there." Then she'd spun her stories about Austin being far away, "sunning himself near the water." *Oh, what a sick story.* Because he had been next to the water. No, *in* it. Tony blew out a breath. "I'll know more once I look at the remains." She let his hand go. Pushed away her covers. Started to rise. "That's why I have to get out of here. Who knows what happened at the scene after we left? I need to see the remains before any additional evidence is lost."

Aiden rose to stand before her. His tall frame towered over her. "You're saying that all this time, two killers were at work?"

"Maybe only one actually killed your brother." She couldn't know, not yet. But her gut told her, "Two hid the body." The problem was that water was unforgiving. Evidence would be washed away. The lake was full of fish. Fish that had lived and died in all the long years since his brother's death.

The fish would have fed on the remains. That was one of the many reasons why so little had been left. Just bones. But she could work with bones.

Pain and grief slid over Aiden's handsome face.

Her eyes closed. "I'm so sorry."

She heard the squeak of the door opening. The soft pad of footsteps. A pad that came to a sudden stop.

"What's happening?" A female voice. "You should be resting."

Oh, right. It probably looked as if she and Aiden were about to make out. Not this time. Her eyes opened as she turned toward the doctor. "I need to get out of here because what I *should* be doing? That's my job. I should be working."

She'd found the missing victim. Now she needed to give him justice.

I need to find the killer.

"Aiden will watch me. He'll stay with me. Observe to make sure I'm good. He'll call nine-one-one immediately if there is any trouble." Her shoulders straightened. "But I feel fine, and I need to get back to my job."

The doctor asked, "Just what is your job?"

Digging up the dead. "You really don't want to know."

***

Tony rushed out of her hospital room like a prisoner escaping from jail. Aiden was right beside her. Sometime during the night, Smith had delivered fresh clothes for them. After the doctor had finished Tony's exam, Tony had changed as fast as she could. The jeans, fresh blouse, and tennis shoes were a whole lot better than the paper gown, but she would have walked out of that place buck naked if necessary.

Aiden had changed, too. No more clothing that smelled of the lake. Jeans. A sweatshirt. Boots.

Aiden reached the elevator before her, and he stabbed the button on the control panel. Tony slanted him a quick glance. There hadn't been a whole lot of talking about the big, emotional reveal the night before. Mostly because she'd been exhausted, and a heavy sleep had pulled her under after his confession.

Part of her wondered if that talk *had* been a dream.

But...no. Aiden had said he loved her.

And, for the first time in her life, she'd told a man that she loved him, too. Terrifying. Because she didn't know what to do next.

Yes, you do. Solve the case. Close it. Then see if this madness between you and Aiden lasts once the danger is gone.

The elevator dinged. The doors opened.

A woman with a big bouquet of flowers walked out. She almost walked straight into Tony.

"Oh, sorry!" The woman blushed and—

I know her. Tony remembered the woman's face peering at her...when she'd been at Levi Russell's vet clinic.

"Sharon," Aiden said softly.

Her hand jerked, and the flowers bobbed. One petal fell to the floor.

Sharon. Right. The woman who was the alibi for Levi.

Sharon lowered her flowers as she gazed at Tony. "How is your dog?" she asked fretfully. "Such a beautiful animal."

"She's good." The scent of the flowers was heavy. Tony's nostrils flared. "Just spoke to the vet in Fairley." She'd snagged Aiden's phone to make that call. Tony had no idea where her phone was. Maybe at the bottom of the lake? "Banshee is making good progress. She should be able to come back to me soon."

A wide smile curved Sharon's lips. "That's wonderful!"

The elevator doors had closed behind her.

Sharon hesitated. "I, um..." Her stare darted to Aiden. Fear flickered in her eyes.

He reached around Sharon and pushed the button on the elevator's control panel once more.

"I'm sorry," Sharon whispered. "I know you loved your brother."

Tony's head tilted. She hadn't braided her hair that day, and her hair slid over her shoulder with the movement.

Sharon lingered. Her stare slowly slid over Aiden's face. There was something almost wistful about her gaze. "It was always so hard to tell the two of you apart. Sometimes, I'd think I was talking to Austin, then I'd realize it was you." Her gaze softened even more as she studied Aiden.

Well, well... "Ahem."

Sharon's gaze whipped to Tony.

Tony wasn't in the mood to play games or to pretend that she was nice. After an attempted murder, nice just wasn't in her vocabulary. "Were you with Levi yesterday evening, right around sunset?"

"Ah...I..."

"Come on. I know the story has been on the news. I was attacked. Human remains were found at the cabin."

More petals fell from the flowers as Sharon clutched them even tighter. "I, um, need to go visit my friend. She's...recovering. Little bit of surgery." Her teeth nibbled on her lower lip.

The elevator dinged.

"Hope your friend recovers fully," Tony returned without missing a beat. "But were you with Levi or not? Because you've already given him an alibi once, and I'm curious to see if you'll do it again."

Sharon's head moved in the faintest of...negative shakes. A *no*.

"Were you with him before?" Aiden demanded. "When Melanie was killed, were you with him then?"

Tears gleamed in Sharon's eyes. "He's a good man."

That was not a yes.

"He wouldn't hurt anyone," Sharon rushed to add. "He helps people. He just—he got involved in a mess with Melanie. But that was over. They were over. And I—" Her gaze darted between Aiden and Tony. "He wouldn't hurt anyone. I-I have to see my friend." She rushed past them, leaving a trail of petals in her wake.

"She lied," Aiden said. "Fuck."

Tony slipped into the elevator. Aiden had thrown up a hand to keep the doors open. "Oh, she definitely lied."

Aiden followed her inside and jabbed the button for the ground floor.

"Probably want to let Barrett know that Levi's alibi won't hold. With a little pushing, Sharon will tell the chief the truth." The truth being that she'd lied to protect the man she loved. "She's worried he's guilty."

Aiden's head turned toward her.

"And I think she might have loved your brother, too."

His brows lifted. "Why do you say that?"

"Because I saw the way she looked at you." Only she didn't think Sharon had been *seeing* Aiden. She'd been looking at Austin.

A shiver slid over her. A few shivers kept coming, every now and then. Leftovers from the drowning? She hated the chill that seemed to cling to her. "Did you and your brother often get confused by people?"

"We were identical." He looked at the elevator's panel and watched as the different floors lit up as they descended. "We got mistaken for each other all the time."

Ask. You have to ask. "Was it ever deliberate?"

He kept staring at the panel. "What do you mean?"

"You know exactly what I mean, Aiden. Twins do it all the time. Especially twins who are perfect matches. Did you ever switch places with him? Maybe to take a math test? Maybe just to see if you could get away with it? To see if teachers would know the difference?" She thought about what Sharon had just revealed, and her stomach twisted. "Maybe even to see if a friend...or a girlfriend would know the difference?"

His head turned. He pinned her with his amber stare. "Yes."

"How often?" Her palms—suddenly feeling sweaty—rubbed against the front of her jeans.

"All the fucking time." The doors opened. He stepped into the lobby.

"Yo!" Smith's voice, calling out before Tony could press for more. She exited the elevator and saw him hurriedly approaching.

Smith shook his head. "Going out the front would be a major mistake. The story has leaked, and reporters are swarming from all over." He stopped near Aiden. His nose wrinkled. "Damn, man. You need a shower. You still smell like the freaking lake." His head turned toward Tony. "No offense, but you do, too."

"*Smith,*" Aiden growled. "Focus."

"Focusing." He turned sharply to the right. "Parked in the employee lot. Come this way. We'll sneak out and miss the crowd. Unless you feel like spilling all to the press at the moment...?"

"Hell, no," Aiden replied.

"Figured that would be your response." He quickly led them through a series of corridors, then they were exiting, going straight to the employee lot. The black SUV waited, and when Tony jumped in the back, she found a small, white bag waiting in the seat for her.

Aiden climbed in beside her.

"Muffins," Smith announced as he took up his position behind the wheel and cranked the vehicle. "Because I'm awesomely thoughtful. Figured you'd be starving, so I picked up some goodies from the bakery in town. You're welcome, by the way." He reversed. Then turned and took them *away* from the front of the hospital and down a snaking alley. "Welcome for the clothes, the deliciously wonderful muffins, and for the swift getaway. All part of my package."

Tony's stomach growled. She'd been given only broth at the hospital, and she was absolutely starving. She snatched open the bag and started to devour a muffin in a very much too-desperate way.

"Give us an update," Aiden directed as he leaned forward and didn't touch the muffins. "What in the hell is happening at the cabin?"

"Oh, the usual. It's crime-scene central. People were there all night long. First it was just the authorities, you know. All official-like. Then the reporters started creeping in. Barrett had to set up a big perimeter and even haul a few of them away for trespassing. The divers finished up. They, um, brought your brother up." His voice deepened. "Really fucking sorry, man. I know we thought he was dead, but there was still hope, right?"

Tony swallowed down a bit of the muffin. The light treat suddenly felt very heavy. "The remains haven't been officially identified yet." Not a question. Even with the ring that had been on the body, an ID couldn't have been made that fast.

"Not yet." Smith braked at a stop sign and turned his head to look back at Aiden. "Heard Barrett say they'd need to get dental records for a comparison. It's gonna take some time."

Yes, it would. But... "I can speed up the process," Tony offered.

Aiden fired her a questioning glance.

"I don't just find the dead. I identify remains. Especially when you're dealing with bones, you're talking about one of my specialties." She wanted to see those bones. "Smith, take me to the police chief. I've worked with law enforcement a million times. This is my job. This is what I do. I can speed the process along and look for things that the medical examiner will miss."

He didn't drive away. Instead, he faced forward and let out a long sigh. "You sure about this? You were nearly killed yesterday. Maybe it's time for you to take a step back from things." A pause. "Aiden, maybe it's time for you to realize what's important right now. And is it her or him? The living or the dead?"

She saw Aiden's jaw harden. Before he could answer, Tony responded, "I'm making the call here, not Aiden. Take me to Barrett." She leaned forward and...

Caught a whiff of herself. Dammit. She did smell like the lake. She hadn't showered at the hospital. They'd been too intent on examining her. Making her *rest*. Her least favorite thing to do. "Maybe a shower, then the police station," she muttered. But to shower, they'd need to go back to the cabin. And the throng of reporters.

"I can help you out on that." Smith finally drove forward. "Aiden gave me orders last night, and like the fantastic head of security I am, I made sure they were executed. He wanted a safe place for you to crash—one away from prying eyes, so I set up a second base of operations. The rental house is about ten miles from here. Secluded. Great security." He turned to the left. "Got the rental from Melanie's assistant. Have to say, the guy was super helpful. And chatty. Turns out, he did not like his boss much."

"Why not?" Tony wanted to know.

"Because he said she spent most of her time, and I quote, 'Fucking clients when she should have been handling her business.'"

Okay.

"Told me that she'd get calls at all hours of the day and night on her phones. *Phones*. As in plural. I thought he must mean her office phone and her cell phone, but he cleared that up for me real fast. Told me that she had *two* smartphones. But the interesting thing is, when I did my dive into her phone records, only one device was linked to her. So that just begs the question...where the hell is her other phone? And who was she calling on it?"

CHAPTER SEVENTEEN

"What's the plan?" Smith pressed his shoulders to the wall near the door and eyed Aiden with suspicion. "I know you have one, you cagey bastard. But I can't help you if you don't bring me in the loop."

Aiden heard the upstairs door click shut. Tony had gone up the steps moments before so she could shower. He intended to join her in that shower, but first... "You have extra clothes waiting for her up there?"

"For her, for you. Yes. Done. Brought them all over just like you asked."

He'd called Smith while Tony slept and had made arrangements. He'd wanted a safe house for her. A place with the best protection in the area. "Additional security is being installed?"

"Yes." A sigh from Smith. "I did everything you wanted. More security is coming. Soon this place will be wired from top to bottom, but...could we get back to my question? *What is your plan?* You have your brother, what's next?"

"We make sure it's him." He needed confirmation on the remains. *But who the hell else would have been tied beneath the pier?*

"So you're back to using Tony again, check."

Aiden glared at Smith. "I'm not using her."

"Yes, bro, you are. You used her to find him. She almost died, but she got the job done." Grim words as Smith shoved away from the wall. "Now instead of taking her out of the line of fire, you're shoving her right back in. Someone else can identify the remains. She can slip back into the shadows. You know she likes those better, anyway. Hell, you know everything about her, remember? You've been choreographing and calculating the whole time, and the poor woman never had any idea just how much she was being manipulated." He stalked forward. "In other words...*used* by you."

***

Tony pressed her shoulders to the wall. She hadn't gone in the bedroom. She'd shut the door, yes, but that had just been a trick. She wanted to hear what the two men below her were saying. Carefully, she inched a little closer to the top of the stairs.

Smith's voice was easy to hear. "*Hell, you know everything about her, remember? You've been choreographing and calculating the whole time, and the poor woman never had any idea just how much she was being manipulated.*"

Her heartbeat kicked up.

Smith added flatly, "*In other words...used by you.*"

Tony shook her head.

***

"You're wrong," Aiden said. He didn't surge toward Smith. Didn't go in with fists flying. He just made the announcement, loud and clear.

"Am I?" Smith didn't look convinced. "You didn't want her to find him? Because I thought that was the whole reason you sent me to meet her in the first place."

"Tony is the best."

"Right. And that's why you wanted her. I get it, I do. *But she nearly died.* Can't you take the freaking win on finding your brother's remains and walk away? Let the local authorities take over. They can handle everything else."

"They aren't as good as she is. They won't see what she does."

"*She was floating in the water.* Face down. She wasn't breathing when you pulled her out. I thought it might matter to you. I thought something might matter. Someone, other than your brother. You've been fighting for a ghost all these years, and you know what? Hate to break it to you, but the guy could be a real sonofabitch. He wasn't perfect. You're not avenging some hero." Smith's jaw hardened. "He partied hard. He used people. Discarded them when he was done. I thought you were different, but you're doing the same thing with her. Using her. Doesn't matter if she gets hurt—"

"It fucking *does*."

"You'll use her, and when she's not useful any longer, you'll toss her to the side."

He took a step toward Smith. "I have no intention of ever discarding her."

"No?" Smith edged closer, jerking up his chin. "Then what the hell are you gonna do, boss?"

"I'm going to marry her."

Smith's mouth dropped open.

***

"I'm going to marry her."

Tony took another small step toward the top of the stairs. She hadn't heard that part right, had she?

***

"Does that clear things up for you?" Aiden asked carefully. "Should I repeat it? In case you missed it?" His voice rose a little more as he said, quite clearly, "I am going to marry her. Spend the rest of my life with her. Have kids if she wants them. Have lots of sex and work hard to make her smile and help her solve as many cold cases as her heart desires. That's what I'm going to do."

Smith just stared at him. After a few moments, he blinked. "Are you bullshitting me right now? Messing with me because I was pushing you?"

"I want to find my brother's killer. I want the bastard *bad* because he's the one who hurt her. *Her*. He tried to take Tony from me." Now rage did stir, but it wasn't flashing hot. It was cold. The death that would come for his enemy. "No one does that. You're right, you see. I'm not so different from my brother. You might have thought I was the good one, but you're wrong. When it comes to someone hurting her, there is nothing *good* in me." He took another step toward Smith. "We find my brother's killer, and we find the bastard who held her under the water."

"Then what do you do?" Smith swallowed. "Hand out your own brand of justice?"

"I do what needs doing." Just like he'd always planned.

"And she's fine with that? The woman who works with cops all over the country is just gonna be fine marrying a guy who plans cold-blooded murder? Don't you see what you're doing? You have a chance here! A chance for more. Let the past go and take what is waiting for you."

"He's not getting away."

"Fuck. You're going to lose her. Tony won't stay when she sees what you are." Smith pointed at him. "You might have fooled a lot of other people, but I always knew, and I still stayed at your side." His lips twisted. "What the hell does that say about me?"

"It says I *can* count on you." A brief hesitation. "I can count on you, can't I, Smith?"

"You're the boss."

Ah, such a flippant response. "Find Barrett. Let him know that Tony wants to see the remains. Don't take no for an answer from him. She has to get access."

Smith swung away. "Oh, sure. I'll just go tell the police chief how to do his job. He'll love that."

"Tell him the other Ice Breakers are coming to town. Tony will have her full team soon."

Smith stiffened. He glanced back. "How soon?"

"By the end of the day."

"Then I guess it's game on, huh?"

"The bastard is *in* this town. He's been hiding here all along. Hell, yes, it's game on. We're hunting him down. He left my brother in a watery grave, and he tried to do the same thing to the woman I love. I don't care if you think I'm a monster—I don't care if I *am* a monster—no one does that to her. *No one.*"

"Just don't make it your funeral." A mutter. "Or hers." He faced the door. His hand reached out—

"Why were you searching the woods?" Low.

***

What had Aiden just said? She strained to hear the men. Aiden's voice had dipped so low on that last part that she hadn't heard him clearly.

But instead of Aiden's voice, she suddenly heard Smith boom, "You're not serious right now!"

"Dead serious." Aiden. "Why were you in the woods near my cabin? You knew Tony was coming back. Why weren't you there to meet her?"

Her palms flattened against the wall behind her.

"Because maybe I'm not fucking useless. Maybe I thought I could help scout the area, too. Figured it was possible the cops overlooked something at Melanie's murder scene. I went back out while it was still light to look around."

"And did you find anything?"

"No. Not a damn thing."

Her breath whispered in and out.

"You saw no one at the pier?" Aiden pressed. "No one running through the woods? No one running away at all?"

"I just saw *you*. When I came out of the woods, you were getting out of the patrol car, then you started yelling Tony's name." A pause. Stiff silence. "What the hell, man? Why are you looking at me that way?"

But Tony knew why, even before—

"Do you think *I* did it?" Smith blasted. "You think I tried to kill your doc? Are you fucking for real? You're grilling *me*?"

"I've been trying to remember," Aiden said, and there was no emotion in his voice, "were you already wet *before* you jumped into the water?"

"You really are a cold sonofabitch."

"*No, she's really that fucking important to me.*" A snarl. Anger now. No, more like rage. "I already had her. You jumping in the water slowed things down. If you'd stayed up on the pier, I could have handed her to you faster. But you jumped in. Why? *To have a reason to be soaking wet?* Because, yes, that suspicion keeps going through my head, and I hate it, but it's there, and I need the truth from you."

"You just told me to go talk to the police chief! Now you're accusing me of—of being Tony's attacker? Her attacker and your brother's killer? That's crazy! You've gone over the edge. That's why I told you to back off this. The obsession is consuming you, man." Tony heard the sound of the door opening. Then closing almost immediately, as if Smith had changed his mind and decided not to exit. "Wait. You were trying to catch me off guard, weren't you?" Smith charged. "Act like things are fine, give me the job with the chief, then hit me with your suspicions when you thought I might trip up. *That's* what you were doing?"

"I don't see you tripping." Aiden's immediate reply.

"Because I'm not going to fall. *I didn't hurt her.* I didn't hurt your brother. Yes, I was pissed as hell at him. He *knew* about my father's business, did you realize that? He and your old man both knew it was a house of cards. They knew everything was falling, and he didn't warn me. Your dad was involved in some shady shit. So was your brother. But I never thought he would hold back on me. I never thought—"

"I knew, too," Aiden announced.

She sucked in a breath.

"My brother and I were trying to get my dad to *help* your family," Aiden continued roughly. "We were putting as much pressure on our father as we could. You want to know why my brother flipped the hell out at school that last time and got expelled? Because he was pissed our dad wasn't doing more for you. We both even gave *your* father our own money. But when *our* father found out what we were doing, he cut us off. That's why we were out here that summer. We had access to nothing else. We both wanted to help, but our dad was stopping us. Austin told me that he had to find a way to get more cash to your family, and the next thing I knew, he was dead, and you were in the wind. I lost my brother and my friend that summer."

"I-I didn't...you never said..."

"You matter to me, Smith. But *she* matters more. That woman upstairs—listening to every word we're saying—"

Tony gasped. *Oh, crap.* Busted.

"She is my world. So, yes, I'm going to question you. I'm going to investigate you. I am going to rip this town apart to find the bastard who hurt her. There is no other option for me. No threat to her can stand. So I will ask you point blank...*Did you hurt her?*"

"No, I swear it. *No.*"

"Then help us to find out who did. Tell the police chief that Tony wants to see the remains. He won't refuse her assistance. She's the best in the nation."

"I...all right. Of course. On it." He cleared his throat. "I never knew. No one told me..."

"You were gone. Off being all you could be. You'd put your old life behind you. It was enough that the ghosts were haunting me." Aiden's voice roughed even more. "Now how about you get the hell out? I need to talk to Tony. Alone."

Once more, the door opened. Shut. Smith got the hell out.

She should move. Aiden had obviously known she was listening the entire time.

A stair creaked. Then another. He was climbing up the steps and coming to her.

She shoved away from the wall and turned toward the staircase.

He kept climbing. Slowly, like he had all the time in the world. A faint smile curved his diabolically sexy lips. "Eavesdropping, my love?"

Hard to deny it when you were caught red-handed. "I thought I might hear something interesting."

He stopped on the landing. Right in front of her. "Did you?"

She had. "You think you're going to marry me?"

"It's on the agenda, provided you say yes."

Her throat felt so dry. Crazy, after she'd swallowed a freaking lake. "And you considered that Smith might have tried to kill me?"

His hand lifted. Stroked her cheek. "Like the thought didn't cross your mind?"

Yes, it had. All sorts of thoughts had crossed her mind.

"You just didn't say it," Aiden murmured, "because he was my best friend, and you worried you'd be making me choose between him and you."

She tensed. She *had* thought it. She'd struggled to remember, over and over, about her attack. And the only thing that had kept coming back to her...

Smith's truck was in the drive. He was there. He'd been at the scene. He had to be a suspect. It would be foolish to overlook him.

"But here's the thing," Aiden continued. No rage in his voice now. Just a dark sensuality. "There is no choice. From here on out, *always,* you will be it for me. Since you didn't want to push me, since you were afraid I'd choose him, I showed you that I wouldn't." He bent and kissed her. Not on the lips, but a tender, careful caress of his mouth against her forehead. "There is never anyone I would choose over you. You own me, love. Body and soul."

Her arms wrapped around his waist. It felt like holding onto an anchor. Maybe that was what he was, and she was just realizing it. An anchor when everything in her life had been churning and storming. He gave her a safe spot to land.

And, in return, she was going to give him what he craved. Justice.

***

"She wants access to the remains." Smith strode toward the rental. Aiden's ride. *I need my truck.* "Did you hear me, Barrett?" Smith scanned the long, twisting drive. No sign of reporters. The guy at the property management firm had better not leak the location. Smith—on orders from Aiden—had paid the fellow a shit ton of money to stay quiet. "Tony is out of the hospital. She's offering her services to ID the remains."

"She's not leaving town?"

Smith snorted. "Hell, no. If anything, I'd say she and Aiden are both even more determined than ever before. They're digging in and not giving up." *He thought it was me. I can't believe the SOB thought it was me.* "She's the best in the nation." Aiden hadn't been wrong on that. "She's offering her services. You refusing? That what I should tell the press?"

"She's a victim. I can't have the case compromised—"

"I'll let the press know those were your exact words. I'm sure they will understand. Or maybe, when the rest of the Ice Breakers roll into town this evening, you can tell them, too. Not like they are media darlings or anything these days. Sure it will all go over great for you."

Silence, then, almost grudgingly, "I'll talk to the ME."

Thought that would be your response. "Wonderful. Thanks for your cooperation. Figured you'd be excited to have a real expert helping out."

"You're a dick, aren't you, Smith?"

"Well, I do have a very large one. Thanks for noticing."

"You ever get tired of being a guard dog for Aiden? Tired of following all his commands?"

Before he could respond, Barrett hung up on him.

Smith glanced back at the house behind him. "Occasionally."

Then he heard a twig snap. He whirled around. Swaying trees stared back at him. He *hated* the wilderness. Give him the city any day of the week.

Another snap. Something—or someone—was out there. Watching. Waiting. Hunting? Screw that. Smith bounded into the woods.

CHAPTER EIGHTEEN

Steam filled the bathroom, drifting lazily in the air. The warm water from the shower pounded down on Tony. The steady stream chased the chill from her body. She'd scrubbed and scrubbed her skin. Washed her hair three times and was on time number four.

She just wanted that lingering lake scent off her.

"Let me."

Aiden was with her. Naked and strong. Aiden's body slid against hers as he sank his fingers into her hair. Carefully, sensually, he stroked her. Almost massaging her hair. Her scalp. Then slowly turning her body and dipping her head so that the spray washed away the lather.

His arms curled around her. His fingers were slick as they eased over her breasts. Teasing her nipples. Then dipping down, down between her legs.

"Just helping to make sure you get as clean as you want to be."

Her back was against his chest. She leaned against him even more, just as his fingers pushed between her legs. A moan trembled on her lips.

His fingers withdrew. Thrust back inside of her.

Tony rose onto her toes. Her muscles went tight. He'd *just* started stroking her. She shouldn't be this turned on already.

His thumb brushed over her clit.

Tony hissed out a breath.

His thumb brushed her again. Again. A little rougher. A little faster. His fingers sank into her. Stretched her. She arched against him and *rode* those fingers.

"So fucking tight," he breathed against her ear. Then his mouth was on her neck. Licking her. Kissing. Sucking. "Like I would ever give you up."

"Aiden." She grabbed for his wrist. Not to pull him away. To urge him on. "I need more."

"I will give you everything. Always." His fingers thrust into her. Withdrew. His thumb kept rubbing her clit. Over and over as he played with her sex. Dipping in. Rubbing. Building the tension as her body was held bow tight.

The water hit her nipples. A sharp surge of sensation just as he drove those wicked fingers of his even deeper in her.

The orgasm hit her hard. A fast spasm of release that had her mouth dropping open as the pleasure soared through her. As the orgasm shook her, he stretched his fingers within her, wringing another gasp of pleasure from her.

The water pounded. She came. And he held her.

Her breath shuddered in and out. In and out. His fingers withdrew.

A protest sprang to her lips.

"Don't worry, baby, we aren't done yet." He reached out and turned off the water. A shiver edged over her as she climbed from the shower, but this shiver wasn't because of the cold or because of fear. Anticipation drove that shiver.

He dried her off, yanked a towel over his own body, and she stood before him, her toes curling into the thick mat that covered the tiled floor, and Tony stared up at him.

His gaze was on her. Taking in every inch of her body. His hand lifted, and his fingers traced over the crescent moon tattoo. "Why the moon?"

"That's what I saw when I got out of that cabin." So long ago. "I looked up and saw the moon and thought it was the most gorgeous thing I'd ever seen in my entire life."

His gaze rose to meet hers. "I'm looking at the most gorgeous woman I've ever seen."

"Sometimes, you can be charming."

"Sometimes, I can be a bastard."

She stepped closer. Closed the distance between them as her arms wrapped around his neck, and she pulled him toward her. "Here's a secret. I happen to really enjoy a charming bastard. Gives me the best of both worlds."

His fingers curled around her hips. "I'm trying to be civilized."

Civilized. "What a boring word. What made you think I wanted that?"

"Tony..."

"Give me everything." She needed it. Couldn't he see that? Didn't he understand?

His mouth crashed onto hers, and she knew that he did. No restraint. No hesitation. He took and tasted and lifted her into his arms as he carried her into the bedroom. Her eyes closed even as her legs wrapped around his hips. His thick, long dick pressed against her, and she knew it would be so easy to arch and take him inside.

So easy...

So she did. An arch of her hips took the head of his cock inside of her.

He froze.

She did, too. Froze as she poised there with the wide head inside of her. Skin to skin. Heat to heat.

"No...condom," he rumbled.

Yes. The condom. They needed protection. She'd never gone without a condom before. Never been so tempted. She arched against him a little bit more.

"*Fuck.*"

"Yes," she said, completely serious. "I do love the way you fuck."

A muscle flexed along his jaw. "When you're ready for me, I will be bare every single time. I will fill you again and again, and you will be so wet with me."

Her breath heaved. She slid down a little more...

"But you're not on the pill, are you, baby?"

Had he found that out when he did his big dive into her life?

"And while the idea of you having my baby just makes me want to fuck you all the more...I want you...*Damn you feel good!* I need you...ready for that."

Her sex had clamped greedily around him. She wanted so much more of him inside her. *All of him. I want him to explode in me.*

She could see an image in her head, too. A family. Aiden. Her. A baby.

"*Tony.*" He lowered her onto the bed. Pulled out.

She cried out in protest.

He yanked open the nightstand drawer. "Better be here. Fucking Smith had better have put—*yes!*" Aiden ripped open the foil packet. Rolled the condom on while she watched and waited, and her fingers slid down her body to touch herself because he had left her on the edge.

He spun around. Saw her. His eyes burned. "I can finish that for you." He caught her hand. Pulled her wrist away. Climbed onto the bed and between her legs. When he lifted her up, she was already reaching for him with greedy hands.

He slammed deep. All the way inside. She cried out because it felt so good but... "I want you with nothing between us. I'll *have you* that way."

His gaze was on hers. She saw the lust take over completely. He withdrew. Drove into her. Her nails scratched over his skin as they fought for release. Faster and harder and stronger. She wasn't thinking about death or fear or the dark.

Passion. Need. Lust. Desire.

She was consumed. The release hit her, and Tony screamed.

The pleasure hit him, and Aiden roared her name.

***

His heart hammered in his chest. The thudding echoed in his ears, a pounding that obliterated every other sound as Aiden heaved up and looked down at Tony.

Her thick lashes slowly lifted. A smile curled her lips. "I love the way you comfort me."

He loved *her*.

He kissed her. Softer than before, but with the same raw need. Aiden suspected that need would never abate. He'd always want her this much. "Tony—"

"*Aiden!*" A bellow from downstairs. Smith's bellow.

Tony's eyes widened, but Aiden was already withdrawing from her body. *Dammit.* He ditched the condom. Jerked on jeans.

"*Aiden!*" Another bellow.

From the corner of his eye, Aiden saw Tony throwing on clothes. He yanked open the bedroom door and rushed for the stairs.

Smith was halfway up, with dirt streaked across his face. *Dirt and blood.* Twigs stuck out of his hair, and his clothes were torn.

"What in the hell happened to you?" Aiden asked.

Smith's breath heaved. "Bastard was in the woods. I saw him. Chased him." He yanked a twig from his shirt. "Then, I fucking fell down a ravine. *He got away.*"

Aiden rushed down the stairs. "Who got away?"

"I think it was that prick Levi. He was here! He was watching the house. He was *here*."

***

"Trespassing. That's what you want me to haul the guy in for?" Barrett sawed a hand over his jaw as he leaned against the edge of his desk and eyed Aiden. "Sounds to me like that's one step away from the man saying the department is harassing him."

"Did you talk to Sharon?" Aiden pressed. He wasn't sitting. He was pacing. Furious energy pulsed through him. "I told you that I think she lied about his alibi." That had been an hour ago. He'd been wasting time in this office with Barrett for a solid hour.

But at least Tony had gotten access to the remains. *Remains. Fuck me. Is that how I really think of my brother now? As remains?* She was working with the ME and Aiden was wasting his time with the chief. "Look, if you aren't going to talk to him, then I will."

"Slow your roll there, Aiden."

He whirled on the chief.

Barrett lifted his hands. "I've got Deion bringing in Sharon right now. We'll talk to her and see what she has to say. If the guy lied about his alibi, *then* I can have cause to *harass* him."

"Why was he at the rental house? Why was he watching us?" *Because he is guilty as sin.* "Look, all the pieces fit. He had access to the drugs used on Banshee. He was involved with Melanie."

"And, what? You think he and Melanie killed your brother all those years ago? Why the hell would they do that?"

Aiden started pacing again. "My brother was desperate for money that summer."

Barrett laughed. "Yeah, right. You two were born with a silver spoon shoved in your mouths."

"No. Dammit. Our father had cut us off. We needed money to—to help a friend." Once more, he turned toward the chief. "I would only realize later that my dad had cut off our money because he'd pretty much lost everything, too. It was all smoke and mirrors." So much suffocating smoke. Aiden had needed to rebuild everything when he took over the family business. "Before he died, my brother told me that he had a way to get some cash."

Doubt covered Barrett's expression. "Levi Russell grew up dirt poor. He worked as a vet tech back in those days so he could save money for college. He wouldn't have been able to give your brother anything." A shake of Barrett's head. "No, look, I know you want justice, but it's not making any sense—"

A knock shook the door. Then... "Chief?" Deion's voice.

Aiden and Barrett both looked toward the door as Deion poked his head inside.

"Chief," Deion said again. "She really wants to talk to you. Says she has to confess..." He swung the door open wider.

Sharon crept inside. Tears trailed down her cheeks. "I-I lied..." Her chin nearly touched her chest. "He wasn't with me when Melanie was murdered. I thought he'd stopped...that he'd changed..." Her hand swiped over her cheeks. "But more are missing. I just checked...more are missing, and it's been happening for so long." Her head lifted. With her lower lip trembling, she murmured, "He's never gonna stop."

Aiden surged toward her. "Stop what?"

Tears trickled down her cheeks.

Barrett closed in. "Just what is it that's missing, Sharon?"

"Drugs," she whispered. "So much ketamine, and it's *gone*. Just like before. Just like all the times before."

"Fuck," Barrett breathed.

Ketamine. Special K. Super acid. Shit. The drug had a ton of street names. Aiden had seen plenty of news stories about the stuff. And Levi had been taking it from the clinic? Aiden locked a hand on Barrett's shoulder. "I think that's reason to haul his ass *in*."

***

"Fractures are noted in both wrists," the medical examiner said as he gestured to the bones that had been carefully arranged on the exam table.

She'd already seen the fractures. No remodeling at all, so they'd either come at the time of death or after. "Could have happened when his hands were tied to the piling. The water would have rocked his body again and again." Easily leading to fractures.

That was why there were other broken bones. Breaks and bends and fractures. The water had been merciless. Every time a storm rolled in, he would have been tossed against the wood. *Over and over again.*

"Dental records won't be here for a few days," the ME told her gruffly. "Not gonna be able to confirm his identity but..."

"We're looking at a male, in his late teens." She could see the growth in his bones. "Caucasian." She studied the skull. Looked beyond bones to see more. "A mix of Spanish and English ancestry." Her finger hovered over his cheek. "I have an artist friend who can reconstruct based on a skull. She can give us his image."

But she already knew it would be an image to match Aiden. Tony had looked at enough skulls that she'd started to be able to see faces, too. When she looked at this skull...

The jaw. The cheeks. The broad forehead.

She saw Aiden.

Sucking in a breath, Tony focused on the rest of the body. Her gloved fingers gripped a magnifying glass as she leaned in closer.

"Looking at the nicks, aren't you?" The ME grunted. "I do know how to perform my job." A sniff. "I saw them, too. Clearly the vic was stabbed."

Her magnifying glass moved over the bones. "Twice in this arm." She looked at the other. "Once here." Defensive wounds that had cut deep?

"Haven't got all the bones up from the lake. We're missing some ribs. Divers are supposed to be out looking again." He grunted once more. "Told them good luck with that. The last thing I'd want to do is be stuck in that cold, black water."

Her gaze lifted to him.

The ME, a slightly balding man wearing an oversized lab coat, widened his eyes as he realized what he'd said. "I, um…"

"I wouldn't want to be stuck in that cold, black water, either." She put down her magnifying glass. Turned away.

"We're supposed to get medical files from the family's old pediatrician later today. The doctor actually had them all boxed up, and when he died, his son took over the practice, so he kept everything." The ME was talking quickly now, nervously. "Barrett said it was a lucky break for us."

"I've already seen those files." She went back to the table. Studied the bones. Felt unease slither through her.

"You have?" Surprise. "When?"

"Before I arrived in North Carolina." Because Saint had gotten access to them. How, she didn't know, but he'd emailed the files to her. She remembered everything that had been in them…

When Austin had been five years old, he'd fallen out of a tree and broken two toes on his right foot.

She looked toward the right foot. Or, rather, where the foot should have been. *Missing. Maybe the divers will get lucky on the search.*

When Austin had been eight, he'd had his appendix removed.

Not like she could tell that by looking at the bones.

When he'd been fourteen, he'd gotten into a fight at school. He'd fractured his left arm because two kids had tried to hold him down. She knew from the school report—again, magically obtained by Saint—that the two kids in question had both wound up with far more broken bones than Austin.

A humerus fracture. That had been in Austin's medical file. But...

Her breath sucked in. She was staring straight at his remains, and while remodeling from the fracture *should* have been there, it wasn't. It wasn't that the fracture had healed. It just *wasn't there*.

But if this man was Austin Warner, the fracture should have been there.

If this man was Austin Warner.

She backed away from the table and remembered questioning Aiden when they'd been in the hospital elevator and a nagging suspicion had slid through her mind...

"Did you ever switch places with him? Maybe to take a math test? Maybe just to see if you could get away with it? To see if teachers would know the difference? Maybe even to see if a friend...or a girlfriend would know the difference?"

And he'd looked right at her. Stared into her eyes without blinking and said, *"Yes."*

"How often?" Her question to him.

She took another step back as his words rang in her head—

"All the fucking time."

Was she staring at the remains of Austin Warner?

Or was she looking at Aiden?

Another frantic step back. She bumped into a tray of instruments, and they clattered to the floor.

***

"You're not coming with me, and I don't care how damn much money you have! Your ass is staying here!" Barrett shoved open the front door of the station and bounded down the steps. He shoved his finger toward the waiting patrol cars. "Deion, I want you on my six, got it?"

"I want to be there," Aiden snarled as he followed them out.

Barrett whirled toward him. He shoved his hand against Aiden's chest. "Civilian." He slapped his own chest. "Police chief. Get the difference? The civilian keeps his ass here while I go confront the suspect. Jesus, man, you assaulted him last time." His voice lowered. "I let you anywhere near him again, I will lose my badge. You don't get to be judge, jury, and executioner."

If that bastard hurt Tony, I will execute him.

Barrett spun back toward his car.

Aiden saw Tony running toward him. The ME's office was in the small building across the street, and she ran straight for Aiden, not even looking at traffic.

"Tony!" Aiden bellowed as fear choked him.

A white car blared its horn and whizzed by her. Tony didn't slow her frantic steps. She raced toward him.

But Barrett stepped in her path before she could reach Aiden. "You found something?" He

282	CYNTHIA EDEN

reached out and curled his fingers around her arms. Excitement filled his voice as he questioned, "You've got evidence I can use? Cause of death? *Tell me!*"

She pulled from him. "Stab wounds. There are defensive wounds on the bones of his arms. Nicks on his ribs."

"Was it the same weapon used to kill Melanie?"

Her stare had been darting toward Aiden, but now it flew back to Barrett. "I can't know that. I-I barely looked at the remains."

"But it's him?" Aiden asked, as he lunged toward her. "Is it my brother?"

Her gaze swept slowly over his face. Pain shadowed her eyes. "It's your brother."

His body jerked as if he'd been hit. He'd known this, deep down. Not like there had really been another outcome but...

She'd warned me. Said that families always had hope even when they said otherwise. They kept clinging to hope when they swore they'd given up.

Aiden swallowed. Twice. A thick lump had lodged in his throat.

"I'm bringing Levi Russell in," Barrett told her. "Think the bastard has been involved in running drugs in *my* town. There's been a steady stream of K in the area for years. And to think it has been coming from that piece of shit who was pretending he was citizen of the year..."

Her attention remained on Aiden. "Lots of people pretend," she said softly.

The chief stepped away from her. "Deion, let's go! The bastard could try to run. We need to stop him! Anders is manning the station and most of my team is back at the lake. We need to haul ass. Let's *go!*"

She didn't once glance at the police chief as he hurried off. Instead, she crept forward. Her hand wrapped around Aiden's wrist. "We need to talk."

His head turned as Barrett and Deion sped away. *You can't be judge, jury, and executioner.* Oh, but he wanted to be.

"Where's Smith?" she asked.

"Staking out the vet clinic." Staking out—searching it. Same thing.

"Come with me. Now." She turned to the right and started dragging him away from the station's entrance and toward a narrow alley. One not big enough for vehicles, barely more than an old trail, really.

"What did you find?" Dread filled his gut. There was more. Dammit. Always—*more*.

She turned onto the little alley. Trail. Whatever it was. He followed instantly, wondering where she—

"*Who in the hell are you?*" Tony demanded as she let go of him.

Frowning, he stepped closer to her. "What? You know who I am."

She pointed to his left arm. "Ever broke it? If I took you in for an X-ray at the hospital, would I see all the remodeling?"

Aiden stiffened. He glanced to the left, to the right. Saw no one. He took a step in retreat, putting his back against the wall of the station while she moved in front of him. "Tony, I don't know what you think is happening—"

"Yes, you do know. Just like *I* know bones. I know them inside and out, and you realized that from the beginning, so you had to understand that I would see the truth eventually. You *had* to know that, and then everything would come crashing down."

Were those tears in her eyes? "Baby..." He reached for her.

She slapped his hand away. "*Who. Are. You?*"

"You know who I am," he responded grimly. "I'm the man who made love to you less than two hours ago. I'm the man who pulled you from the lake. I'm the man who was ready to kill to protect you at the rental house in Biloxi."

Another tear tracked down her cheek. "If I take you to the hospital and X-ray your left arm, what will I see?"

Fucking hell. "It's not what you think."

"*Are you Aiden or are you Austin?*" A ragged cry.

He opened his mouth to tell her the truth.

"That's what I was wanting to know, too." A male voice announced. "Fucking twins. Guess I got the wrong one before. Realized it when you gave me that punch. Never forgot that hook..."

Tony's eyes widened as she stared up at Aiden. Horror flashed on her face.

"This time, I'll get the right twin."

Aiden's gaze flew over her shoulder. He saw Levi barrel forward, with a gun up and aimed. He knew the bastard was going to fire the shot, but Tony was standing between him and the sonofabitch. When Levi fired, it was going to hit her first. "No!" Aiden thundered as he shoved her to the side.

The gun blasted.

The bullet tore through him, and his shoulders slammed into the wall of the police station.

CHAPTER NINETEEN

Bam. Bam. He fired two times more as Tony screamed. The bullets thudded into Aiden's body. His blood spattered onto her, and she could feel hell opening up right in front of her.

Aiden is shot. Levi is killing him. Aiden is dying.

"Stop!" she screamed. Where were the cops? They were right outside the police station. Someone *must* have heard the shots!

Levi aimed the gun at her. His glasses sat askew on his nose. "Why aren't you dead?" He shook his head, seeming genuinely confused. "I felt you stop fighting in that water. You were *gone.* But now you're back, and I'm just going to have to kill you all over again."

"Go..." Aiden rasped. "Baby...*go*..."

"Shit. The boyfriend is still alive. Got to finish him first." Levi swung the gun back toward Aiden.

He was going to fire. She jumped on top of Aiden, flattening her body against his because if Levi took one more shot...

Aiden is barely alive. He's dying. I'm losing him.

Levi laughed. "Oh, right, like that will stop me. Bitch, you weren't making it out—"

"Levi?" A woman. Stunned. "Levi, what are you—"

"Get back, ma'am!" A thunderous order.

Tony's head whipped to the side. She saw Sharon gaping at them, but a cop had just caught her and was dragging her behind him. He grabbed his weapon and hauled it out with shaking fingers. "I want you to drop the gun, Dr. Russell. Drop it now!"

Levi blinked. "I...they attacked me."

Oh, the hell they did. Her hands flew over Aiden's chest. Blood pumped too fast from his wounds. "He needs an ambulance, *now!*" She tried to stop the blood flow.

"They came at me!" Levi continued doggedly. "I had no choice but to defend myself!"

"Drop the weapon," the officer blasted. "Drop it, *now*." Another cop appeared behind him and rushed Sharon toward safety.

Levi looked back at Tony. At Aiden. Rage twisted his face. He wasn't going to drop that weapon. She knew it with certainty. He would squeeze the trigger and take them out.

"I told them!" Sharon suddenly cried as she broke free of the cop who'd been leading her away and ran back to the mouth of the alley. "That's why you followed me to the station, isn't it? You knew I was done! Done with your lies. You've been selling drugs since you were a teen. You're always acting like you're good, a person who helps others, but you just destroy!"

Tony's hands flew around Aiden's waist. No holster. She couldn't remember the last time she'd seen him with a gun. *When we found Melanie?* And, dammit, not like he would have been able to take one into the police station anyway. "You hold on," she whispered to him. "Don't even think about dying. You saved me, and now it's my turn to save you." If she could just get a weapon. Her hands slapped on the ground beside him. Behind Aiden. And...

A brick. Her fingers shoved against the thick surface of a brick that rested on the ground near the wall of the station. She heaved it up and looked back at Levi.

The veterinarian still had his gun turned toward her, but he was looking at Sharon.

"I thought you were screwing Melanie." Sharon shook her head. "But she was working with you, wasn't she? You guys were using Aiden's cabin. Dropping the pills off, picking up payments. Why? *Why?* You had a great life. You had me. You had so much—"

"How the hell do you think I got that life?"

The young cop was sweating as he kept pointing his weapon at Levi. With one hand, he pointed the weapon, with the other, he pushed Sharon back. Once more, the other cop—a fellow with dark brown hair—curled his hands around Sharon's waist and tried to pull her away.

Just two cops.

There was probably only a skeletal crew at the station, Tony realized. Some of the cops must be at Aiden's cabin. And the chief had just left.

Any minute, she expected Levi to pull the trigger.

Slowly, she rose to her feet. She inched forward while Levi's attention was on Sharon, even as the cop kept trying to haul her away from the danger.

"I *got* this perfect life because I fought for it! I didn't grow up rich like the Warner brothers! I fought for everything! When I was a teen, that vet tech job—that's how I got my start. The pills were just right the hell there for me to take. Nobody even noticed! Not until Austin."

Tony inched forward a little more. The rough edge of the brick bit into her hands.

"Austin *knew!*" He jerked the weapon forward and pointed it at the cops and Sharon. "He found out. He saw me at that stupid damn party. Saw me and Melanie and said he wanted in on the cut. The fuck I was dealing him in on *anything*. So *he* got cut!" Spittle flew from Levi's mouth. "Oh, hell, yes, he got cut, and he didn't tell *anyone* about what he'd seen. Bastard. I wasn't going to lose my life for him. I wasn't going to lose my plans, but I can't be sure which one I fucking killed! So I have to kill them both—Austin, Aiden—they just have to die!"

The cop suddenly screamed, "Lower the weapon!"

Levi didn't. He fired.

Sharon cried out and dove for the ground. The bullet hit one cop in the shoulder, and he fired back, but the bullet went way wide and blasted into the side of the building. Levi prepared to fire again.

But Tony kicked him in the back of the knee. His leg immediately gave way, and he staggered, lowering his body just in the range she wanted. She brought her brick down hard on the back of his head.

Thunk.

He fell forward, and the gun flew from his fingers.

"That's for Aiden," she yelled at him.

He rolled over, tried to shove up and attack her—

So she slammed the brick down on his face. Bones crunched and blood flew. "And that's for my dog, you bastard."

***

"Wakey, wakey, sleeping beauty."

At the amused voice, Aiden's eyelids slowly lifted. He frowned as the room came into focus. Lots of white. Bright white. Blinds. Beeps. The smell of antiseptic.

"You're not in hell, if that's what you're thinking. It's a hospital. Though I have heard they can be pretty comparable."

His head turned toward the voice.

"I'm Saint," the tall, dark-haired man said as his lips twisted into a smirk. "But I'm guessing you already know that, don't you? Seeing as how your nosey, billionaire self just thought it would be helluva fun to dig into Tony's life."

Saint.

"And that's Memphis." He jerked his thumb over his shoulder to indicate the other brooding man who sat in the corner. "He does silent and intense well."

"No, I don't," Memphis denied. He rose to his feet. Stalked forward. There was a similarity in the features of the two men. Dark. Strong. Something around the eyes and mouth.

Or maybe they just looked similar because they were both glaring at him.

Aiden attempted to sit up, but pain immediately flew through his chest.

"Bad move." Saint whistled. "When you take three bullets to the chest, you aren't supposed to try and jump out of bed the next day. You're not some superhero, you know."

His teeth snapped together at the pain.

"Do you think he's about to pass out again?" Memphis wanted to know. "Should I call someone?"

"Nah. If the man's gonna be rolling with Tony, he needs to know how to take some hits and keep on going." Saint quirked a brow. "Are you about to vomit on me? Kinda looks that way."

No. *Maybe.* His nostrils flared. "Where. Is. Tony?"

"She and our friend Lila are talking to the police chief. She's making sure the bad guy is in custody. Hugging her dog. Doing important stuff like that. I stopped and brought Banshee over, by the way. Figured Tony would be going crazy missing her. That's just the kind of awesome friend I am."

Memphis elbowed him. "Stay on topic."

"Right. Topic." Saint's eyes narrowed. "Just what are your intentions with Tony? Because it's not every day that a woman beats the shit out of your sworn enemy—"

"With a brick," Memphis inserted.

Saint nodded. "Right. Beats the shit out of your sworn enemy—*with a brick*—for you. So I hope you appreciate just how awesome she is, and you get ready to do some serious groveling for her because the woman is freakishly pissed at you, and honestly, I can't figure out why." His gaze raked Aiden. "I mean, I read the initial report she gave to the chief. You pushed her out of harm's way. Took bullets like a boss for her. But...something is off."

"Way off," Memphis agreed grimly. "Because instead of being grateful, she's furious."

They both leaned over the bed, looking menacing. "So what the hell did you do?" Saint asked.

He stared at them both. Nodded. "I'm glad she's got good friends. Truth be told, I didn't think I'd like you two at first. Worried you were too close to her."

"Oh." A nod from Memphis. "It's because you heard I was stunningly gorgeous, and you worried I had a thing with Tony? Don't worry. I'm taken."

"Good to know...because she's taken, too. My intentions are to marry her. To take her off into the sunset and never, ever look back." Of course, there was just one small problem with that plan...

He could remember exactly what had happened before the shooting, and he knew just why something seemed...*off*. Because Tony wanted to know who he was.

Are you Aiden or are you Austin?

"I need to talk to her."

The hospital room door swung open. He looked toward the door eagerly, hoping it was Tony.

Barrett marched inside. "We need to talk."

But...tailing Barrett...

Tony.

Her gaze darted to Aiden, then away.

He stiffened. Oh, yes, something was definitely *off*. Fuck. No wonder groveling had been mentioned. Tony seemed to be freezing him out. There was no way he could let that happen.

"We love talking," Memphis announced. "Do it all the time, don't we, Saint?"

"Every damn day," he agreed.

They made no move to leave.

Barrett sighed and glanced at Tony. "A little help?"

"Will you guys please head down to the cafeteria? Lila is there. I think Smith might be, too. Not sure you've met him yet."

Memphis squinted at her. "If we leave, will you nearly get killed again or can we trust the police chief?"

Barrett's chest puffed out. "I'm one of the *good* guys!"

"No such thing," Saint told him. "Why lie to yourself?"

"It's okay." Tony's voice was soft, but firm. "*I'm okay.* Thanks for staying with Aiden. I appreciate you watching him."

Wait. They'd been *babysitting him?* Jesus.

"No problem." Saint headed for the door, and Memphis trailed him. "But the dude called out for you like six times. Totally tragic. He's got it bad."

Fuck.

The door closed. Barrett grabbed a nearby chair and hauled it toward the bed. His worried stare swept over Aiden. "The doctor said I wasn't supposed to tire you out, but I have questions I have to ask."

Aiden couldn't look away from Tony. *She* was looking everywhere but at him.

"Levi Russell is on the floor below you. Guy got, uh, some face fractures. A broken nose. Suffered a severe concussion. All when Tony—"

"I shoved a brick into the back of his head and then hit him again in the face." She shrugged. "I had to make sure he wasn't going to get up again."

He's on the floor below me? Rage stirred. The machines near Aiden beeped faster.

Tony's gaze immediately cut to those machines. "Easy," she chided.

He didn't feel easy.

"Problem is..." Barrett cleared his throat as he perched in the chair. "He's saying that *you* are Austin. That Aiden died years ago. I don't know what the hell is happening, but when we get the dental records, I'm sure we can clear things up. Still, I thought it would be best if I just talked to you, and you went on the record as saying—"

"Did you take an X-ray?" Aiden asked Tony. "Of my left arm? Did you do it?"

"Buddy, you were shot in the chest, not the arm. I'm sure you're a little groggy coming off the meds," Barrett added with a sympathetic nod.

"But you weren't hit in the arm. You can take a breath on that one."

The hell he could. "Did you do it?" he asked Tony once more.

Her gaze finally met his. Those deep, dark eyes of hers cut right through him. "Why would I do that?"

Fuck me.

"Yeah, why the hell would she do that?" Barrett rubbed a hand over the back of his neck. "Not to pressure, but, ah, I need to move things along. So if you could just tell me the guy is being a crazy bastard, that you are Aiden Warner—"

"I *am* Aiden Warner," he said, never taking his eyes from Tony. "And Levi Russell is not crazy. Don't let him pull some BS that gets him out of prison in any way. I want him rotting there for what he did to my brother."

"Well, there's your brother's murder—which we are still working on—but right now, we have him for *your* attempted murder. Should be a slam dunk considering that Tony was a perfect eyewitness. We also have him for *her* attempted murder since he confessed to my officer. We can also tie him to Melanie's murder because we got an anonymous tip that there were bloody clothes hidden in the storage room of his vet clinic. Betting that blood will be hers. *Ahem*." He cleared his throat.

Very, very reluctantly, Aiden glanced his way.

Barrett wiggled his brows. "Pretty sure that anonymous tip came from Smith. Did you, by any chance, send him over there to rip the place apart?"

"I have no idea what you mean."

"Right." Barrett rubbed the back of his neck again. "I'm suspecting Levi and Melanie met out at your cabin and left the Acepromazine in the dog food. Then maybe Levi realized Melanie was a loose end who needed eliminating."

So he stabbed her seven times.

A brisk nod from Barrett. "Evidence is piling up left and right. We should be able to bury the guy."

Bury the guy. "Exactly what I wanted."

"Thought you might like to know that we also found the second phone Melanie used. It had been smashed to hell and back and thrown in a dumpster behind Levi's vet clinic. Doesn't matter how smashed it was, though. We can still access the info we need from the company, and I'm sure we'll find calls and texts between Levi and Melanie. A whole lot of them. By the way, I suspect it was Levi who ripped up the flooring in your cabin before you arrived."

"You think there were drugs beneath the floor?" Was that what this really had all been about? A drug ring that Levi had been running since he'd been a teen? A fake life he'd built over the years.

A shrug of one shoulder as Barrett considered Aiden's question. "I think there might have been some, yes. Could be he did a lot of damage to that room in order to try and cover up after himself." His attention shifted to Tony. "When Aiden called Melanie and said he was coming back, maybe she panicked and contacted Levi. Aiden had been all over the tabloids with you and that info about the

Biloxi shooting, so it stood to reason he'd be bringing you to town with him. If you were here, maybe Levi had something in the house he thought your dog would sniff out."

"Banshee flunked when it came to drug sniffing," Tony replied. "She only finds the dead."

"But he didn't know that," Barrett said. "Or maybe he just trashed the room to try and scare you both off. Like I said, there were plenty of stories about Aiden saving you in Biloxi. And when Dr. Antonia Rossi comes to town, clearly, she's there to do one thing." A pause. "Stir up the dead."

That was exactly what she'd done.

Barrett's gaze darted between Tony and Aiden as the chief rose from his chair. "Um, yes, so I have about a million other questions for you, but your doctor says you need your rest. As soon as you're feeling up to it, I will need a statement from you."

"I can give you one right now." He wanted out of that bed. He wanted to be touching Tony. Once more, his gaze slid to her because she was the only thing he wanted to see. When he'd been in that alley, he'd been so afraid she'd get shot. "Levi Russell shot me. He told me that he'd killed the wrong brother before. So I take that as a confession that he murdered my twin. He's a drug dealer, a killer, a cold-blooded bastard, and he belongs in a cage for the rest of his life." The machines beeped steadily. "That a good enough statement for you?"

"I, ah, I'm sure we'll get a more formal one from you later. You and one of your lawyers can come down to the station. Rest now and I'll see you again soon." Barrett bobbed his head toward Tony before he backed out of the room.

Tony watched him go. When the door closed, it was only then that her head slowly turned back to Aiden.

He'd been waiting for her to look at him. "You didn't tell him about the broken bone."

"The humerus fracture that your brother doesn't have, but you do?"

"Yes."

A shrug of one shoulder. "Didn't see the point. He'll know one way or another when he gets the dental records back." A pause. "Won't he?"

He pushed aside his covers. Sat up even as pain burned through him, and Aiden began to swing his legs to the side of the bed.

"What the hell are you doing?" Tony's frantic voice. "You'll break open your stitches!"

He was pretty sure he'd done just that to a few already. He still tried to stand up.

Tony jumped in front of him. Her hands flew to his shoulders. "Stop it!" She pushed him back down. "I'm calling a nurse!"

He stopped trying to get out of the bed. After all, he now had what he wanted. Tony, close to him. Tony, touching him. "There was never a good twin or a bad one."

Her brow crinkled.

"Dad always said that bullshit. It wasn't true. My brother wasn't bad, and I wasn't magically good."

When her hands started to fall away from him, he caught her right wrist. Kept her close.

"Aiden..."

"That's my name. But I went by his. He went by mine. We started swapping lives when we were three years old. Thought it was a game at first. Only it was one we never stopped playing. He could be me. I could be him. No one could tell the difference between us. They saw what they wanted to see."

"A good twin and a bad one."

He nodded. "You know who hit Levi all those years ago? When the sonofabitch was getting angry with Sharon? It was me. I did that, but everyone thought it was my brother. He was the one who always took the swings. Who always struck out so quickly." A shake of his head. "No, we *both* struck out. It was always both of us. But the world thought it was just him."

She inched ever closer to the bed. "You were the one who got the broken arm in school. Those boys jumped *you*."

The bitter memory pulsed through him. "They thought I was Austin, too. They were mad at him for something, and they tried to jump him after basketball practice."

"Only they jumped you instead."

"I made them sorry. I could fight just as hard and dirty as he could."

Her stare dropped to his chest. "You're bleeding through the bandages. I need to call a nurse."

"I'm Aiden. I didn't take my dead twin's identity all these years. I didn't lie about who I was to you. Or maybe I did." Hell, he didn't know. "Because I'm still not good. I'm not the good one."

There is no good one. "Doubt I'll ever be good. All along, I intended to find the person responsible for my brother's murder and kill him."

She licked her lower lip. "Is that still the plan?"

"Levi didn't just kill my brother. He tried to kill you. Twice." He stared straight at her. "What do you think the plan is?"

"He also shot you. Murdered Melanie. And tried to kill Banshee. The cops have a ton of evidence against Levi. He's going to be locked away. He'll lose everything he loves and spend the rest of his life in jail. Those long, agonizing days will be hell for him."

Levi deserved some hell. Aiden didn't mind some payback torture at all.

"You pushed me to the side," Tony accused.

His fingers slid over her inner wrist. "Damn right, I did."

"You knew he was going to shoot. I had my back to him, I couldn't see the gun. *You pushed me to the side,* and all the bullets slammed into you."

Yes.

"Why?" Ragged.

"I told you before, if there's ever a choice...you or anyone else, it's going to be you, baby."

"The choice was me or your own life! You're not supposed to sacrifice yourself for me! And dammit, you are bleeding too much. I'm calling the nurse." She pulled from him and pushed the call button. Her breath came faster. Harder. "I thought you were going to die next to the police station." She wrapped her arms around her stomach. "I wanted to *kill* him, and I was terrified you'd die before medical help could arrive."

"I'm not dead."

"Yes, that's only because he was a shit shot." She rocked back onto her heels. "I realized something in that stupid little alley."

He waited. Ignored the burning in his chest. His stitches had definitely torn open.

"I didn't care what your name was. Aiden. Austin. Didn't matter. *I loved you.* Dangerous, unpredictable, maddening *you.* Loved you so much that nothing else mattered. It wasn't the name I fell in love with. It was just you."

"I am Aiden."

"And I'm T—" She stopped. Released a long breath. "I'm Antonia. *Antonia.* And people don't take things from us, not anymore. They don't take names. They don't take lives. They don't take *anything.*" She crept back toward the bed. "I love you, but don't you dare try dying for me ever again, understand?"

He caught her hand again. "I'd die a hundred times for you."

She choked out a laugh. Or maybe it was a sob. "Do not say sappy crap like that. Because I think you actually mean it, and that terrifies me." She leaned over the bed. "*I want you around for a very long time.* When I think about my life, you're what I see. I need you."

Her hair had been twined into its usual braid. The braid hung over her shoulder, and carefully, he caught the thick edge of it. Using his hold, he tugged her closer. "That's good. Because you are my life. I love you."

She kissed him. Pressed her lips frantically to his, and he was so happy. He wanted to haul her into the bed and hold her close against him. Tony was safe. Alive. And she loved him. Sins and secrets and everything in between—she loved him.

"Oh!" A startled female cry. "I—did someone hit the call button?"

The nurse.

Tony lifted her head. She smiled at him. "He broke his stitches."

The nurse bustled closer. "And you're smiling...like that's a good thing? *Hmmmph*." A glower covered her face.

But Tony kept smiling. One of her real, rare smiles. The smile that made her dark eyes sparkle. "It means he's back in fighting form."

Hell, yes, he was. He'd fight for her every day of the week.

He'd gladly spend the rest of his life fighting for her.

CHAPTER TWENTY

"He's gonna be transferred soon," Smith said as he paced near the small window in Aiden's hospital room. "They kept him here because of the concussion and because, you know, Tony seriously fucked up his face when she slammed her brick into it like a badass."

Aiden shoved aside the tray of food that had been brought to him. Like he cared about broth and Jell-O.

"Cops will be with him every step of the way." Smith grabbed the blinds and peered outside. "A transport will probably be arriving within the next hour."

That didn't give them much time. "Then I guess if I'm going to enjoy a private chat with Levi, it needs to happen now."

Smith glanced over his shoulder at Aiden. "Can you even walk right now?"

Aiden considered the matter. His body was incredibly weak. "No, but I've got this great best friend who can probably find me a wheelchair..."

A long-suffering sigh. "The fucking things I do for you."

***

The parts of Levi's face not covered with white gauze and bandages were bruised and scraped. He lay on the hospital bed, one hand cuffed to the railing, and the bastard had no idea what was waiting for him.

Time for him to figure it the hell out. "Wake the fuck up," Aiden snarled.

Gasping, Levi woke the fuck up. His cuffed hand jerked against the railing, and he instantly tried to sit up. But Smith was there, and he shoved the guy right back down. He also pulled out a scalpel he'd borrowed from an exam room, and he put it against Levi's throat. "Nope. Shouldn't do that."

"What the hell?" Levi went very, very still. "Y-you can't be here! There's a cop—"

"On break," Aiden supplied helpfully as he wheeled closer to the bed. "And lower your voice or Smith will cut your throat."

Levi's breath shuddered out.

"Your face looks like shit," Aiden told him. "Pretty sure Tony broke your nose and your cheek bones. Every time you look in the mirror, I bet you'll be remembering her."

Levi gaped at Aiden. "How are you...alive?" A hoarse whisper.

"Turns out, you can't shoot worth a damn." Aiden stopped his wheelchair at the edge of the bed.

"Y-you can't be here..."

"Who the hell do you think *paid* for this hospital? I can do anything I want, and the people here—people who are plenty loyal to me—will look the other way. Just like the cop looked the other way when I wanted to come and have this little chat with you." Deion was gonna have one hell of a vacation fund coming his way.

Levi laughed. "Y-you're throwing away your case...this is just going to h-help me. I'll get off..."

Aiden shook his head. "No, you won't. Because this meeting never happened. You try to say it did, and people will just think you're stirring up shit. See, I have four nurses who will tell everyone that I've been in my room the whole time." He smiled. "You're not the only one good with alibis."

"B-bastard..."

"You've got so many cuts and scratches on you already," Smith noted with pursed lips. "Another one won't be a big deal. I am so tempted to add a new one to your collection."

"Smith's mad," Aiden explained. "Because he happened to be friends with my brother. You know, the guy you tied beneath a pier and left to rot?"

Levi's chest heaved with his desperate breaths. "You...you're going to kill me?"

Oh, someone was finally getting the picture. "Not today. Today, you're being transferred to a cell. You'll be put on trial eventually, and you will be found guilty." He leaned forward in his chair. "I will make absolutely certain of that. If you think my money can't buy you a ticket straight to hell, you are dead wrong."

Levi shuddered.

"I'm not killing you. Tony said staying in a cell and losing everything will be the fate you hate the most. So I'll just let you rot there for a while."

Levi's eyes swept over him. Rage burned in his stare. He was missing his glasses, not like he could wear them with all that crap on his face, but Aiden knew the jerk saw him perfectly.

"Funny thing about prison," Aiden continued as he looked right at the man who'd taken his brother's life. *Who tried to take Tony's life*. No, there would never be a second chance for Levi. No promise of freedom down the road. "The people there are so unpredictable. Violent. If I were you, I'd always watch my back. Maybe the first year locked away won't be so bad. Maybe you'll start to adjust. Maybe by the second year, you won't miss fresh air so much. Maybe you'll get used to being someone's bitch. And then that third year...a fight could break out. You could get caught in the middle. Or maybe you just piss off the wrong person...and you wind up gutted and bleeding out on the floor." He snapped his fingers. "Just like that, you're gone from this world."

"*Fucking...b-bastard...*" A rasp from Levi. But he didn't move. Smith kept the scalpel right against Levi's jugular.

"I am a bastard. Good of you to notice."

"You're Austin...I'll tell everyone...you're really—"

"Good luck with that. Good luck with prison, too. Like I said, you never know when you're gonna piss off the wrong person." He turned the chair around. Wheeled for the door. Stopped before he left. "I am that wrong person."

"*I know why you don't remember!*"

Aiden's shoulders stiffened.

"I slipped something into your drink. You thought you were so big and bad, punching me when Sharon started crying. The Warner brothers always thought they were so untouchable! Fuckers! I saw you at the party. You weren't paying attention, so I slipped one of my mixes into your drink, and your ass was *out!* That made it easy to take on your brother. Austin—Aiden— whoever the fuck he was—it made it easy. He came to me, saying he wanted a cut in on *my* ring. On the business *I'd* created. If I didn't deal him in, he threatened to go to the cops. The hell he would! So I handled him. I took care of the big, bad, rich bastard. You weren't there when he needed you, you weren't there, and he died alone and—"

"If I cut his throat, he'll stop talking," Smith offered.

Smith. Always the helpful one. Aiden looked back. "You're going to enjoy prison," he told Levi. "I'll make sure of that. Those years will roll by."

Until the end. Just like I warned you. One day, you'll turn around...

And be dead.

Aiden opened the door. Wheeled out.

"*No!*" Levi yelled after him. "I want to make a deal! Where's Barrett? I want a deal! I want protection! I want—"

The guy should really watch that screaming. Patients were resting.

The nurse didn't even look up from her station when Smith joined Aiden, and they headed toward the elevator.

As soon as they got inside...

"You're bleeding again," Smith noted.

He didn't feel the pain.

"Guessing there will be no deals from Barrett?"

"There will be no deal on anything." Why would there be? Too much evidence existed. As for protection, that was laughable. There would never be enough protection in the world to shield Levi from the justice that would come his way.

An eye for an eye.

A life for a life.

"I knew you two used to swap places," Smith murmured. "You thought you were so good at fooling everyone, but there were occasionally some tells."

Surprised, he glanced over at Smith.

"You always had a better right hook than your brother." His hand clamped over Aiden's shoulder. "He used to say you were smarter, too. That you could do anything with numbers. Wasn't that why he'd get you to slip into his math classes?" His Adam's apple bobbed. "So be smart now, man. Don't throw your life away for something that happened in the past. You've got a whole lot to live for. Look forward. Hold tight to what matters."

The elevator doors opened. Tony stood there. With her arms crossed over her chest. "Feel better now?" she asked sweetly.

Because, of course, she'd known what he was doing. He planned to keep nothing from her. Not ever. Tony was the one person in the world who would know everything about him.

Even the dark parts.

He wheeled out of the elevator. He'd be glad when he was strong enough to stand, but as it was...

Tony came toward him. She leaned over and put her hands on the armrests of his borrowed chair. "That was very risky."

He'd needed to look in the bastard's eyes. "Never happened." Even the security footage would be gone. A side effect of having more money than God, as Smith would say.

"Do you feel better?"

He was staring at his forever. She was safe. Hell, yes, he felt better. Smith didn't need to worry. The past wasn't going to drag him down. He'd put terror into Levi. No matter what else happened, Levi would always be looking over his shoulder. Always wondering if an attack was coming.

He would never know peace.

As for Aiden, he had peace right in front of him. Peace, happiness, love. And he would never let her go.

Her fingers reached out and touched his cheek. The softest silk. He turned into her touch. "Baby, I feel fantastic."

Or as fantastic as he could feel with all the bullet wounds in his chest.

But when she pressed her lips to his...

Screw the bullet wounds.

He had her.

Fantastic.

***

"So you suspected that I'd tried to kill you." Smith stood in the foyer of Aiden's Miami home. "That hurts." He put his hand over his heart. "Right in here."

Tony spared him a brief glance. The last few weeks had passed in a whirlwind of activity. Levi had been charged with a slew of crimes, the remains taken from beneath the pier had officially been identified as belonging to Austin Warner, and Aiden had been released from the hospital. It had taken a bit of time for him to recover from the gunshot wounds, and he had *not* been the best patient in the world. But he was alive, he was safe, and they were home.

A home that was overwhelmingly *huge*. The Miami mansion looked over the glittering water, and the place felt surreal to her.

"You were on my list of suspects, but so was the police chief. And even Sharon." She shrugged one shoulder. She'd just come inside after having a meeting with the vice-president at the University of Miami. He wanted her to teach classes, and, since she was planning to stay in the area for the foreseeable future, she'd agreed.

"I can't believe you thought I was a killer."

That was adorable. Tony turned toward him, even as she heard Aiden climbing down the stairs. "You *are* a killer, Smith."

He pouted. "Lies. Rumors. Innuendo."

"You think the Ice Breakers didn't tell me about the work you and Aiden have been doing? The two of you set up your own rescue operation after Aiden's attempted kidnapping in Mexico all those years ago." She'd known many of these details for a while. But why show all her cards too soon? "You made it your mission to rescue others who'd been taken." All over the world. In some of the most dangerous cities out there. "That work isn't pretty. It's not easy. And it certainly is not for the faint of heart."

He brushed his nails over his suit coat. "I like to stay busy." His gaze flickered past her, toward the staircase. "We both do."

Oh, she knew Aiden certainly liked to keep his hands in all sorts of interesting activities. That was why she had a proposition for them both. "You ever think of being an Ice Breaker?" Tony asked Smith. "Because I think you might be one fine asset."

He blinked. "Huh. I *am* always up for trying new things..."

She turned to glance back at Aiden.

A faint smile curved his lips. "Are you trying to steal away my head of security?"

Tony crossed the marble floor of the foyer so she could stand in front of him. "Not steal. I'm no thief. Just trying to convince you *both* that maybe you could use some of your ample skills to help my team."

"Use me any way you want," Aiden assured her. "I'm yours."

She knew he wasn't teasing. He was hers. Just as she belonged completely to him.

A quick bark drew her attention to his side. Aiden hadn't come down those stairs alone. Banshee was at his side, grinning up at Tony. A full recovery. For Banshee and Aiden. Her family was right in front of her, and she absolutely loved them both.

No darkness. No fear. For the first time in longer than she could remember, Tony was looking forward to the future. She had hope. She could see joy.

"I'll just slip out for a bit," Smith announced. "Think you two might want some alone time. Hey, Banshee, want to go for a walk?"

Banshee bumped her head against Tony's palm, but then happily trotted toward Smith. He opened the door, pulling in the scent of the water. "I'm interested in your offer," he said, voice deepening. "But you should know I don't always work well with a team."

"I'll consider myself warned," she said, not looking over at him.

The door closed.

Aiden's grin stretched. "Your clothes arrived. Your boxes. You are officially moved in with me now."

Her hand rose to press to his chest, and her diamond engagement ring gleamed. Normally, she didn't care at all about jewelry. While she was sure the ring had been stupid expensive, it wasn't the price that mattered to her. What mattered was that Aiden had given her the ring. He'd gotten down on one knee, had Banshee standing close at his side, and he'd proposed to her.

They were going to get married in a month. All the Ice Breakers had already RSVP'd. The press kept saying it was going to be the wedding of the century.

She didn't care what the press said. When it came time for the wedding, Tony planned to just be on a beach, with Banshee and her friends watching as she took her vows with Aiden. Soon, she'd be holding a bouquet and promising that she'd love Aiden forever. An easy promise to make considering she could not imagine her life without him.

"Have I ever told you just when I fell in love with you?" Aiden asked her.

The question caught her off guard, and Tony laughed.

"There. There it is." His hand lifted, and his index finger gently traced her smile. "The one that lights your eyes. God, I want to make you happy every single day. I want you always smiling."

Once, smiles had been hard for her. But with Aiden, they came easier and easier. "When did you fall for me?" She expected something sexy, a reference to the first time they'd made love.

"When we were in my casino and you dumped all the chips into my hands and walked away."

Her eyes widened.

"Knew right then that you couldn't be bought. You weren't interested in my money or power. You were the sexiest woman I'd ever seen, and all I could do was chase helplessly after you."

"You...you came after me because you wanted me to take your case. To find your brother."

An incline of his head. "And you did, but, baby, I would have chased after you regardless." His amber eyes gleamed. "When you find someone worth keeping, you don't let go. You fight like hell, and you pray that you won't screw up too much with her. You hope that one day she might feel the same way about you."

She wanted his mouth. "Want to know when I fell in love with you?"

His head had started to lower toward her. "Was it when I bravely saved you at that house in Biloxi?"

She inched closer. "No."

"Was it when I breathed for you after pulling you from the lake?"

"You like to hit your hero highlight reel, don't you?" Tony pressed onto her toes. *So close to his mouth*. "But, no, that's not it, either."

"When?" His breath teased her. Delicious peppermint.

"When Banshee was hurt. When you rushed her out of the cabin and carried her to your SUV. You were willing to do anything to help me save her. You were willing to do all of that, just because you knew how much she meant to me."

"I would do anything for you," he said. So simple.

She knew he meant that vow. *Anything*. And that was why she loved him. He wasn't completely good. Wasn't bad, either. A bit of both. Just like she was. Dark places in their souls, but light, too. More and more light when they were together.

Tony couldn't stand the distance between them any longer. Her hands flew up to curl around his neck as she pulled him toward her. She kissed him with all her passion and all her love.

She was a woman who hadn't believed in happy endings. The world had been far too dark and twisted for them.

But she and Aiden were going to create their own ending, and she *knew* it would be amazing.

THE END

A NOTE FROM THE AUTHOR

Thank you so much for reading TOUCHED BY
ICE! I have to tell you, I am cold case obsessed. I
have been for years. I watch way too many crime
shows, and I am always rooting for the missing to
be found. The Ice Breakers grew out of my love for
cold cases, and I've had such an incredible time
exploring their world.

If you'd like to stay updated on my releases and
sales, please join my newsletter list.

https://cynthiaeden.com/newsletter/

Thank you, again, for reading TOUCHED BY ICE.

Best,
Cynthia Eden
cynthiaeden.com

ABOUT THE AUTHOR

Cynthia Eden is a *New York Times*, *USA Today*, *Digital Book World*, and *IndieReader* best-seller.

Cynthia writes sexy tales of contemporary romance, romantic suspense, and paranormal romance. Since she began writing full-time in 2005, Cynthia has written over one hundred novels and novellas.

Cynthia lives along the Alabama Gulf Coast. She loves romance novels, horror movies, and chocolate.

For More Information

- *cynthiaeden.com*
- *facebook.com/cynthiaedenfanpage*

HER OTHER WORKS

Wilde Ways: Gone Rogue

- How To Protect A Princess (Book 1)
- How To Heal A Heartbreak (Book 2)

Ice Breaker Cold Case Romance

- Frozen In Ice (Book 1)
- Falling For The Ice Queen (Book 2)
- Ice Cold Saint (Book 3)
- Touched By Ice (Book 4)

Phoenix Fury

- Hot Enough To Burn (Book 1)
- Slow Burn (Book 2)
- Burn It Down (Book 3)

Trouble For Hire

- No Escape From War (Book 1)
- Don't Play With Odin (Book 2)
- Jinx, You're It (Book 3)
- Remember Ramsey (Book 4)

Death and Moonlight Mystery

- Step Into My Web (Book 1)
- Save Me From The Dark (Book 2)

Wilde Ways

- Protecting Piper (Book 1)
- Guarding Gwen (Book 2)
- Before Ben (Book 3)
- The Heart You Break (Book 4)
- Fighting For Her (Book 5)
- Ghost Of A Chance (Book 6)
- Crossing The Line (Book 7)
- Counting On Cole (Book 8)
- Chase After Me (Book 9)
- Say I Do (Book 10)
- Roman Will Fall (Book 11)
- The One Who Got Away (Book 12)
- Pretend You Want Me (Book 13)
- Cross My Heart (Book 14)
- The Bodyguard Next Door (Book 15)
- Ex Marks The Perfect Spot (Book 16)
- The Thief Who Loved Me (Book 17)

Dark Sins

- Don't Trust A Killer (Book 1)
- Don't Love A Liar (Book 2)

Lazarus Rising

- Never Let Go (Book One)
- Keep Me Close (Book Two)
- Stay With Me (Book Three)
- Run To Me (Book Four)
- Lie Close To Me (Book Five)
- Hold On Tight (Book Six)

Dark Obsession Series

- Watch Me (Book 1)
- Want Me (Book 2)
- Need Me (Book 3)

- Beware Of Me (Book 4)
- Only For Me (Books 1 to 4)

Mine Series

- Mine To Take (Book 1)
- Mine To Keep (Book 2)
- Mine To Hold (Book 3)
- Mine To Crave (Book 4)
- Mine To Have (Book 5)
- Mine To Protect (Book 6)
- Mine Box Set Volume 1 (Books 1-3)
- Mine Box Set Volume 2 (Books 4-6)

Bad Things

- The Devil In Disguise (Book 1)
- On The Prowl (Book 2)
- Undead Or Alive (Book 3)
- Broken Angel (Book 4)
- Heart Of Stone (Book 5)
- Tempted By Fate (Book 6)
- Wicked And Wild (Book 7)
- Saint Or Sinner (Book 8)
- Bad Things Volume One (Books 1 to 3)
- Bad Things Volume Two (Books 4 to 6)
- Bad Things Deluxe Box Set (Books 1 to 6)

Bite Series

- Forbidden Bite (Bite Book 1)
- Mating Bite (Bite Book 2)

Blood and Moonlight Series

- Bite The Dust (Book 1)
- Better Off Undead (Book 2)

- Bitter Blood (Book 3)
- Blood and Moonlight (The Complete Series)

Purgatory Series

- The Wolf Within (Book 1)
- Marked By The Vampire (Book 2)
- Charming The Beast (Book 3)
- Deal with the Devil (Book 4)
- The Beasts Inside (Books 1 to 4)

Bound Series

- Bound By Blood (Book 1)
- Bound In Darkness (Book 2)
- Bound In Sin (Book 3)
- Bound By The Night (Book 4)
- Bound in Death (Book 5)
- Forever Bound (Books 1 to 4)

Stand-Alone Romantic Suspense

- It's A Wonderful Werewolf
- Never Cry Werewolf
- Immortal Danger
- Deck The Halls
- Come Back To Me
- Put A Spell On Me
- Never Gonna Happen
- One Hot Holiday
- Slay All Day
- Midnight Bite
- Secret Admirer
- Christmas With A Spy
- Femme Fatale
- Until Death

- Sinful Secrets
- First Taste of Darkness
- A Vampire's Christmas Carol

CPSIA information can be obtained
at www.ICGtesting.com
Printed in the USA
LVHW041211080323
741118LV00001B/138